PRAISE FOR SOUND

Excellent dystopian sci-fi.

— Amazon Reviewer

Brilliant writing, fantastic story . . .

— Goodreads Reviewer

Survival Aptitude Test: Sound will be tough to top.

— Amazon Reviewer

I didn't want to put it down.

— Amazon Reviewer

Highly recommended for anyone looking for a fast-paced, thought-provoking book.

— Amazon Reviewer

SURVIVAL APTITUDE TEST: SOUND

MIKE SHERIFF

THE EXTINCTION ODYSSEY - BOOK 1

This book is a work of fiction.
Names, characters, places, and incidents are
products of the author's imagination or are used fictitiously.

Edited by Bobbie Jo Reid

Cover Design by Wicked Good Book Covers

Cover Art by Tom Edwards

Published by The Appended Press
41 Craig Street, Suite 4
London, Ontario, Canada N6C 1E9
ISBN-13: 978-0-9952766-7-3

For Bob and Asia-Lee.

FOREWORD

700 years After the Cycle of Extinctions,
life offers little hope for Earth's last species . . .

And so the journey begins. A wise author never stands in the way of a good story, so I'll keep this short and to the point. Let me start by offering you my heartfelt thanks for picking up this book, the first in The Extinction Odyssey series.

The pages that follow will transport you to a stark and sterile future where one terrifying truth reigns supreme: *Extinction is the Rule; Survival is the Exception*. I'd like to say you're reading a work of fiction, but recent events around the world have left me wondering whether the title should be listed in the *non*-fiction section of bookstores. Time, I suppose, will tell.

Six books are planned for the series—assuming we survive that long—and five are complete at this time of writing (*Sound, Fury, Rise, Fall*, and *Life*). Depending on when you're reading these words, the last title (*Death*) might be available. If you'd like to keep up-to-date regarding my latest releases and upcoming sci-fi series, be sure to join my Readers' Posse using the info provided at the end of this book.

Okay, I've droned on long enough. It's time to step aside and let you plunge into the odyssey. I hope you enjoy reading this book as much as I enjoyed writing it. And I fervently hope it will forever remain a work of fiction.

Mike Sheriff
    London, Ontario

1

700 A.C.E.

THOUSANDS OF RAWBONED bodies packed the Center's northern stairway. Thousands more glutted the transway two flights below.

Daoren clenched his jaw and balanced on the landing's edge atop the second flight. He kept his spine as straight as a sparring staff to minimize the risk of contact with the writhing, murmuring horde. He loathed crowds for one reason.

It wasn't the shorn scalps or smug self-righteousness worn by Daqin Guojin's denizens, though the two attributes proved as loathsome as any. It wasn't the bulging waistlines, triple chins, or other displays of wealth touted by the entitled elites. It wasn't even the endless chatterwailing spewed by the malnourished masses.

It was the smell of hunger.

Not the physical hunger caused by a shortage of grooll, but a *psychic* hunger caused by hopelessness. The miserable scent soured every gathering he'd encountered. Life seven hundred years After the Cycle of Extinctions made it impossible to escape, just as life in a city-state of fifteen million made it impossible to avoid. Still, he took every measure to shun crowds, which made standing amid a crush of humanity doubly loathsome.

The crowd cast particularly cruel shadows in the morning twilight. The *shenyi* garments favored by most denizens spanned the spectrum, slathering the stairway in a smear of color—minus shades of green. The clothing mirrored the styles of Mother China's imperial dynasties; stiff tunics with billowy sleeves and broad sashes draped knee-length trousers and skirts. Each of the stairway's eight flights also bore ample swaths of dull, white *pienfu*—the mandated garb of the city-state's prospects.

The quality of the apparel reflected wide disparity, announcing the wearer's social status without a wasted word. So did the pinched faces above the *quju* collars and *zhiju* lapels; they represented the different lineages of all fifty Chengs.

Daoren maintained his balancing act, but contact was unavoidable. Every random rub of a shoulder or careless brush of an arm made his skin shrink and throat itch. Mercifully, the nearby crowd settled down, congealing into clumps of four or five. Islands of families formed on the Center's stepped shores, adrift in their thoughts. Few among them spoke, praise be to Sha.

His gaze settled on his own island. Its inhabitants included Lucien and Cordelia—he hadn't called them Papa and Momma since he was ten—and Mako. Daoren stood at arm's length while his parents closed ranks around his brother, and so they should.

Today was the day of Mako's S.A.T.

Lucien wore a purple shenyi woven from the finest gleam-glass filament. The color and quality suited his position as a member of the Cognos Populi—and the Cognos Populi was all about appearances. Unlike most members of the bloated forum, his body retained its youthful leanness. He placed a steady hand on Mako's shoulder. "Once you're inside the Center, get to your seat right away. Give yourself time to settle in before the test starts."

Daoren grunted. The pang of hunger in his father's eyes clashed with his pragmatic tone. Lucien had vaulting ambition, but his lineage served as a crippling anchor. Caucasoids whose ancestry traced to the ancient western continent were a distinct minority in Daqin Guojin. Asianoids, Indonoids, Africoids, and Eastern Caucasoids like the Slavvs enjoyed the majority. They also enjoyed the benefit of multi-generational wealth on which to mount their social ascent.

"You must remember to breathe," his father continued.

Mako's head bobbled as if on a spring. His glassy eyes remained static.

His brother was easier to decipher than Lucien. Despite years of counseling, Mako hadn't learned to hide his emotions. They always clothed him, and none fit his wiry frame better than anxiety. Though ten months older than Daoren, he stood three inches shorter and weighed fifteen pounds less. He overcompensated for the genetic slight, hence the aggressive patterns of glass implants in his face and arms. His expression—what could be seen of it beneath a tangle of black bangs—displayed ill-disguised dread.

Daoren pivoted away, unable to stomach the smell of his brother's angst. The landing atop the second flight provided a view of architectural splendor that all but the most jaded eyes would find mesmerizing.

Zhongguo Cheng's administrative district basked in sunlight. Its towering edifices integrated every geometric shape imaginable. Trapezoids. Toroids. Icosahedrons. Polygon meshes. Their sprawling spectraglass façades glistened, reflecting yellow, orange, and red hues. Blue, crystalline transways threaded the structures, mimicking the serenity of ambling, ancient rivers.

The visual effect was a lie, of course; the city-state restricted flowing water to decorative fountains and waste chambers. Distant levitrans navigated the transways, their teardrop hull-forms riding on proud cushions of compressed air. They transported society's elites in the kind of style the masses might dream of possessing, but never own.

The majestic vista offered little relief. Daoren put his back to the splendor. He glanced up the stairway and took in a more bitter view.

Six flights above, an archway gaped like a starving mouth in the Center's columned façade. The structure's domed roof consumed at least one hundred acres of bone-white, shock-fused ceramic. The cost of the roof alone would have fed ten thousand families for a year, but the old rulers of Daqin Guojin had needed a suitable abode for their new test.

"Slow, deep breaths will help calm your mind and sharpen your focus."

"I know, Papa. I know."

"Heed your father, Mako," Cordelia said, brow folding into shallow creases.

It was a Slavvic brow; broad due to her cropped hair, but statuesque even when furrowed. She'd selected an azure shenyi with gold trim and matching wrist rings for today's test. The wrist rings were ordinary ceramic—moldable crystal jewelry cost a hundred times as much. His mother restricted her glass implants to the helices of her ears. The five studs mirrored the custom of the ancients, starting with violet devices in the crowns and ending with red ones in the lobes. A tiny hole pierced the center of each helix; she'd stopped wearing the green studs at his father's insistence.

"Do you have enough grooll?" Lucien asked.

Mako clenched his hands. His gaze panned the lower flight.

Daoren read the restive signs as easily as a glass scroll. "I thought you said she wasn't coming."

"She isn't."

"Then why do you look for her?"

"I'm not looking for *her!*"

"It's obvious you're looking for someone."

"Teimei, Bushudo, and Zilian," Mako said, spitting out the names. "We agreed to meet on the northern stairway half an hour before the test."

Daoren snorted. "They're probably on the other side of the Center. Your friends couldn't tell north from south with a compass and a plasmonic map."

"At least I have friends!"

"What use will they be to you today? You'd better focus on whether the test's passing score is still twenty thousand points."

"Daoren!" Cordelia said. "Your father told you there's no truth to that rumor."

"And we know how much the Cognos Populi values the truth." He glared at his father. "How many times have they raised the S.A.T.'s passing score in the last thirty years?"

Lucien buried his fingers in Daoren's lapel. "Tread carefully, boy," he said, twisting the burrglass material. "You sound more and more like a dissenter every day."

Daoren shrugged off the insult. "Funny how the simplest questions ring as dissent in the ears of the ruling caste." He pulled free from his father's grasp. "Forget your friends, Mako. You're on your own in this world. The sooner you accept that truth, the better."

"Pay your brother no mind," Cordelia said. "I'm sure your friends are here."

Mako wrung his hands. "Then where are they?"

"You know Teimei," Lucien said. "That boy's always running late."

HEAVING BREATHS SCORED Teimei's windpipe, like he was inhaling two grains of sand for every molecule of air. Knotted bangs flayed his eyes raw with each stride. Cramps wracked his muscles, but he was close to the objective; closer than he ever imagined he'd get.

Behind him, the slap of sandals announced Bushudo and Zilian's pace. Their distant footfalls rebounded off the glass walls bracketing the concourse, doubling and redoubling, making the two sound like twenty.

The flutter-echo faded when he hit the end of the concourse and burst onto a stark plane of white glass. Five hundred feet farther, the objective soared skyward.

The Great Northern Border.

Teimei stopped, ignoring the instinct to cross the cull zone as fast as his legs could carry him. How could he not?

To look upon the border wall was to look upon the mythic. Legendary battles had been fought in its shadow; battles whose heroes were immortalized in sculptglass dioramas throughout the city-state; heroes whose exploits were embedded in the cultural scrolls of the Spires.

Sheer mass gave the wall an air of permanence. It fanned east and west, stretching one hundred fifty-five unbroken miles to the Eastern and Western Seas, bisecting the peninsula. Its cylindrical watchtowers topped three hundred feet, their crystalline shafts as gray as mourning shrouds. Archways penetrated the wall's base at two-mile intervals, too many to count.

There was a purpose in their design, his tutors at the Librarium had once said. Each archway could accommodate the passage of a Jireni column, their heavy weapons, and their Hexalite levicarts. To the north, far beyond the wall, lay the mongrel colonies.

Teimei pushed aside all thoughts of the mongrel incursions of yore. To the south, somewhere *within* the wall, lay another enemy made more ominous by its proximity and ruthlessness. He resumed his sprint and crossed the cull zone.

He reached the closest archway two hundred feet ahead of his friends. He sank to a knee, wheezing, and watched their approach.

Bushudo had ten paces on Zilian—not surprising given her trimmer frame and love of physical conditioning. Zilian's complexion matched the ruddy morning twilight, his mouth a black pail for scooping oxygen. White pienfu clung to their bodies, wrapping them from neck to knees in coarse burrglass. Snarls of matted hair bounced in time with their bounding strides. At ten times the distance, anyone would recognize them as prospects for denizenship. The plain garments and unruly hair were dead giveaways.

There was a purpose in that, too.

They thumped to a stop before the archway's entrance and folded over, panting. Teimei scanned their route for pursuers, but the view seized his attention.

Daqin Guojin's expanse of multicolored glass and crystalline structures glittered. The skyline fused scintillating geometries at dizzying angles and stupefying heights, radiating harmony, balance, and strength. Red cupolas with flared, golden eaves topped many of the structures.

The Imperial Regalia.

A vestige of Mother China's lineage, the regalia served as the signet of the Cognos Populi. It also served as the signpost of civilization's last oasis on the sterile Earth.

The sight stung his eyes. Forty miles to the south, Mako would be standing on the steps of the northern stairway, wondering where they were, unaware that he'd never see them again.

Teimei pushed that thought aside as well. He rose and focused on his friends. "We don't have much time. The watchtowers will have noted our arrival."

Bushudo raised her head, hands pressed against her thighs. She gulped air like a fluid. "You're . . . sure . . . about . . . this?"

Sunlight kissed the glass implants adorning her cheeks and

neck. The spiraling ocher studs sparkled, setting her skin afire. Her Asianoid beauty stilled his breath at the worst of times. In this moment, she shone more radiant than ever—but glass glinted brightest before it shattered.

She straightened and pinned him beneath one of her searching gazes. "Are you sure this is the right decision?"

Teimei willed himself not to cry. He was sure Bushudo would fail the S.A.T.; her previous prep-test scores left no room for doubt. He was sure Zilian's inability to think clearly under stress spelled his doom. He was sure his own chances of passing were null. Yipsing had failed the S.A.T. two years ago, and his sister had been blessed with much stronger aptitude for the required technological knowledge.

"Teimei! Answer me!"

He swiveled away from her, not trusting his stinging eyes to stay dry. His gaze tracked through the darkened archway to the desert beyond the wall.

Mountainous dunes heaved and swelled, their razorback ridges bleached like skeletal remains. The sea of sand stretched to infinity, starved of color, moisture, and life.

He shivered. A month ago, they'd agreed the northern desert held their salvation. Seeing it now only strengthened his conviction. "I won't be harvested," he said. "No other way is this quick or this painless. Isn't that right, Zilian?"

Zilian fixed his wide-eyed gaze upon the sandy void. He fingered the black studs stippling his forearm.

The stud pattern mimicked the crystal daggers carried by the Jireni. Teimei had played *Jireni and Slags* countless times with Zilian as a child. His friend was never a slag. Now the security force he so admired and so longed to join was hunting him.

Zilian's eyes pleaded. "You're certain it's painless?"

A shrill hiss leaked across the cull zone—the unmistakable acoustic signature of highly compressed air. It came from everywhere and nowhere.

Zilian's panicky gaze locked onto the structures to the south. "Merciful Sha!"

Bushudo snatched Teimei's hand. "Are they coming?"

Teimei detected no movement across the cull zone. "Zilian! Where are—"

Zilian bolted through the archway without saying another word. He reached the desert in three seconds. The instant his sandals touched the sand, a jarring screech radiated from his head.

Zilian clapped his hands over his ears—ruddy mist sprayed between his fingers. He staggered and collapsed onto a dune. Blood oozed from his ears and blotted the sand.

What little grooll Teimei had in his stomach climbed his gullet. He gagged and gaped at his friend's motionless body, willing it to move.

"We can't let them take us alive!"

He tried to process Bushudo's plea, tried to translate her fear into action, but his mind and body no longer occupied the same vessel. He sensed her tugging his hand, pulling him through the archway. Faster and faster, as if compelled by an invisible force, Teimei swept toward his salvation . . . toward the wind-spun sand . . . toward Zilian's corpse. . . .

His muscles froze. His legs stopped functioning, halting him steps from the desert.

Bushudo's fingertips slipped across his palm. Her body broached the archway's mouth.

Another horrid screech slashed the air, its ultra-high frequency identical to the first.

Without uttering as much as a whimper, Bushudo dropped to her knees and slumped face-down next to Zilian. White sand lapped up the blood streaming from her ears.

Teimei cradled his head, eyes awash. He opened his mouth, scouring his soul for words to beg her forgiveness.

The shriek of compressed air slammed his mouth shut again. He whirled to the din.

A hulking black form hovered in shadow at the far end of the archway. Other figures flanked it, cloaked by swirling gray mist. The shrieking din ceased.

The silence triggered a clamor of conflicting thoughts. One thought alone gave him any hope of survival. "I'll go back to the Center!" he said. "I'll take my chances on the test!"

The black form extended a needlelike appendage. A chilling voice drifted through the archway. "That aerostat has sailed, prospect."

Of all the thoughts that might have ushered him out of existence, Teimei never imagined it would be a simple accounting of the date. He was going to die today, seven hundred years After the Cycle of Extinctions.

The appendage recoiled. Two percussive reports smacked the archway's crystalline blocks.

Two shimmering objects hammered Teimei's legs. He gasped and lowered his chin.

The fluted end of a glass dart jutted from each kneecap. Their blood-streaked tips pierced the back of his knees.

Teimei blinked, unable to fathom why he felt no—

Slag-hot pain incinerated his thigh muscles. It arced into his hips and spine, melting his bones.

He flopped onto his back. His mouth stretched. It didn't close again until his lungs had emptied, the scream amplified tenfold by the archway.

The form advanced, cacklebracking a guttural growl stripped of humanity. "I'd wager they heard your yowling inside the Center."

Teimei's vision grayed. Consciousness seeped away, then flared back on brilliant waves of saw-toothed pain. The form appeared above him, its eyes numb orbs behind a black helmet's slotted faceplate.

Beneath the agony, Teimei wondered how Zilian had ever wanted to be one of these *things*. "Cull me," he said. "For Sha's mercy, Jiren, cull me!"

"No, slag," the Jiren said, his tone almost melancholy. "I'm going to do far worse than that."

2

SPEAK OF THE UNUM

RESTLESS DENIZENS JOSTLED Daoren from all sides of the stairway's landing. He held his ground and cursed under his breath.

Over the last ten minutes, the approaching test had churned the sea of humanity into a simmering froth. Empty conversations bobbed along its surface; final words of advice from parents to their children, fervent petitions to Sha the Sapient for good fortune, frantic pleads for postponement of the inevitable.

A few prospects waded through the agitated waters in silence, gazing up at the Center. Most looked like they were encountering an apparition from their worst nightmare.

The Center dominated Zhongguo Cheng's administrative district like a festering boil on a fevered forehead. Constructed from cold-rolled crystal, the octagonal structure perched at the apex of eight terraced stairways. Two hundred years ago, designers had taken great pains to orient them to within one arc-second of the compass' cardinal and inter-cardinal points.

The purpose for the alignment escaped Daoren; the decisions of the Cognos Populi tended to defy logic. On their orders, the stairways had been built to equally exacting standards. They comprised eight flights, each measuring eighty steps high and eighty feet wide, and separated by generous horizontal landings. If the fixation on multiples of eight held special meaning for the old rulers of Daqin Guojin, it escaped him as well.

Panicky cries rang out near the upper archway. They broke over the lower flights like acidic waves on a sun-parched shoreline. Mako shrank at each one.

Daoren kept a watchful eye on his brother. If a prospect for denizenship was going to break, this was the moment.

The moment when reality could no longer be denied.

All prospects, regardless of wealth or lineage, had to sit the S.A.T. within one year of their nineteenth birthday. The edicts of the Cognos Populi granted an exception to those with mental or physical impairments. The small mercy was a hollow comfort for the few to whom it applied—they were culled upon the determination. Each year, five hundred-thousand prospects sat the test. Each year, half of them failed. For some, the one-in-two odds of survival proved too much to bear.

Another panicky cry drilled down the stairway, much closer than the others. Mako shuddered and released a whistling breath.

"Stay calm," Lucien said. "Do you have enough grooll?"

Mako patted the opaque pouch clipped to the receiver loops on his waist. Bruised knuckles marred the back of his hand.

Daoren eyed the swollen welts. Mako must have struck a solid object . . . and done so within the last twenty-four hours. "Your hand!"

Mako covered the bruises with his other hand. "It's nothing."

It wasn't nothing. A thousand snares could trip up a prospect during the S.A.T. Inadequate preparation and insufficient technological knowledge were the most common snags, but innocent physical ailments could also be fatal. A few years ago, a prospect with laryngitis had found it difficult to voice his answer confirmations. According to the cautionary tale, he wasted too many precious minutes on repeating muted *yeses* and *noes* and didn't complete the test. He failed by less than a thousand points.

The hand injury might hamper Mako's ability to manipulate the touch-screen inside the Center, but its further discussion served no purpose. It was too late to seek medical attention, and his brother had enough worries choking his mind. Cordelia had other ideas though.

"Let me see it," she said.

Mako muttered a brief protest before lifting his hand.

She peered down her nose at the welts. "How did you do this?"

"An accident. It doesn't hurt."

Cordelia kissed each angry knuckle.

Mako blushed and yanked his hand back. "I'm not a child!"

"You're my child and don't forget it. If you run out of grooll, seek the Libraria inside the Center. They can—"

"I have more than enough for the eight hours, Momma."

"You're certain?"

A throbbing drone drowned out Mako's response. Daoren craned his neck skyward.

A Jireni aeroshrike sailed overhead, one thousand feet high. Sunlight rippled off its black, ceramic-armor panels. Six contra-rotating airscrews, blade-like airfoils, and triple-barreled turrets fouled its streamlined shape. Two more aeroshrikes orbited a mile to the east, maneuvering among the Cheng's tallest structures. Their enormous gas envelopes blotted the sun.

Daoren grunted. The Jireni were showing their strength for a reason; they loathed crowds as well.

He glanced up the stairway, knowing they'd be up there. Sure enough, a dozen of them skulked in the archway's shadow.

The Jireni's black, studded chest plates and segmented body armor paid homage to the Terra-cotta warriors of antiquity. Their name harkened from the same time period. *Ji* referred to the dagger-axes once carried by Mother China's imperial armies.

Collectively, the men were known as *Jireni*—men with dagger-axes. The security force had long-since abandoned the weapon and broadened its ranks to men and women, but the name persisted like a chronic disease.

Today, each Jiren carried a crystalline dart gun. Its needlelike appendage fired eight-inch darts with a variable muzzle velocity of up to 3,200 feet-per-second. Flex-hoses connected the guns to conformal air packs on their backs. The packs held enough high-pressure air to fire two hundred darts. Depending on the skill of the Jiren, that could translate into as many as two hundred culls.

Daoren lifted his chin in their direction. "Will they also be inside the Center?"

"Never mind the Jireni, boy. They're only here to maintain order in case . . ." Lucien shifted his attention to Mako. "If you need anything once the test starts, look to the Libraria."

Cordelia cupped Mako's chin. Her finger traced the contours of a face she likely knew better than her own.

Daoren suppressed a pang of envy—when had she last touched *his* face like that? He couldn't recall, but one thing was certain. Mako's face honored obedience and brought harmony to the family. *His* face questioned everything under the swollen sun and cultivated discord. At times he forgot they were related.

Cordelia lowered her hand, the tracing complete. "This day has come too soon."

"As it comes for us all," Mako said.

"And once it's finished, you'll be a denizen," Lucien said.

A lone, violet stud glinted in the notch beneath his father's lower lip. As a young prospect, his face had boasted garish glass implants that pushed the limits of good taste—Daoren and his brother had rasplaughed many times at the old quantum images. Lucien opted for the single, sober stud twenty-five years ago when he ascended to the ruling caste; the Assembly of the Cognos Populi frowned on limit-pushing.

Daoren frowned on the ornamental custom. Unlike his family

and the other inhabitants of Daqin Guojin, he wore no implants. The habit reeked of superficiality. Years ago, prospects at the Librarium had offered him suggestions on stud shapes, patterns, and body placement. In time, they stopped. He'd abandoned them to embark on independent study when he was eight years old. Mako, on the other hand, had excelled under the tutelage of the Libraria, finishing at the top of his cohort thanks to his impressive prep-test scores.

"A *denizen*, Mako," Lucien continued. "Do you understand what that means?"

Daoren grunted anew. Of course his brother understood. For every prospect, passing the S.A.T. and attaining denizenship meant the right to life. For his father, it meant much more. Upward mobility in the city-state required two virtues; a stellar S.A.T. score and an obscene amount of grooll. Lucien had only the former, but if Mako received a high enough score to join the Cognos Populi he'd have a crucial advantage—a father in the Assembly to help lift him higher. Lucien had blathered about little else for the past six months.

"Score high enough and you may be in contention to become Unum one day."

"Lucien!" Cordelia said. "Let him concentrate on passing this damnable test first!"

Daoren rolled his eyes. "Even if he ignored half the questions he'd still pass, Cordelia. Maybe attain a perfect thirty thousand points if he's not careful."

Mako lunged forward. "I don't want to be Unum!"

The shove caught Daoren off-guard. He teetered on the edge of the landing, a hair's breadth from falling down the flight. For all his militant implants and truculent posturing, Mako never used physical force. Bruised knuckles and now this act of aggression? The stress of the S.A.T. must be playing havoc with his mind. Was he seeking confrontation as a means of distraction?

Daoren primed his muscles, keeping his intent hidden from his eyes, but a quivering hiss preempted his retaliatory shove.

On the transway at the base of the stairway, five bulky levitrans whisperglided to a stop. Red cupolas with flared, golden eaves etched their gloss-black doors; the Imperial Regalia of the Cognos Populi.

Unlike civilian levitrans, those of the regal fleet shunned teardrop hullforms in favor of brute protection. Anechoic wedges coated their outer skins. Their glossy finish masked a serious purpose; the wedges were designed to deflect kinetic blasts and absorb acoustic energy. Judging by the plumes of compressed air jetting from the gimbaled varinozzles, the vehicles countered their mass with far fewer hydrogen-infusion cells than their non-regal counterparts.

The compressed-air plumes thinned. The levitrans settled onto the transway.

The leading and trailing vehicles disgorged squads of armed Jireni. Red-and-gold regalia emblazoned their chest plates, marking them as members of the personal guard. They converged on the middle levitran and cordoned it off. One guard opened its rear door.

The Unum of the Cognos Populi hauled his bloated body out of the levitran. His purple *mianfu* strained mightily at the waist, but the eight layers of gleamglass garments played a minor role in producing the bulge. A stud-encrusted *zhaoshan* topped the layers, its side panels vented from ribs to thighs to enhance freedom of movement. Cropped hair revealed a bulbous skull that grew larger and redder by the day. Two pyramidal studs erupted from the Unum's forehead, positioned over each eye. He tended to change their color to suit the occasion. For some reason, today's S.A.T. warranted black.

"Speak of the Unum and he appears," Daoren said.

"*Quiet, boy!*" Lucien said, the words more growled than spoken.

Below, the Unum adjusted the red sash draping his chest. He positioned its embroidered gold cupola over his heart and waved. A smarmy smile softened his brittle Slavvic features. Behind him, a prospect exited the levitran.

The prospect's aura of aloofness earned a snort of disdain from Daoren. Although Julinian wore a white pienfu to signify her social status, its luster indicated it wasn't the itchy burrglass variety that swaddled her cohorts. Her coiffed hair confirmed another difference; wealth and lineage allowed her the occasional styling without fear of punishment. Her belly also suggested she never ran short of her monthly grooll ration. Every nuance of the Unum's niece reeked of privilege, but none was as offensive to the senses as her smug bearing.

Surrounded by his Jireni guard, the Unum led Julinian up the stairway. The masses parted. Most bowed with spineless admiration, others with unthinking obedience. A rare few offered stunted nods, making little effort to conceal their contempt.

A minute later, the regal entourage halted before Daoren and his family. Lucien, Cordelia, and Mako folded at the waist in unison, bowing so low they could have kissed the Unum's knees if they'd chosen. Daoren dipped his chin while they groveled.

"Survival through sapience, Unum," Lucien said after he straightened.

The Unum pulled him closer until they touched foreheads. "And to you, Lucien." He flashed his version of a winning smile. "Cordelia, you look as lovely as ever despite the circumstances. Your Mako sits the S.A.T. today?"

Cordelia answered with a fretful nod.

"As does Julinian." The Unum gripped Mako's shoulder. "It's good to know she'll have such intelligent company inside the Center. How do you feel, boy? Confident?"

Mako's head bobbled. His glassy eyes remained static.

Daoren cringed at his brother's timid posture. He shifted his focus to Julinian.

Purple implants outlined her lips, extending their corners to the outer limb of each eye. The pattern gave her smile a disturbing prognostic quality—like she could see into the future. Her smugness persisted until a biting squeal made her flinch.

On the flight above, the crowd edged away from an Indonoid prospect. The girl struggled to break the grip of an older Indonoid denizen. "I can't do it, Papa! I'm not ready!"

The father grabbed his daughter by both arms and shook her. "If you try to run they'll cull you!"

She warped her body from side to side. The convulsions threw her father off-balance. She squirmed free and bolted down the steps.

Prospects and denizens gave her room to pass. The gesture had nothing to do with courtesy.

Fifty feet above her, a Jiren hoisted his dart gun. He pressed its crystalline stock into his shoulder and steadied his aim.

Three glass darts spat from the gun's muzzle. They streaked arrow-straight down the flight and pierced the girl's back.

"*Nnnnnnnn . . .*"

The girl launched forward, clearing a dozen steps before thudding onto the stairway. She tumbled downward, legs pinwheeling, sandals sailing into the air, before coming to rest on the landing separating the two flights. Her dying moans drifted over the crowd's murmurs. They blended with her father's tortured cries.

Whether either heard the other, Daoren didn't know, but the girl wouldn't be harvested. Grooll production required sanitary deaths. The father would have to pay for her body's disposal, a service that might cost more than a year's grooll ration depending on his vocation.

The Jiren on the upper flight lowered his dart gun. "Any prospect who attempts to evade the edicts will be dealt with as a dissenter!" he said, addressing the crowd. "Don't repeat her mistake! Remain calm, sit your test, and place your trust in Sha."

The Indonoid father stumbled down the steps to his daughter. He wavered over her body, hands wringing a sand-tone shenyi embroidered with gold, corkscrew-shaped columns. The garment's embroidery and quality suggested he was a senior silica engineer—the body's disposal would likely claim less than two months' worth of his grooll ration. He crumpled to his knees and rocked his daughter in his arms. The dart tips jutting from her chest complicated the act.

The Unum released a drawn-out sigh. "Every year we lose more prospects before they sit the test."

"Maybe the Cognos Populi should stop raising the passing score," Daoren said.

Lucien's face paled to the color of shock-fused ceramic, but the barb didn't earn a verbal rebuke. It stung the Unum into speaking though.

"It isn't something we take lightly, Daoren. We only raise the passing score to make up for grooll shortfalls."

"Yet millions still live on the cusp of starvation. Why is that?"

"Enough, boy!" Lucien said. "Please forgive him, Unum. He knows not what he—"

"Narses is the same age," the Unum said. "I'm well acquainted with the impudence of youth." He sized up Daoren, eyes glinting like glass darts. "You've applied to sit the May S.A.T.?"

Daoren sized up the Unum. The man had a habit of turning factual statements into questions. He used the tactic to pull sensitive information from people. He also used it to test whether they'd tell him what he already knew to be true.

Daoren had applied to sit the test in May—Lucien must have mentioned it to the Unum in passing—but didn't see the need to confirm it. As the son of a member of the Cognos Populi, he'd been in the Unum's presence often enough to know that silence was the best answer.

"Perhaps I'll take your advice on the passing score," the Unum said. "For your sake."

"No need."

"Oh? You're a genius like your brother?"

"Just well prepared," Daoren said.

Gruff laughter shook the Unum's belly. "Such a spirited boy! Now if you'll excuse me, I need to speak with Julinian before she goes into the Center."

"I'd wager you would," Daoren said, censoring a smile. Julinian was as thick as the crystal columns gracing the Center's façade. The fid's odds of surviving the S.A.T. were slimmer than the most malnourished inhabitants of Daqin Guojin.

"Of course, of course," Lucien said, oozing the irritating eagerness he reserved for the Unum. "Good fortune this day, Julinian."

The smug fid ignored the platitude and plodded off with her uncle. Daoren caught a foul look from his father before it freshened and shifted to Mako.

"You'd best get inside now," Lucien said, taking Mako's hands. They leaned together and touched foreheads. "I am your father."

"And I am your son," Mako said, voice breaking.

Cordelia clutched Mako's hands and gazed upon her firstborn. Her eyes welled.

Next to the prospects, the S.A.T. was hardest on the mothers. Many refused to attend their children's tests, leaving it to the fathers to bear the emotional burden. Whatever her past failings, Daoren admired Cordelia's strength for being here—even when her tears flowed.

She touched her forehead to Mako's. "I am your mother."

"And I . . . I am your son."

Daoren squared off with Mako and pushed him backward. The challenge wasn't a delayed retribution for the earlier shove; it was meant to rally his brother's inner strength.

The tactic failed. Mako swiped away his own tears, sniffling.

Daoren masked his pity and leaned in to touch foreheads. Mako held on to a rigid, upright posture, leaving him hanging. Daoren raised his head and stared into his brother's eyes.

They brimmed red with raw emotion, but which emotion he couldn't put a finger on. Was it anger? Resentment? Jealousy? Was it *his* fault Mako had to sit this damnable test today? His own S.A.T. was four months away, then it would be Mako's turn to watch *him* sweat.

"Mako, trade farewell with Daoren."

Daoren bristled at his mother's intervention—ever the peacemaker—but her gentle goading worked. Mako leaned forward.

Daoren leaned the rest of the way to make the connection. "I am your brother."

"And I am your brother," Mako said, forcing the words through his teeth like crystalline bricks. He broke contact and trudged up the stairway.

Daoren watched him pass families engaged in the same ritual of farewell—and the Indonoid father still rocking his daughter's dead body. Beyond the pair, weeping parents and siblings looked on while their kin climbed toward the darkened archway. Other parents had to drag their children up the steps.

The prospects clawed, kicked, and screamed all the way.

3

THE JANUARY S.A.T.

MAKO EMERGED FROM the archway and halted beneath the brightest light he'd ever encountered. Despite fifteen years of preparation, countless interactions with high-fidelity plasmonic reconstructions, and numberless hours of visualization therapy, stepping into the Center for the first time culled his breath.

This was real.

This was happening.

This was his S.A.T.

Climbing the northern stairway, he'd thought only of finding Teimei, Bushudo, and Zilian before finding his seat. He wanted no more than a brief encounter with his friends and enough time to wish them good fortune. The sight before him smashed that hope and slammed home the scale of the coming challenge.

A translucent floor supported forty thousand transparent seats arrayed in a two-hundred-by-two-hundred grid. Eight feet separated each row and each seat to prevent sneakcheating. Tens of thousands of prospects, Jireni, and Libraria filled the void spaces, venting a burble of tense chatterwailing, curt commands, and calm reassurances. Above them, cubic chronoglyphs strobed below the enormous convex ceiling. Their square, blue faces identified row numbers.

Mako picked his way forward, threading pockets of weeping prospects. Hundreds more filtered through the eight archways encircling the floor. Jireni corralled the ones who tarried or succumbed to emotion and dragged them to their seats. He refused to suffer that indignity. He'd find his seat on his own, as would any man worthy of denizenship.

It didn't take long. He'd been assigned Seat 12 in Row 110 upon his application to sit the test. It was located in a central row, favoring the floor's north end. Red letters floated over its integrated touch-screen.

Mako al Lucien.

He gazed at the hovering name, entranced by its naked luminance.

This was real.

Every drop of saliva in his mouth evaporated.

This was happening.

His heart's accelerating contractions pummeled his eardrums.

This was his S.A.T.

The floor seemed to split open and swallow him.

Mako clutched the seat-back. A vague clot of dread thickened, congealing to the certainty of impending doom. The primal urge to flee the Center, to remove himself from the environment, threatened to overcome his reason.

He couldn't let it win. He needed to fight through the panic. He needed to—

"Are you Mako al Lucien?"

He spun to the gruff voice.

A Slavvic Jiren towered over him. Crosshatched scars and menacing black studs blighted the brute's jaw and eye sockets.

His heart rate doubled. He tried to respond—he *wanted* to respond as a man worthy of denizenship—but his desiccated tongue couldn't form the words.

The Jiren leveled her dart gun. She stabbed its muzzle into his chest. "Are you Mako al Lucien?"

"Y-y-yes."

She thrust the dart gun forward. "Then for Sha's sake, sit."

Mako keeled backward. He grabbed the touch-screen and swung into the seat with a jolting *oomph.*

The Jiren secured flexglass restraining straps around his chest and legs, anchoring him in place, but leaving his arms free. She detached a halo from the back of the touch-screen and waggled it. "Don't forget your crown, my princeling."

The halo inched down his forehead, stopping in line with his temples. Ten ounces of hardened glass compressed his skin. It felt more like ten pounds.

The Jiren cinched the chest strap tighter and straightened with a joyless smile. "Only one way out of this seat now, prospect." She slung her dart gun. "Oh, and don't remove the halo before the test ends and the restraints unlock, unless you *want* to set off the nanocharges in your head."

The brute cacklebracked and lumbered away.

Mako sucked shallow, rapid breaths, struggling to draw air past the chest strap. A familiar taste fouled his mouth, scorched and toxic. Tingling pinpricks numbed his hands and feet, divorcing them from his body.

He squeezed his eyes shut. He needed to slow his breathing. He needed to calm his—

"By Sha's silica fingers, if it isn't Mako al Lucien!"

Mako opened his eyes.

A craggy Asianoid face loomed above him. Silver-gray studs extended each eyebrow. They swept up and over the temples of a shorn scalp, lending an air of unbounded curiosity. A wispy gray beard veiled the lapels of a yellow *lanshan* tunic.

Mako knew the face—he *knew* he knew the face—but the name took an eternity to pass his lips. "Laoshi."

Laoshi's smile hiked his beard off his lapels. "So quickly this day arrives, my young pupil. So much at stake."

Mako swallowed. His throat burned slag-hot.

"Did Heqet wish you good fortune before you came inside?"

Mako shook his head. The motion served to remind him of the glass halo circling his cranium. "She didn't come."

Laoshi's smile dimmed. "She locked herself in her sleeping chamber when she returned from your abode last night. No amount of my coaxing could draw her out again. I trust there's no problem between you two."

Mako tried to voice an articulate answer. The partition erected between his mind and mouth prevented one. "I don't . . . she isn't . . . we aren't—"

"It's none of my concern," Laoshi said, waving off the stammering response. His smile rekindled, lighting up his eyes. "Did I mention I've been studying a most fascinating collection of artifacts?"

"Um . . . no."

"An incredible find. A silica-sourcing team discovered the cache in the Great Eastern Regolith, six months ago. Can you guess what it contained?"

Mako stammered anew. Laoshi had the vexing habit of injecting random, unanswerable questions into his meandering, free-flow conversations.

"Artifacts made from carbon-based synthetic polymers," Laoshi said, not waiting for a guess. "They have the highest molecular mass of any synthetic polymers ever encountered. And despite being exposed to the elements, they show remarkable resistance to decay."

"They weren't cryocached?"

"No, boy. They were buried under six hundred feet of compacted sand."

"That's, um . . . fascinating."

"Such wondrous resources the ancients possessed to

construct their world, hmm? How limited ours seem in comparison."

"If life gives you sand . . ."

"Make glass," Laoshi said, completing the famous dictum. He leaned over and leveled a hypnotic stare. "That's excellent advice, isn't it?"

Mako nodded, grasping the anecdote's point. The old Librarian was telling him to make the best of an ill situation.

"Remember my teachings and trust your instincts." Laoshi straightened and tousled Mako's hair. "And before you know it, this mop will be a memory."

"You promise?"

"I'll see you after the test," he said, winking. "Your parents, Daoren, Heqet—we'll celebrate your denizenship together."

Laoshi advanced up the aisle, pace brisk in spite of his limp. He paused here and there to comfort distraught prospects.

Mako focused inward and cycled through his self-checks. The tightness in his chest had eased. The numbness in his extremities had faded. The depth of his respirations had increased. Laoshi's calming manner and distracting anecdote had worked; the panic attack had subsided. Seeking any diversion to keep the anxiety at bay, he absorbed the setting.

An equal split of male and female prospects resided in his vicinity, heads crowned with glass halos. The majority were Asianoids from Zhongguo Cheng or the eastern districts. The second-largest contingent boasted darker skin tones that pointed to Indonoid and Africoid lineage; they'd harken from Yindu Cheng and Feizhou Cheng, the city-state's southernmost districts. A handful with Slavvic features hailed from Nansilafu Cheng or the other northern districts. He recognized no other prospects from Meiguo Cheng in the immediate area.

Different lineages, different Chengs.

The lesson had been pounded into his head at the Librarium. Daqin Guojin embraced the whole of civilized humanity, but held it in segregated districts that fostered little intermixing.

Meiguo Cheng occupied a nine-square-mile footprint within the borders of Zhongguo Cheng, making it more like an island canton than an independent district. Ringed by four million Asianoids of the city-state's most populous Cheng, Mako and his family were among sixty thousand Caucasoids who charted their origins to a nation that once existed in the west, across a body of water whose vastness eclipsed the Sea of Storms. The ancients had called it the Atlantic Ocean. Today, it was a sterile, acidic expanse whose name escaped him.

A smaller, acidic expanse gurgled, demanding his attention. Mako slipped his hand into his waist pouch and pulled out a piece of grooll.

He squeezed the springy torus between his fingers, reassured by its gritty texture and flesh-tone hue. He popped the piece into his mouth and let it sit on his tongue, allowing what saliva he could muster to break the bonds between the powdered silica and bitter macronutrients.

An uneasy flutter buffeted the walls of his heart.

The macronutrients had been harvested from prospects who once occupied these same seats.

The flutter intensified and spread to his lungs.

Whose flesh, bone, and tendon was he sucking on?

Mako extinguished the thought before it flashed into another attack. He refocused on the surrounding prospects.

Most had their eyes closed, lips moving as though offering petitions to Sha, the Sapient, Heuristic, and Adaptive. Some wept, stifling sobs with their hands. One prospect seated three rows away was the picture of serenity.

Julinian yawned, hands folded atop her touch-screen like an elder riding a levishuttle on a hazy summer night.

He shook his head. How could she be so calm? You'd think she was—

A soothing, maternal voice filled the Center. *"Welcome, prospects. Your Survival Aptitude Test will commence in one minute. A score of twenty-two thousand points is required to pass and confer upon you the rights of denizenship."*

Despairing groans escaped the adjacent prospects. The morose chorus swelled and resounded off the ceiling.

Mako sucked a breath to fend off the icy tongues licking at his fingers. Daoren had spoken the truth—the passing score had been raised by two thousand points. Why had his parents denied it? Why hadn't his father warned him before he was strapped into a transparent seat, head girded with a halo of conductive glass?

The icy tongues lapped his hands and slathered his forearms. Mako lowered his gaze to his bruised knuckles. Fixating on a single point sometimes helped to mute the anxiety. "Focus . . . focus . . . focus . . ." He flexed the hand, making a fist, and repeated the mantra in his head.

He could do this.

He could write a stellar S.A.T.

He could prove to Heqet that he was Daoren's equal.

The technique worked. His nerves relaxed, freeing his mind from their all-powerful grip. He raised his head, took another deep breath, and found Julinian staring back at him.

She smirked, as calm as before, but her bestudded, upturned lips carried another emotion.

It took a moment for Mako to recognize it.

Smugness.

MAKO SWIPED HIS forehead and looked up from his touch-screen.

Thousands of prospects manipulated their own screens, faces frozen in concentration. A few buried their heads in their hands and wept. Knots of Jireni hurled taunts at them, encouraged by their colleagues' cacklebracking. Libraria strolled the aisles, but none stopped to defend the prospects. Above them, the chrono-glyphs relayed a countdown. Blood-red digits ticked off the seconds.

04:00:56 . . . 04:00:55 . . . 04:00:54. . . .

Mako lowered his gaze and ran a finger across the touch-screen, skimming the eighth set of equations. He tapped the screen; another set of equations opened. As he proofed the solu-tion, a chucklebuck shook his body. He knew there'd be a ques-tion on Zhaoling's Fractal Conjecture for Shadow Analysis on the test.

Why the archaic method for determining latitude and longi-tude using localized dune shadows was considered valuable tech-nological knowledge in modern times wasn't his concern. He simply needed to make sure he'd selected the right datum and sun angle and calculated the correct dune heights—accurate to seven decimal places—to earn the two hundred points assigned to the question.

His finger traced the last line. Another tap brought up a new screen.

Submit Answer?

Mako flexed his hands. For the hundredth time today, he asked the question. Was he sure? For the hundredth time today, he gulped a spine-bracing breath. "Yes."

A new question opened on the touch-screen, its glut of text too compact to take in all at once. He glanced up at the nearest chronoglyph.

04:00:02 . . . 04:00:01 . . . 04:00:00. . . .

The maternal voice filled the Center. *"Four hours remaining."*

He refocused on the screen and scanned the question. It listed five endothermic processes used for sintering liquid hydrogen from low-pH water and asked for a rigorous proof of which was most efficient. The last line triggered a shiver.

The question was allotted thirty minutes and worth nine hundred points.

———

TWO WORDS FLOATED over the touch-screen.

Test Complete.

Mako smeared his hands against his face, rubbing them up and down and back and forth, massaging away eight hours of stress. He plucked a piece of grooll from his waist pouch and placed it onto his tongue. A smile formed while he chewed.

After nineteen years, eleven months, and six days of preparation, it was over.

A mouthful of grooll couldn't block the mirth bubbling up from his belly. Its effervescence jetted from his nose.

Not only was it over, *it was easy.* The four prep-tests he'd completed last year had been much harder. Laoshi had prepared him well.

He searched the floor for his tutor, but the restraining straps restricted his movement and limited his field of view. No matter; they'd soon be celebrating his denizenship together.

Another bout of rasplaughter rocked his body. Heqet would change her mind once she learned of his score! It had to be at least twenty-nine thousand points out of the thirty-thousand maximum. None of his prep-tests over the past five years were any lower.

With such a stellar result, he'd be guaranteed entry into the Cognos Populi. He'd also earn the right to union, unlimited reproduction, a private abode, an abundant grooll ration, and much more. Filtered through that shining lens, Heqet would see him anew. She'd realize what a glinty life they could build together.

The maternal voice revived its soothing strains. "*The Survival Aptitude Test concludes in five, four, three, two, one . . .*"

Forty thousand touch-screens turned black, triggering a crescendo of anguished howls. A few nearby prospects wore satisfied smiles. Most exhibited crushing tension, their foreheads scored like wind-rippled dunes. Two rows away, an Africoid girl tore at her restraining straps, spittle spraying from her mouth. Her test obviously hadn't gone well.

Beyond the spastic prospect, Julinian's posture displayed perfect serenity until she caught sight of Mako. Serenity morphed to smugness with a curl of her lips.

"Now tabulating scores."

Mako left Julinian to her smugness and stared at his touch-screen, taut with anticipation. It flared to life, dousing him in blood-red light.

. . . FAIL . . .

. . . FAIL . . .

. . . FAIL . . .

The single word strobed, scribed in grotesque red letters. Below it, an accusing score flickered.

9,462.

Mako squeezed his eyes shut. What in Sha's name was happening? He rattled his head, trying to shake loose the misfiring neural connection playing tricks with his vision. He opened his eyes with deliberate slowness.

The *FAIL* strobed as before. The score flickered, unchanged. It wasn't a trick. It was—

A joyous whoop penetrated the muddling fog.

Three rows away, Julinian thrust her arms toward the ceiling. Her glass halo projected an interlaced white globe around her head. The globe scintillated with blue, inward-directed light pulses. Her hair vaporized in a smokeless flash, leaving black stubble in its place.

Throughout the Center, thousands of restraining straps unlocked with a double-click. Julinian and legions of close-cropped denizens sprang to their feet and rushed for the archways, sandals slapping the floor. Their shouts faded, exposing the pleas of the failing prospects still anchored to their seats.

Mako didn't cry out. He could barely breathe.

There had to be a mistake. He'd answered every question, proofed every answer, verified every proof. Failure wasn't possible. It wasn't possible. It—

"—isn't possible!"

His shout echoed in the half-empty Center. Libraria ambled toward the archways. None glanced his way.

"Tarry!" he called to them. "There's been a mistake! I know I passed!"

A voice rumbled behind him. "Time to leave, old man, lest you want to join him on his journey."

Mako reefed his head to the side.

Laoshi stood next to the seat. A bewildered gaze erased every sign of warm curiosity from his face.

"This can't be happening!" Mako said. "I remembered your teachings and trusted my instincts! I answered every question!"

Laoshi touched Mako's hair. "There's nothing I can do, boy."

The Slavvic Jiren with the scarred jaw strode into view. She aimed her dart gun at Laoshi. "You can leave before you're harvested, Primae Librarian. That's one thing you can do."

"No! Don't leave!"

"I'm so sorry, Mako."

"Don't leave me here! Please!"

Laoshi limped toward the nearest archway. The Jiren trailed him by two paces until they disappeared.

Mako and twenty-thousand hysterical failures had the Center to themselves. A subtle, almost subliminal whir wafted through the air, growing louder by the second. Lights recessed into the ceiling grew dimmer by the second, power draining in tandem.

The skin on the back of his neck dimpled. Nearby prospects thrashed in their seats, prying at their restraining straps. A few wrenched off their glass halos—ruddy mist erupted from their ears and eyes. Their heads lolled forward, chins flopping onto blood-stained lapels.

He lost control of his bladder. Involuntary spasms huffed his chest.

The whir reached the amplitude of a thunderclap, drowning out the screaming. Light bled away, occulting the terror etched on the surrounding faces.

Mako voiced the one thought he had left. "I don't want to be harvested! I don't want to be harvested! I don't—"

An almighty zap pierced the darkness.

Ferocious heat coursed through his temples, then—

OUTSIDE THE CENTER, Daoren watched from a new vantage point while thousands of ecstatic, newly ordained denizens reunited with their families.

Over the eight-hour vigil, he and his parents had picked their way up the northern stairway. They'd stopped on the landing beneath the uppermost flight, eighty vertical feet below the darkened archway, when the first wave of survivors gushed from its yawning mouth.

The wave had since slowed to a trickle. Above and around him, delirious fathers and mothers embraced their children, rubbing their cropped scalps and kissing their tear-stained cheeks. Other childless parents searched the throng, crumbling faces registering their worst fears.

Two steps below, Lucien and Cordelia scanned. Cordelia clutched Lucien's tunic. Her white-knuckled fingers crumpled its gleamglass fabric. "Where is he? Where's my Mako?"

A skirmish line of Jireni formed outside the archway. They donned helmets and lowered their faceplates. An unheard order brought their dart guns to the ready position across their chest plates, muzzles raised at a forty-five-degree angle.

Crystalline shards needled Daoren's gut. Mako should have come out by now.

He turned to his parents. "He may have come out another archway," he said, neutralizing his expression and filtering his words to remove any signs of worry. "You know what he's like when he's under stress."

Cordelia grabbed onto the suggestion as tightly as Lucien's tunic. "Yes! We should check the other exits. Check all of them until we—"

Lucien's moan cut her off. He pointed up the stairway, hand trembling. "Look to Laoshi."

Daoren tracked his father's trembling hand up to the archway where Laoshi lingered behind the line of Jireni.

The old Librarian's gaze locked onto Daoren. His eyes communicated a solitary, unmistakable emotion.

Remorse.

Crystalline shards shredded Daoren's gut. No . . . no . . . no. . . .

"No . . . no . . . no . . ." Cordelia whispered behind him, mirroring his thoughts. "This can't be. This can't be!"

Enraged shouts punched down the stairway. At the top of the upper flight, ranks of grief-torn parents surged toward the skirmish line. The Jireni aimed their dart guns at the mob.

Molten glass flushed Daoren's veins. The muscles in his legs hardened, ready to propel him up the steps. His hands curled into fists, ready to strike. A singular impulse burned slag-hot in the most primitive part of his brain. *Join them.* This injustice called for—

An azure figure streaked past him.

"Cordelia!" Lucien said. "Stay here!"

Daoren blinked. Two precious seconds passed before he realized the azure figure was his mother . . . and she was rushing up the stairway to join the mob. He bolted after her.

Above, the mob advanced toward the archway, fists shaking, shouts taunting. The Jireni issued no warnings.

A fusillade of razor-sharp darts tore into a wall of unprotected flesh. Impaled denizens pitched backward and toppled down the flight. Innocent onlookers gathered below the mob collapsed and screamed, struck by stray darts.

Daoren's sandals pounded the steps. He leaned forward, hand outstretched to snag Cordelia's billowing tunic. His fingers brushed its fabric.

She veered to the side, skirting a cartwheeling body. He leaped to clear the tumbling form.

His foot struck a lifeless limb—he thudded face-down on the steps. He raised his head, dazed and winded.

Cordelia barreled at the Jireni as if intent on suicide. The Jireni trained their weapons, ready to oblige her.

Daoren planted his feet and pushed off. He mounted three steps at a time, arms and legs pumping, muscles searing.

The Jireni triggered their weapons. A volley of percussive reports rippled down the flight. A lethal grouping of darts homed in on Cordelia's chest.

Daoren dived forward. His hands found the back of her shenyi and clamped on, dragging her onto the steps.

The darts flashed overhead. Their supersonic shockwaves crackled, caressing his cheek.

He covered Cordelia with his body, one hand raised to the line of Jireni. "I have her! Hold your fire! Hold your fire!"

The Jireni held their fire.

Daoren lowered his hand and rolled to the side, fighting for air. Lucien arrived seconds later, pale and gasping. He fell with a wrenching groan next to Cordelia. They buried their faces in each other's tunics, wet sobs bursting from their mouths.

Daoren had to look away.

Down the blood-spattered stairway, the Unum and Julinian sauntered toward the regal fleet, laughing and well clear of the carnage. They climbed into the middle levitran. Their Jireni guard clambered into the other vehicles. The fleet whisperglided away.

Daoren's numb gaze swept over a mass of impaled denizens. Asianoids, Indonoids, Africoids, Caucasoids—the glass darts hadn't discriminated in their gruesome harvest. His parents' wails blended with those whose kin lay dead or dying.

A harmony of hopelessness.

The stench stung his eyes. He grunted to release the pressure constricting his throat.

It didn't work. The one certain cure was crying, but he'd long since forgotten how to invoke his tears thanks to Daqin Guojin's ruling caste and humanity's future.

Another grunt echoed behind him. He twisted to the archway.

Laoshi stood there still. His sullen nod acknowledged Daoren and perhaps reflected the same painful condition.

4

SPARRING

D AOREN SPUN TO the left and raised the staff with both hands, careful to align his palms with its knurled grips.

Fifteen minutes of air-sparring in his abode's courtyard had generated a slick sheen of sweat. The last thing he needed was to send a twelve-pound, combat-hardened glass rod sailing through the door leading into the parlor. He took a wide-legged stance and chose his target—an imaginary head four feet away.

To whom the head belonged changed depending on his mood. On one day it might be a brutish Jiren who'd detained him for biometric scanning. On another it might be a pompous Librarian who'd long ago dismissed his ideas. Some days it was his father's imperious head, conjured up in the aftermath of a heated argument. Other days it was the Unum's, but not today.

Today's imaginary head belonged to the Unum's niece.

The staff's beveled tip carved a semi-circle. Daoren checked the swing after it passed the point in space where Julinian's suitably smug jawline resided. He spread his hands apart and hoisted the staff to a blocking position. Without pausing, he crouched and raked the staff outward at knee level.

He repeated the fluid pattern until shortness of breath forced him to stop. The pause gave him an opportunity to stretch; a week of inactivity had left his muscles tight.

A week had passed since Mako's harvesting. For seven days he'd observed the customs expected of a grieving family member. For seven days he'd worn a mourning shroud, offered the requisite petitions, avoided physical activity, and fasted.

Today he returned to living on his own terms. A white pienfu once again chaffed his skin, Sha was pushed to the dark recesses of his mind, and he was back to his daily sparring routine. The one routine he hadn't resumed was eating; a casual glance at the urns of grooll in the pantry thirty minutes ago had soured his stomach. He'd retreated to the courtyard, eager to convert exercise into appetite.

Recovered, he launched into an eight-move defensive *taolu* designed for multiple opponents, maximizing his use of the courtyard. Its frosted-glass walls blocked the outside world and muffled the mid-day din of Meiguo Cheng. Their height and alignment let morning sunlight flood the twenty-by-twenty enclosure, but provided welcome shade in the afternoon. It was his favorite place in Daqin Guojin; four hundred square-feet of ceramic-tiled tranquility.

Today its tranquility competed with a mosaic of disturbing echoes from a week earlier.

Mako's sullen words.

The Indonoid prospect's dying gargles.

The Jireni's blood-soaked volleys.

His parents' sobs.

Julinian's callous laughter.

Daoren stumbled, mid-pivot. The sparring staff's whirling tip clipped a wall; its stinging vibrations focused his attention onto the most troubling echo.

Julinian's smug look had been bothering him all week. Why would a prospect with such obvious intellectual shortcomings, moments away from sitting the S.A.T., show such an obvious lack of concern for her fate?

He lowered the staff, chest heaving. Maybe she'd concealed her concern, adopting a brave face to mask a cowering heart. While possible, the explanation rang false. Julinian was brash and prideful, but not so much that she could overcome the fear of her imminent death. It would have shown itself in other ways, divulging telltale signs.

He leaned on the staff, gaze tacked onto the tan tiles beneath his sandals. But what if she felt no fear? What if she'd known she was destined to pass *despite* her shortcomings, no matter the tally of her final score? If that was the case, it raised a more distressing question.

How did she know?

The sun-drenched courtyard held no answers nor tranquility. He turned to the parlor door.

Inside the parlor, Lucien and Cordelia inhabited opposite sides of a square table. Both wore mourning shrouds. The sheer fabric dulled the sheen of their shenyi. Their faces cast an equally gray pall. Crystal tongs, bowls, and cups glinted atop flex-glass napkins set before the four chairs surrounding the table.

Daoren set the staff against a wall and entered the parlor. Suffocating heat struck him—the inductive panels embedded in the walls had been activated. "May I switch off the panels?"

"Your mother's cold."

"That's because she hasn't eaten."

"She can't eat."

Daoren wasn't surprised. The sparring routine hadn't sparked his appetite; Mako's harvesting was still too fresh. "It's been seven days. Are you going to remove your shrouds?"

"Soon," Lucien said.

Cordelia fingered her shroud. Her statuesque face showed signs of severe erosion.

Daoren couldn't deny that his mother's physical and

emotional qualities resembled a living statue. The physical quality had figured into Lucien's decision to ask for her hand in union, twenty-three years ago. *It wasn't for your dowry*, was his standard response whenever she asked why he'd chosen her. Lucien usually smiled when he said it. Cordelia, more often than not, rolled her eyes.

At the moment, her sunken eyes reflected boundless pain, but —as Daoren knew too well—her personality muted her ability to share it.

"We've been talking," Lucien said after an uncomfortably warm silence.

"About what?"

"About you returning to the Librarium."

"Why would I do that?"

"To complete your tutelage before your S.A.T."

Daoren snorted. "I don't need the help of the Libraria to pass."

"You can't take that chance!" Cordelia said, flaring to life. "I won't lose another son to that damnable test!"

"I'm not going to fail, Cordelia. You've seen my prep-tests results. They—"

"Mako's prep-tests were stellar," Lucien said. "There's more to passing the S.A.T. than technological knowledge."

Sweat tracked down Daoren's forehead, rimming his eyebrows. He wiped it away with his sleeve. "I have all the tools I need. There's nothing the Libraria can teach me."

"They can impart techniques that maximize the chances of success," Lucien said. "Techniques to handle stress, manage time, and more."

"What use were they to Mako?" Daoren asked.

The question bounced off the parlor's tiled walls. It grew hotter with each reflection.

Cordelia smothered a sob. Lucien flexed his hands as though grappling with the reality in which they now lived. "You're going back to the Librarium," he said, hurling the pronouncement across the table like an inflexible edict. "That's the end of it!"

For seven days Daoren had bottled his rage over Mako's death. His father's dictatorial stance and the parlor's oppressive temperature combined to uncap it. "Why didn't you tell Mako before the test?"

"Tell him what?"

"That the Cognos Populi had raised the passing score! Maybe it upset him enough to ruin his focus! Maybe you're to blame for his failure!"

The violet stud quivered beneath Lucien's lower lip. "You think I would have kept it from him if I'd known?"

The tortured response appeared to be aimed more at Cordelia. She must have been asking him the same question since learning of the raised score from Laoshi.

"How could you not know?" Daoren asked.

Lucien's mouth twisted. "The Assembly didn't raise the score."

"What?"

"The Unum raised it . . . on his own."

"He can do that?"

"He's the Unum."

Daoren sank into his chair with a jarring *oomph*. The jolt to his mind was just as violent.

Even the dimmest prospects knew the Unum was the most powerful man in Daqin Guojin, but none would suspect he had the power to raise the S.A.T.'s passing score without consulting the Assembly. What else could he do without their knowledge?

"And Julinian?" Daoren asked.

"What of her?"

"She receives a passing score?"

"She's the Unum's niece."

"So?"

Lucien averted his gaze. "So she's subject to a different set of rules."

The dots fell into place like waypoints on a plasmonic map. The conclusion they led to culled Daoren's breath. "You don't think the Unum manipulated the test scores..."

"Don't even suggest it, boy!"

"I'm not saying he manipulated them with his own hands, but what if he arranged for them to be switched between Mako and Julinian?"

"No son of mine would dare speak such heresy!"

Cordelia reached for Lucien's hand. "Tread carefully, Lucien."

Daoren stabbed a finger into the table. "It's the only explanation that makes sense. The Unum must have—"

Lucien hammered his fist into the table. The crystal abodewares rattled. "Leave it alone!"

Cordelia flinched and drew her hand back.

"How can you say that?" Daoren asked. "We're talking about the sanctity of the S.A.T.! We're talking about Mako's life!"

Lucien craned forward. Veins bulged over his temples "I said leave it alone, damn you!"

The shout struck with the force of a sparring staff. The parlor's heated walls shrank inward, squeezing the oxygen from Daoren's lungs. Numbness invaded his fingers and advanced up his arms. He searched for a focal point on which to fix his attention. His gaze found the abodewares across the table.

Mako's place setting.

Lucien placed his hand atop Cordelia's. They sat in silence, heads bowed by grief, hands clasped before a set of tongs, a bowl, a cup, and a flexglass napkin that would never be used again.

Sweat trickled into Daoren's eyes. He squeezed them shut and focused on his breathing to dampen the tremors of anxiety wracking his body.

The last thing he'd do was leave it alone.

LAOSHI ROCKED BACK and forth in his chair in the Temple's parlor. Movement eased the numbness in his lower back and the ache in his right knee; the remnants of old wounds, aggravated by sitting for prolonged periods. For the past seven days he'd done little else but focus on the quantum tile embedded in his desk's glass surface.

The tile air-linked to the data repositories below the Spires. They stored the quantum images, genetic sequences, scroll-access records, prep-test results, S.A.T. scores, and patterns of movement of millions of prospects. The data's collection had been facilitated by the spintronic diodes injected behind the eardrums of every inhabitant born in Daqin Guojin since 669 A.C.E.

He traced a finger across the tile, scanning a dataset. It belonged to Bushudo alum Ventis, an Asianoid prospect from Riben Cheng near the Eastern Sea. She was one of a dozen of Heqet's friends who hadn't survived the January S.A.T., albeit not due to failing the test.

Born in 681 A.C.E., Bushudo had spent most of her waking life on the grounds of the Librarium in Zhongguo Cheng according to her pattern of movement. That was typical. Although situated in Daqin Guojin's most heavily patrolled district, the Librarium represented a rare haven for prospects. A sacred edict separating the functions of rule from the functions of sapience prevented Jireni from entering its grounds.

He spent a few minutes reviewing her scroll-access records. They ceded insights into her interests; a mere caricature, to be sure, but insights nonetheless. The records sketched a picture of a young woman who'd divided her time in equal measure between the A and B stacks within the Spires.

That wasn't typical. Most prospects discounted the cultural scrolls of the B stacks. Instead, they invested their time in acquiring technological knowledge to maximize their chances of passing the S.A.T. In Bushudo's case, a fascination with cultural history may have led to her downfall. Her prep-test records captured a litany of poor results.

He navigated to the dataset's quantum images. A tap of the tile converted them to plasmonic projections. One after another, three-dimensional transcriptions of Bushudo's head assembled above the desk. Every curve of her face, every strand of her hair, and every facet of her glass implants rendered with lossless accuracy.

Her eyes gleamed with unsettling sentience, fusing an odd mix of openness and wariness. Though smiling in most of the projections, she didn't show her teeth. Perhaps they were misaligned, but it would take more than crooked teeth to detract from her beauty.

Laoshi leaned back and winced. It wasn't the old wounds that bothered him. It was the sense of violation emanating from the disembodied heads.

The Cognos Populi had enacted the spintronic tagging program following a short-lived civil insurrection. Two years prior to the program's introduction, a sizable faction of prospects had taken up arms in response to the doubling of the S.A.T.'s frequency. The diodes helped enforce new edicts that stripped the caste of all rights and privileges. Thirty-one years later, the diodes and the edicts remained in place.

Prospects could still be detained without formal charge. They were forbidden to own property, enter union, or engage in coitus. Their movements were severely restricted. Daqin Guojin comprised fifty Chengs, but a prospect today would be lucky to visit two Chengs beyond her home district. Far more disturbing, any prospect who ventured beyond the city-state's borders invited instant death.

The last edict was enforced by clusters of sonic nanocharges that accompanied the diodes. For those carrying the deadly microscopic cargo, a single step beyond the border before gaining denizenship would trip the bandnet surrounding the city-state and trigger the nanocharges.

He deactivated the plasmonic projections and scanned the final biometric entries recorded in Bushudo's dataset. They mapped her journey from the Librarium to the Great Northern Border, a journey that ended on the morning of the January S.A.T. when she stepped beyond the wall. The entries on the tile's screen represented a desperate but deliberate choice; the girl had chosen suicide over harvesting. She was the same age as Heqet.

The entries also represented a perversion of three technologies. The diodes had tracked transshipments of grooll and glass products throughout the city-state for centuries. Medical practitioners had developed the nanocharges generations ago to eliminate metastatic calcifications in soft tissues. The ultra-high-frequency bandnet had been installed in 558 A.C.E. to detect incursions by the mongrel colonies. None had been introduced to restrict the freedoms of Daqin Guojin's inhabitants. A capricious man's suspicious mind had contrived that aberration.

Laoshi closed Bushudo's dataset. He shifted his attention to the data-mining program running on the quantum tile.

It accessed datasets containing encrypted prep-test and S.A.T. scores dating back to 501 A.C.E., the inaugural year of the test. Thankfully, it didn't need to dig that far into the past. The program confined its interest to the previous thirty-one years, coinciding with the reign of the current Unum. Even then, the resulting data-points numbered in the millions.

The program's heuristic algorithms could compile and cross-reference the data-points a million times faster, but he'd opted for manual processing. Despite enormous advances in quantum computing, human intuition couldn't be coded. His intuition told him something abhorrent had happened at the January S.A.T.

Never in his twelve years as Primae Librarian had a prospect with such dismal prep-test scores achieved a stellar score in the

S.A.T. That made the January S.A.T. an anomaly. One prospect had pulled off a result that bordered on miraculous. The prospect's lineage made the anomaly all the more ominous.

It connected to the Unum.

So far, the individual scores in the datasets showed no signs of overt tampering. That wasn't surprising. Evidence of manipulation would only disclose itself in the aggregate. Recognizable patterns would emerge—as clear as fingerprints on a crystal dagger. Uncovering them might take weeks, perhaps months, but he could afford the time.

He couldn't afford the visibility. Manipulation of S.A.T. scores carried one punishment—death. Anyone taking part in such a scheme would have no compunction with using an equal measure to prevent discovery. For reasons both fortunate and tragic, the past five years had given him abundant opportunities to perfect the art and craft of secrecy.

A knock on the main door lured Laoshi's attention from the desktop. He powered off the tile. "Come."

Gustar entered the Temple. An enormous yellow lanshan encased his body, filling the door's threshold. A patchy gray-black beard mottled the Slavv's bulging cheeks. His smile revealed tapered eyeteeth that abutted his lower lip.

If it wasn't for the needling smile, Laoshi would be hard pressed to recognize the senior datakeeper anymore. Once tall and scrawny, Gustar's body had been transformed by fate. A wealthy relation in Nansilafu Cheng had passed away five years ago, leaving him a small fortune in grooll. Not enough to retire from his position, Gustar always complained, but adequate to fend off malnutrition. More than adequate, Laoshi reckoned.

"Ah, the Temple of the Primae Librarian," Gustar said, flitting his gaze about the parlor. "Every time I come here, I expect to see it furnished."

Except for the desk and two nearby divans, the parlor was empty. No sculptures or decorative wares dressed its perimeter.

The walls could display a variety of colorful geometric patterns, but Laoshi lacked any appetite to activate the program. The windows bracketing the door provided an unbroken view of the Librarium grounds to the south. It lent a pleasing aesthetic touch to the space, and an authentic one.

"Too many denizens exchange too much grooll for useless abodewares," he said. "I have no desire to mirror their example."

"We can't all be ascetics," Gustar said. "Besides, it's the peoples' right to trade grooll for whatever pleases them."

"The people also have responsibilities. A society that places vapid style over fulsome substance is one that flirts with doom."

"How so?"

"Resource allocation."

"We have plenty of sand," Gustar said. "Glass production has never been so high."

Laoshi harrumphed. "Yes, we have more than enough sand to weave fibrous gleamglass into glittering shenyi, fashion pressure-shocked ceramic into transparent armor, and erect cold-rolled crystal into towering structures."

"Then why the concern with resource allocation?"

"We also fashion glass, ceramic, and crystal into levicarts, abodewares, and countless frivolous adornments."

"Surely we can divert some production to items that help smooth life's rougher edges."

"Sand isn't the only resource we need for survival," Laoshi said. "How much grooll is exchanged for these baubles and trinkets? How much intellectual capital is wasted on their creation and pursuit?"

Gustar sighed. "I was commenting on your decor. I wasn't trying to start a philosophical debate."

"That's the problem, Gustar. No one wants to discuss it. A people so enthralled by superficialities can't carry out their responsibilities to the planet, the city-state, or each other. The cultural records are filled with examples of failed societies that lost sight of what matters. They might teach us that extinction isn't limited to plant and animal life—if we have eyes to see."

Gustar waddled forward. His gaze panned. "Well, my eyes see a depressing parlor. No wonder you spend most of your time in your underground lair."

"Then allow me to expedite your visit. What can I do for you?"

Gustar halted a few feet from the desk. Sweat glistened on his shorn scalp. So, too, did an elaborate design of red and black studs.

The fractal pentagram was new, and must have taken weeks to implant. Laoshi could only imagine how much grooll Gustar had exchanged for the crowning work.

"It's come to my attention that you've been accessing the datasets for prep-tests and past S.A.T. scores," Gustar said.

"I have."

"May I ask why you didn't coordinate it through me?"

Laoshi squinted. The question's polite veneer clashed with its surly undertone. "I'm conducting a study on scoring trends. I want to know which subject areas show weaknesses in our collective knowledge."

"A noble aim, but one that will take time to bear results."

"I don't mind the effort if it allows us to give better tutelage to our prospects."

Gustar scraped his fingertips across his whiskered chin. "And you felt no need to enlist your senior datakeeper's help?"

"I know how busy you are."

"Never too busy to aid the Primae Librarian. We need to look after one another, don't we?"

"Are you suggesting I need looking after?"

"I am." Gustar tugged a quantum tile from his tunic's outer pocket. "Your recent writings could be misconstrued by the wrong people."

"Misconstrued as what?"

"Criticism," Gustar said, waving the tile. "You've written about the ill treatment of prospects, misplaced social values, and the past conditions that led to civil insurrection."

"Those aspects of our society deserve criticism."

"You've also criticized the shortcomings of the Cognos Populi." Gustar tapped the tile's screen. "This excerpt from your latest scroll, for example, in which you discuss the Cycle of Extinctions."

"I know my own writings," Laoshi said. "I don't need you to recite them."

Gustar ignored the warning. "Allow me to quote you." He read from the tile's screen. "The human migrations that marked this era were the largest and most chaotic in recorded history. They were also the costliest in terms of the preservation of knowledge. Some societies managed to transport their technological and cultural histories with them, preserving their treasures for future generations. Others weren't so fortunate or far-thinking. As a result, countless insights and innumerable discoveries have been lost to the sands of time."

"Hardly revolutionary."

"Discussion of the Cycle of Extinctions is forbidden," Gustar said without looking up, "but you didn't stop there. In the next paragraph you write, 'The edicts of the Cognos Populi have forbidden tutelage on crucial topics and locked millions of scrolls to prospect access. No longer can they study the role played by chlorophyll in photosynthesis. Or the number of offspring produced over the lifetime of a lesser-striped swallow. Or the pollen-collecting methods used by honeybees. This cheapens our repository. It also ensures that these insights, too, will be lost to the sands of time.'"

"Those words are true."

Gustar lowered the tile. His eyebrows arched, rumpling his fractal pentagram. "Those words could be interpreted as outright dissension."

"I was pointing out the parallel between historical forces and social forces in suppressing knowledge."

"A fine point, Laoshi. Perhaps too nuanced for the ruling caste to discern?"

Laoshi's lower back issued another protest. He had no time for this nonsense. "And what's *your* point?"

"Only that we walk a delicate line between independence and domination," Gustar said. "A sacred edict separates the functions of rule from the functions of sapience. The ruling caste places such importance on it that no Jiren has ever set foot within the Librarium's grounds. It would be a tragedy if your ill-advised writings gave them cause to rescind the edict."

"Exchanging critical thought for imaginary independence would be a greater tragedy. If we don't hold the Cognos Populi to task, who will?"

"Another noble aim, but one that's misplaced, I fear. I've locked the scrolls in question to prospect access."

"Then you can unlock them!"

"Scrolls that touch upon forbidden subjects, however lightly, must be locked." He pocketed the tile. "I'm bound by the edicts, not your requests."

"It isn't a request!"

"Yes it is. And one I can't fulfill." Gustar strode toward the door. He halted at its threshold and turned back. "I have your best interest at heart."

"I'd prefer you to have Daqin Guojin's best interest at heart."

Gustar flashed a needling smile. "In this world, the Libraria must look after one another."

"In this world, *every* life is precious!"

Gustar's shoulders brushed against the door's threshold as he exited the Temple. "So you keep saying." The door swung closed, muffling his clumpy chucklebucks.

Laoshi grunted; the only interest the senior datakeeper had

ever taken to heart was his own. He powered up the desk's quantum tile and navigated to a new dataset.

It belonged to Daoren al Lucien.

GUSTAR ENTERED THE data repository through the northwest door, still chuckling over the Primae Librarian's parting words.

In this world, every life is precious.

What world was Laoshi talking about? The one orbiting the swollen sun had done its best over the millennia to cull off every life form. Daqin Guojin annually slaughtered hundreds of thousands of its young to survive. The mongrel colonies embraced even darker deprivations. Only a sanctimonious cudd would call any of those worlds precious.

He shook his head. Laoshi may be a sanctimonious cudd, but he had courage. A Librarian willing to voice grievances against the Cognos Populi—to embed them in scrolls under his own name no less—was as rare as rainfall in the high summer. But such courage had a downside.

Gustar descended a flight of stairs and stepped onto the repository's main floor. It covered more than three hundred-thousand square-feet, making it the largest of the twelve housed beneath the Spires. And the coldest.

He quickened his pace to offset the chill. Quantum-computing cradles partitioned the floor into narrow rows, creating a labyrinth that flummoxed every new datakeeper. Most kept site maps on their tiles to assist with the navigation.

Gustar had long since memorized the myriad routes. He stalked up a row, following a path he'd walked a thousand times.

The cradles bracketing him supported massive slabs of translucent glass. The slabs measured seven feet high, seventy-five feet long, and one-inch thick. Each contained numberless miles of optical channels for tracking the quantum states of numberless electromagnetically suspended ions. The cradles themselves were decoupled from the environment to mitigate decoherence.

He resisted the urge to touch the slabs as he walked. The storage capacity they provided was virtually unlimited. This single data repository contained the contents of more than eight billion scrolls on technological and cultural knowledge. It also housed the datasets of every prospect who'd lived in Daqin Guojin since 501 A.C.E.

Not long after joining the datakeepers, he'd examined some of the earliest datasets out of curiosity. An Asianoid prospect named Qinbao al Diyong bore the distinction of being the very first entry. He was the eldest son of Diyong al Shunyi—the Unum responsible for instituting the S.A.T. In a cruel twist of fate, Qinbao became one of the first prospects to be harvested in the grooll mill.

That was another era. Since then, an unbroken sequence of prospect datasets had been created. They now numbered in the hundreds of millions. The data they stored had also grown exponentially following the inception of the tagging and tracking program in 669 A.C.E. Despite the proliferation, the repository operated at only thirty-eight percent of its capacity. A smaller repository located in the Spire's southern sector replicated each dataset, providing a measure of redundancy. In a testament to the quantum engineers who'd originally designed the cradles, not a single qubit of data had ever been lost.

Gustar reached the end of a row of cradles and veered left. Fifty feet ahead, a dozen datakeepers toiled in the alcoves lining the eastern wall. Most didn't look at him as he approached. Those that did make eye contact didn't bother to acknowledge his presence.

The acrid aftertaste of resentment seared Gustar's throat. As far back as he could remember, his fellow datakeepers had treated him with indifference. Few Slavvs wore the yellow

lanshan, and even fewer graced the inner sanctum of the repositories. Most senior datakeepers traced their lineage to the
Asianoid and Indonoid families that had founded the city-state.
They regarded the position as a hereditary right. The arrival of a
scrawny Slavv from a poor family in Nansilafu Cheng had represented an unwelcome rift in the natural order.

The pall of indifference had steadily thickened since his
change in fortune five years ago. He now possessed more grooll
than the next one hundred datakeepers combined. A few weeks
ago, he'd given tangible expression to that fact when he walked
into the repository sporting his new implants. None of his
colleagues had commented on the crowning fractal pentagram—
then or since.

Outwardly, he denied them any signs of caring. Inwardly,
their apathy chaffed him. It was a continuation of the coolness
he'd experienced as a prospect. During his time at the Librarium,
he'd tried to make friends and get closer to those in his cohort.
But no matter how pleasant he was or how helpful he tried to be,
his peers had spurned and ignored him. Worse, they'd teased
him about his pointed eyeteeth, his scruffy pienfu, and his infe-
rior implants.

No one teased him anymore. Now that he carried the heft and
adornments of the affluent, no one dared. But he still felt their
judgments pressing around him as tangibly as the repository's
chilled air.

No matter—he had a pleasant thought to warm him. In a few
more years, he'd possess enough grooll to leave the Librarium
and fund his return to Nansilafu Cheng and his own kind. Of
course, that depended on the test-manipulation scheme operating without interruption.

Gustar reached his alcove along the eastern wall. For the past
seven years, the ten-by-ten workspace had functioned as his
second abode. More than his second abode if he weighed the
number of hours he spent in there each day.

The alcove housed a desk with an integrated touch-screen and some personal items from his childhood abode. An army of miniature denizens stood post in the nooks beside his desk. Nooks in the opposite wall held a smattering of crystal sculptures.

The figurines had belonged to his mother; she'd curated them from all fifty Chengs during her travels as a silica engineer. His father had preferred geometric sculptures, especially toroids. Like many older men in Nansilafu Cheng, he saw the divine in the torus—a beginning without end. Whenever Gustar stared at the shape, all he saw was grooll, praise be to Sha.

His parents had left him the collections when they died. The few dozen pieces were all that remained to testify to their—

A hushed voice leaked from the adjacent alcove. "Did you hear the latest edict?"

Another hushed voice followed. "Which edict?"

Gustar grunted. The Indonoid brothers spent twice as much time babbling as they did performing their datakeeping duties. Were it within his power to do so, he'd have them removed from the Spires and sent to work scrubbing serving pans in the Librarium's messing facilities.

"The latest one," the younger brother said.

"You'll need to be more specific. The Cognos Populi produce edicts like my wife produces children."

"They're offering huge rewards for reporting dissension."

The older brother sighed. "Wonderful. Now anyone who has an issue with his neighbor can settle the score for a profit."

"Still, it might be worth reporting that couple."

"Which couple?"

"The one that lives across the transway. Their abode's windows are always tinted. And have you noticed how they never talk to anyone on distribution days?"

"So?"

"Maybe they're hiding something."

"Like what?" the older brother asked. "The fact that they're introverts?"

"Or dissenters. "

"I'll have no part in it."

Gustar sneered. Of course he wouldn't—the man had no backbone. None of the datakeepers had backbones—or the courage to act on the foreknowledge their unique vocation granted them.

He settled into the seat at his desk. Ordinarily, he'd air-link to the repository using its touch-screen, but this was no ordinary query. He pulled the quantum tile from his lanshan's inner pocket. The tile had the benefit of being unregistered.

It took a few seconds to establish a connection. Once confirmed, he typed in a new access code using a different scrambler key. The extra encryption was superfluous, but one couldn't be too cautious when masking one's fingerprints.

A new interface opened on his tile's screen. It air-linked to every scroll record residing in the Spire's A and B stacks.

Gustar keyed the tile, entering two simple search metrics.

New data flooded the screen. Excerpts streamed from more than one hundred scrolls, all written within the past five years.

They belonged to Laoshi al Euclidius.

5

PROMISES

D AOREN SWIPED HIS brow and surrendered a weary sigh to the afternoon's cloying humidity. It had already taken him three minutes of brisk walking to reach the open square's mid-point.

Three minutes.

And that was despite going unchallenged by the Unum's personal guard stationed along the square's ample length and width. To a casual observer, the scattered Jireni might appear random. Closer inspection, however, revealed a more purposeful deployment; the checkpoints represented the outermost shell of a layered defense. The Assembly of the Cognos Populi was a hardened target.

Daoren kept his gaze fixed forward. He diverted his focus onto the clip of his sandals against the square's red and yellow ceramic tiles. The steady cadence helped mute his angst.

He didn't know which was more unsettling; walking into the nexus of all that was contemptible about Daqin Guojin, or walking around with the knowledge that something vile had infected the S.A.T.

He stalked past another group of Jireni. They issued no challenges. Another half-dozen checkpoints lay between him and the Assembly's eastern entrance; he'd undoubtedly be stopped and bio-scanned before reaching the structure. So be it. The news he had to deliver was worth a bio-scanning or two.

He'd spent the last three weeks studying the outcome of the January S.A.T. The city-state's datakeepers usually released the posting within two days of a test's conclusion. It only indicated whether a prospect had passed or failed—individual scores were never revealed. Luckily, other data sources existed to infer the results.

Seven days after each test, the datakeepers started posting updates to the various vocational rolls. Those with the lowest barriers to entry trickled out first. The passing scores needed to join the city-state's artisans, industrial engineers, and Jireni were lower than those needed to join its medical practitioners, quantum programmers, and Libraria. The data was considered public domain, but few outside the Librarium paid attention. For those that did, patterns and trends could be uncovered. He'd found several disturbing anomalies.

Some of Mako's closest friends had failed the test despite their above-average affinity for technological knowledge. Others had achieved stellar results and joined loftier vocations despite displaying no prior prowess. One or two unexpected failures and inexplicable successes might be dismissed as coincidences—the results of ill nerves or good fortune—but these inflated numbers smacked of correlations.

Over the last week, he'd expanded his investigation to the three previous S.A.T.s. One correlation stood out like a blood pool on a sand dune; the wealthier a prospect's family, the higher the chances of passing and the loftier the vocational placement.

As disturbing as that discovery may have been, it paled in comparison to the one he'd made this morning. The datakeepers had finally posted the Assembly's updated roll. The Cognos Populi represented the pinnacle of Daqin Guojin's social castes.

The S.A.T. score needed to ascend to its ranks was higher than any other vocation. Only the most technologically gifted prospects made the cut.

Julinian's name was on the roll.

Daoren had paced the courtyard at his abode, quantum tile in hand, and rechecked the roll three times. Three confirmations were necessary to convince himself that he hadn't confused her with another prospect. There was no mistake. Julinian alum Petravic had joined the Cognos Populi.

The revelation had driven him from the courtyard to seek out his father at the Assembly. He couldn't recall the last time he'd made the journey, but the ill news needed to be shared—and shared immediately.

He reached the edge of the massive square without being stopped by any of the Jireni checkpoints. It buoyed his mood—until he glanced up at the Assembly.

It stood three hundred-fifty feet high and extended twice that distance along its major axis. Muscular mauve columns buttressed a two-level roof finished with flared, golden eaves. Secondary columns supported balconies along the imposing façade. The lower balconies were the shortest. Their length increased with height. The uppermost balcony was by far the longest, easily spanning a tenth of the Assembly, leaving no doubt it belonged to the ruler of Daqin Guojin. The structure was rumored to be modeled on an ancient fortification from Mother China's imperial past—Zijin Cheng.

The Forbidden City.

He shivered. *Forbidden* was an accurate descriptor. The Cognos Populi preferred to conduct their affairs with minimal outside observation. The Assembly discouraged casual visitors like no other structure—except for the Center, which lurked fifteen miles to the west. He recalled seeing its bone-white dome from the Assembly's roof during one of his childhood visits.

Daoren pushed the recollection aside as he reached the tiered staircase—he wouldn't be visiting the roof today. He climbed two flights and entered the structure.

Inside, a vaulted nave enclosed exquisite crystal sculptures, a hundred visiting denizens, and dozens more Jireni whose chest plates bore the Imperial Regalia. They guarded the access points to the structure's stairways and elevating chambers. Some thirty levels comprised the Assembly. His father's chamber resided on the twenty-fourth.

Daoren angled for the nearest elevating chamber. Ordinarily, he'd have chosen a stairway to make the ascent, but his impatience outweighed his discomfort.

An Asianoid Jiren held up his hand as he approached. "What's your business in the Assembly, prospect?"

"I'm here to see my father, Lucien al Braccus."

The Jiren extracted a probe from his quantum tile. The thin, tubular device glinted. "Come, then. You know the routine."

Daoren raked his hair from his ear and stepped closer. The Jiren inserted the probe.

It emitted a series of bright chirps, air-querying the tracking diode implanted behind his eardrum. The bio-scan lasted three seconds.

The Jiren consulted his tile. "I see your brother was a regular visitor." He looked up. "You've not been here in six years."

"Is that a problem?"

The Jiren stowed the probe and waved him past. "Not for me it isn't."

Daoren stalked into the elevating chamber. He took a deep breath, steeling his nerves for the ascent, and petitioned Sha to close the doors before anyone else joined him.

The doors swished closed, sealing him off from the bustling nave. The chamber ascended. He closed his eyes and resisted the urge to scream.

Ten seconds later, the doors swished open. He opened his eyes and surged into a hallway lined with clear glass.

Assembly members in purple shenyi filled it, flitting to and fro. A meeting must have adjourned a few seconds earlier. Their raucous conversations saturated the air.

The clamor and congestion triggered a shudder. He dredged his memory for the route to his father's chamber. It had been so long since he was last here, he couldn't—

"Lost, boy?" a passing Africoid elder asked.

"I'm looking for Lucien al Braccus."

The elder leaned closer and squinted. "You're his youngest, aren't you?"

Daoren nearly said yes before a morbid thought stilled his tongue—he wasn't his parents' youngest child anymore.

The elder must have drawn the same conclusion. "My sorrow for your brother. He was a fine boy." He cocked his head. "You know, you look nothing like him."

"So I've heard." Daoren pointed down the hallway. "This way?"

The elder pointed in the opposite direction. "Take your first left. Your father's chamber is the second on the right."

"My thanks."

Daoren darted down the long hallway, dodging purple clumps of prattling members. Two minutes later, he stood outside his father's chamber. He rapped the door's thick glass.

"Come."

He edged through the door and basked in the chamber's relative calm. Twenty feet away, Lucien sat behind a transparent desk. The floor space matched that of the abode's parlor, but its minimalist aesthetic made it seem all the larger. A ceramic water fountain gurgled in the center of the chamber. His father must have installed it within the last six years.

Lucien looked up from his desktop. He frowned.

Daoren noted the look of disdain. Doubtless his father had offered Mako a more welcoming expression whenever *he'd* visited.

"What brings you here?" Lucien's body stiffened, causing his shoulders to rise. "Is your mother all right?"

Daoren gathered his thoughts. He'd expended hours of effort to come see his father, but hadn't given a second's thought to broaching the findings of his investigation.

"Answer me, boy! Is your mother all right?"

"Yes," Daoren said. "Did you hear about Julinian?"

Lucien's shoulders slumped. "Sapient Sha—*that's* what this is about? You scared me half to death."

"Did you hear?"

"I saw the Unum earlier this morning. He's ecstatic about the news."

"*That's* all you have to say?"

"What else is there to say?"

Daoren stalked closer and tugged his quantum tile from his tunic. "I've been looking into past S.A.T. results. I found something you need to see."

"Just a moment," Lucien said, raising a hand. "What do you mean you've been looking into S.A.T. results? Those results are secret."

"Not the actual results. The pass-fail postings and vocational rolls."

"Why the vocational rolls?"

"I used them to extrapolate the results." He tapped the tile's screen. "Take a look at—"

"I thought I told you to drop this."

"I know, but if you'll look at what I've uncovered."

"Do you think I enjoy saying no to you?"

Daoren held out the tile. "Just look, will you?"

Lucien rose from his seat and leaned on the desk. "This is exactly the kind of activity that can get you culled! Who else have you told?"

"No one."

"Keep it that way." Lucien swiped his desktop, closing an

array of documents. "I have a meeting to attend in five minutes. I suggest you go back to the abode and start making plans to attend the Librarium."

Daoren squeezed the tile to stop his hand from shaking. Slag-hot ire welled up from his gut and spewed from his mouth. "What's the meeting about? More useless discussion on banning the color green?"

Lucien pointed at the door. "Get out."

"Maybe if the Cognos Populi spent less time worrying about which color represented dissension and more time worrying about the sanctity of the S.A.T., the city-state would be better off!"

"Out!"

"Gladly." Daoren rammed the tile back into his pocket and turned to the door. A bright chirp from the desktop made him turn back.

Lucien lowered his gaze to the desk's embedded tile. His brow creased.

Daoren glanced at the desk. Its glare obscured whatever his father was reading, but it couldn't hide his trembling hands. "What's wrong?"

Lucien's gaze remained fixed on the desktop. Color bled from his cheeks.

"Lucien, what is it?"

His father didn't look up. He mumbled as if talking to himself. "Someone . . . someone just forwarded me five years of prep-test results."

"Mako's results?"

Lucien shook his head.

"Mine?"

"No."

A chill crested on Daoren's skin. Though prep-test results were commonly shared within families, they were never publi-cized to outsiders. The Libraria had unrestricted access to them, but they were bound by the edicts to safeguard their confidentiality. "Whose results are they?"

Lucien tapped the desktop and powered off the embedded tile. "It doesn't matter."

"It does judging by the look on your face."

"Get yourself home, boy. We'll talk more about this later."

Daoren evaluated his father's lighter tone. Was he saying that just to get rid of him?

"I promise we'll talk," Lucien said, motioning to the door. "But for now, *go*."

LAOSHI KNOCKED ON the door a third time. The sharp-edged raps echoed through the parlor, but elicited no response from within the sleeping chamber. He knocked again, harder and longer.

"Go away!"

He allowed himself a cautious smile. Her shout was a welcome addition to the Temple's ambience, even if its timbre was less-than-pleasing to the ear. "When's the last time you ate?"

"I'm not hungry."

He could tell she was still lying in bed—likely face-down given the muffled quality of her reply. "You can't stay in there forever."

She didn't respond.

He leaned against the doorframe. His granddaughter had been locked in her sleeping chamber since Mako's S.A.T. No amount of coaxing could draw her out. The best he could accomplish over the last few weeks was drawing her into curt conversations. Those conversations spoke of a young woman mired in pain and self-loathing.

He placed his mouth next to the door's seam and softened his tone. "It's not your fault, child."

Muffled sobs ebbed through the door. Obviously, Heqet felt otherwise.

Her misery sliced into him like shrapnel. "I saw Mako inside the Center. He wasn't upset. He wasn't distracted. He did his best on the test and failed. That's all that happened."

The sobs grew in clarity and intensity. "You're just saying that to get me to come out."

"I'm speaking the truth," he said. "I promise. You're not to blame for the outcome."

The sobs receded over the next minute. He took that as a good portent. "I know it's difficult, but you need to get on with life. Why don't you call him?"

"He won't want to see me."

"How will you know unless you call?"

"Because I know Daoren!"

Laoshi grinned. His granddaughter was never more responsive than when provoked. He stripped every hint of compassion from his voice. "Your mother and father didn't raise you to sit and sulk in a sleeping chamber, and I'll be damned if I'll start now!"

"I'm not sitting and sulking! I'm lying down and crying!"

"Regardless, this behavior isn't worthy of their memory."

"Don't throw their memory at me! Who do you think you are?"

Her rage warmed his heart—he had her now. He summoned a commanding tone he hadn't used since his youth. "I'm your grandfather. This is my abode. Come unlock this door or I swear I'll break it down!"

"You're an old man! You'll only break your shoulder!"

He stifled his amusement—she was a sharp one, his granddaughter. He needed to maintain the façade of anger a little longer to prod her out of her cave. "I used to be a Jiren, child! This door stands no chance against me!"

Heqet responded with silence. Laoshi put his ear to the door.

Beyond it, the patter of footfalls grew louder. A second later, the lock's latch clicked.

He stepped back. The door opened a crack—not far enough to see her, but far enough to know he'd succeeded in his mission. "Thank you."

On the other side of the door, Heqet sniffled. "I didn't want you to hurt yourself."

"Would you like some grooll?" he asked.

The answer took a long time coming, but it was worth lingering for. "Yes."

Laoshi turned from the door.

"And grandfather?"

He turned back. "Yes, dear?"

"Could you bring me my tile?"

"Of course."

He limped away, beaming. It was a small victory, but a victory nonetheless.

DAOREN SHOVED THE door open and exited the Assembly's alcove. His heartbeat thumped his eardrums—an aftereffect from the elevating-chamber's descent and the argument with his father.

Why was it so difficult to talk to him? Why wouldn't he ever listen? Lucien had hung on every word Mako had ever spoken. Of course, his brother had mostly gushed about joining the Cognos Populi and following in Lucien's footsteps. Even as a child, Mako had embraced the political and social norms of Daqin Guojin. Daoren had always held them at arm's length—the better to inspect their many blemishes. Why couldn't his father accept that both stances were equally valid? Why did he have to treat one son as a perpetual outsider?

He descended the steps. On the open square, a few dozen

Assembly members in splendid purple shenyi complemented the mix of armed Jireni.

One of the members waved as she paced closer. "Daoren al Lucien!"

Daoren halted on the landing dividing the two flights. A tingling chill shrank his skin.

Julinian climbed the first flight and stopped before him. Cropped hair shortened her stature and framed a flushed face. Like her power and promise for the future, her waistline had expanded since their meeting on the steps of the Center.

Her studded lips stretched in a cryptic smile. "What brings you to the Assembly?"

Daoren searched for a suitable response. The sight of Julinian in the garb of the Cognos Populi culled his voice; the cognitive dissonance was too great.

She dipped her chin. "My poor prospect. You look so confused. Can I be of any assistance?"

He clenched his hands at his side, resisting the urge to drive a fist into her smug face. As satisfying as the act might be, it would also be his last.

"I mourned your brother." Julinian lowered her clouded gaze to the landing before raising it again. "I was sitting near him in the Center. You should know he met his end like a man worthy of denizenship." She shook her head. "Such a pity. Was it his nerves, do you think?"

He didn't dare open his mouth and speak his mind.

Julinian smirked. "Quite the conversationalist, aren't you?" She placed a hand on his arm. "I hope your nerves are more settled. You sit the the May S.A.T., right?"

Daoren yanked his arm away. He found his voice. "What concern is that to you?"

She stepped closer, putting her face within inches of his, and lowered her voice. "It's of no concern at all, slag. I only like to plan my mourning in advance."

He craned forward—the tip of his nose nearly touched hers. "And I like to plan my culling in advance."

Julinian didn't back away. She leaned forward until their noses touched. "Is that a threat?"

Her stale breath brushed his lips. "It's a *promise*."

"Is there a problem up there?" a Jiren called from the square.

Julinian pulled her head back and waved at the Jiren. "I think this prospect only wanted to kiss me." She shifted focus to Daoren and offered a smug grin. "Best run along before you get hurt, boy. Say hello to your mother and father for me." She ascended the second flight. "Oh, and good fortune on your S.A.T."

Daoren watched the smug fid enter the Assembly. He whirled and stormed down the steps. He made it ten paces across the square before his quantum tile vibrated. He pulled it from his pocket.

The name on its glass screen made him halt once again.

6

THE HOLLOWS

DAOREN TARRIED BEFORE the Hollow's crystal plinth. Sunlight flared off the waist-high surface, highlighting the inscription on its angled face.

For Those Who Gave Their Lives That We Might Live.

On the other side of the plinth, millions of slender gray-glass tubes erupted from gray-ceramic slabs. The tubes stood five-feet tall and filled a cloister spanning one square-mile in the heart of Zhongguo Cheng. They swayed in the wind, emitting a mournful *om* that hung in the air like an aural mist.

To the north, the Center's domed roof filled the oval hole of an elliptical torus that loomed a half-mile beyond the cloister. The alignment between the structures resembled an eye, albeit one with a white pupil and black sclera.

He'd often wondered if the configuration had a purpose. Did the designers intend for visitors to stand before the plinth and see a prying eye staring back at them? Was it a random quirk of geometry? Humans were good at finding meaning in patterns, but they were infinitely better at giving meaning to patterns when none existed. Some saw portents in lunar eclipses. Some glimpsed the face of Sha in striated sandstone deposits. Some heard voices in resonating glass tubes.

Daoren surveyed the field of tubes, known to inhabitants as the Hollows—Daqin Guojin's most hallowed ground. In their youth, he and Mako had stopped at this spot more times than he could count. They had to pass it on the way to the district's glass market, and their parents were always sending them there to trade grooll for one vital abodeware or another.

The Hollows never failed to terrify Mako. Twelve times a year, coinciding with each S.A.T., the field of tubes grew larger and denser. The growth gave it the quality of a living organism—one that might eat an unsuspecting observer. But it wasn't the memorial's ever-expanding size that had troubled his brother for so long.

It was the *om*.

How many nights in the past five years had Mako awakened from an auditory nightmare, hyperventilating and crying out in fear? The resonance had never fazed Daoren, not even as a child. He understood the physics of acoustics.

They were here two months before the January S.A.T. Daoren could picture him now, standing before the plinth with his anxious gaze locked onto the cloister, clenching his hands whenever the wind stirred up a haunting moan. He could picture Heqet as well, twisting her hair braids, micro-studded cheeks shimmering in sunlight. The humid November afternoon marked the last time the three of them—

A northerly wind ruffled the tubes. They swayed and released another *om*.

The hairs on the back of his neck stood. Acoustic resonance didn't cause the reaction—someone was standing behind him. A grief-tinged voice cut through the mournful mist, confirming his suspicion.

"My grandfather says the moans are the departed prospects, lamenting the lives they never lived. What do you believe?"

Adrenaline spiked his veins. He shouldn't have agreed to the meeting; he wasn't ready to see her. He waited until his throat relaxed before answering. "I believe nothing a Librarian says."

The patter of sandals on ceramic drew closer. The outline of her body, refined and petite in the periphery of his vision, halted beside him. The rustle of burrglass fabric against her skin vied for his attention. Still, he kept his gaze fixed on the cloister.

"I fasted for Mako," she said. "All seven days."

So did he, but she wasn't beholden to observe the custom. "You needn't have. You aren't part of his immediate family."

Out of the corner of his eye, he glimpsed her shoulders rise and fall.

"But I hoped to be one day."

Daoren didn't share her attachment to hope. Hope was a useless gamble—an emotional investment with no chance of a return. That people still clung to it baffled him. Didn't they have eyes to see the world? Didn't they know humanity would soon follow every other life form and complete the Cycle of Extinctions?

"I don't understand how this happened," she said.

A gust buffeted the cloister, bending a few tubes toward them. He grabbed one and pulled it closer.

White letters inscribed the tube's gray glass.

Fiarina alum Claudius.

He ran his thumb over each letter. "I used to tease Mako that there was a memorial tube in here with his name on it." He let the tube go; it sprang back and rejoined the others. "I never dreamed it would come true."

"Did I have anything to do with it?"

He turned to her.

Heqet's twin hair braids shone, the color of polished sandstone. They spilled down the front of her white pienfu, flowing over her breasts and terminating below the grooll pouch on her hip. Her cheeks were drawn taut as if she was sucking on a piece of grooll, but the pucker did little to dim her radiance. Hundreds of clear micro-studs speckled her cheekbones. They cascaded like starfalls to her jawline.

Now that he gazed upon her, Daoren found it impossible to stop. She was a Hyphenoid—a child of mixed lineage. Her finely proportioned Asianoid-Caucasoid features had entranced Mako for years. They weren't the only qualities; her unswerving curiosity, her unassuming grace, her unsparing sense of humor . . . his brother would run out of fingers ticking off the attributes that had ensnared his heart. But that was Mako—always ruled by his heart.

"Why would you have anything to do with it?"

She shrank from the blunt question, as fragile as whisper-glass. He wished he'd softened its delivery. By the look in her eyes, she risked fracturing before the most muted syllable.

"I mean how could he have failed the test?" she asked, twisting her braids.

"He couldn't have."

"Then how did—"

"It's obvious," he said. "His score was switched."

Heqet's hands dropped from her braids. "What are you saying?"

"I'm saying Mako couldn't have failed unless his score was switched with another prospect."

"Which prospect?"

"Someone who had the right connections to sneakcheat fate."

Her cheeks flushed beneath the micro-studs. "Who is the prospect?"

"Someone who couldn't have passed the test," he said. "According to the most recent Assembly roll, that person's now a member of the Cognos Populi."

"Who is the prospect?" she repeated, voice rising to a shout.

Daoren weighed the benefits of blurting out the name. He chose not to for Heqet's own protection. "Let's just say the prospect is a close relation of the Unum."

Her hands shot up to her mouth. "To suggest such a crime is heresy!"

The tubes swayed in the wind, emitting their moans.

Millions of them.

The hairs on the back of Daoren's neck stood. For a fleeting moment, he swore he heard Mako's voice in the mix. He shrugged off the ridiculous notion. "Then I'd wager I'm a heretic."

"TREAD CAREFULLY, LUCIEN. You're flirting with heresy."

The Unum rested his elbow on the desk and loosened the stud above his right eye to ease its pinch. He'd selected the ash-gray set to show solidarity with those grieving the loss of their loved ones in the February S.A.T. held three days ago. Not that he shared their pain—pinching forehead studs aside—but one had to look the part.

Lucien stood before the desk, a depleted shade of his former self. Grief leadened his skin. Bloodshot eyes hinted at a month of sleepless nights. He'd probably spent most of them commiserating with Cordelia, helping her come to terms with Mako's harvesting.

The Unum had heard through back-channels that she hadn't ventured into public since the boy's S.A.T. and that she may have stopped eating grooll. There were past cases of mothers—it was always mothers—who'd chosen starvation over the risk of ingesting their own children. He'd always assumed Cordelia alum Dominus possessed stronger fortitude.

The toll it had taken on Lucien was obvious, but that didn't excuse his behavior. Heresy was heresy, regardless of the source, and his accusing finger still hung in the air. It pointed at the seat of power in Daqin Guojin, in the Unum's own chamber.

No other forum conveyed the gravitas of his position like the chamber. No other space within the Assembly of the Cognos

Populi surpassed its grandeur. The crystal ceiling's bas-relief panels depicted stirring scenes from the *Siege of Havoc* during the resource war of 462 A.C.E. Luminescent glass walls displayed an ever-shifting parade of vivid geometric patterns. The finest sculptures by the city-state's finest artisans accented the perimeter of its expansive, sunlit floorspace.

Lucien's strident tone carried its solitary dark note. "Then explain how Mako excelled on every prep-test and still failed!"

"The pressure may have got to him," the Unum said. "He was such a skittish child."

"Impossible! I demand to see his S.A.T. scoring."

"You know that's privileged data, exclusive to the Libraria. The edict separating the functions of rule from the functions of sapience must be obeyed—even by those who write the edicts."

"And I demand to see Julinian's scoring."

The Unum folded his hands on the desk. He'd perfected the art of inscrutability long ago, but in his gut a knot of concern tightened. Lucien wouldn't voice such an unorthodox demand unless he had foreknowledge of what he might discover. His innate caution precluded reckless accusations.

Ten feet from the desk, Julinian and Narses fidgeted on a transparent divan. They'd received strict orders to hold their tongues in Lucien's presence. Threats, in fact.

Julinian's purple shenyi cast the awkward sheen of newness, her eyes the glaze of rising panic. Her scalp gleamed as bright and pink as a newborn's bottom, a common trait among fledgling denizens whose hairless skin had been introduced to the swollen sun.

Narses' shock of red hair extended well past the collar of his white pienfu. His eyes wore the drab patina of incompetence under a protruding brow. He'd inherited the physical and mental traits nineteen years ago from his mother, Sha rest her immaterial soul. Two pyramidal studs jutted from his forehead, emulating the Unum's appearance. In Narses' case, the studs suffered from misalignment; the one over his right eye sat a quarter-inch higher than its twin.

The Unum shuddered. He oft-wondered what traits of his own had found a sticking place in his second-born and whether the rumors of infidelity that prompted his wife's ritual suicide were true. He abandoned the musings and returned his focus to the most immediate problem.

"Why do you want to see her scoring?" he asked.

Lucien glared at Julinian. "*She* earns a score high enough to gain entry to the Cognos Populi? How were your prep-tests, prospect?"

Julinian jumped to her feet, flushed face matching her tunic. "I'm not a prospect! I'm a denizen, and you'll address me as such!"

"You're no more a denizen than this chamber is an aerostat. I've seen your miserable prep-tests, *prospect*. You failed every one of them!"

The Unum launched out of his chair. "Who gave you access to her prep-tests? I'll have them culled for violating the edicts!"

Lucien directed a pleading glance to the opposite side of the desk. "You have to investigate, Pyros."

Pyros crossed his arms. He assumed a look of careful contemplation.

The Unum masked his relief; Lucien might actually think the Primae Jiren was considering the request.

Despite his Africoid lineage, Pyros had soared through the Jireni ranks. The Unum appointed him head of the security force four years ago, over the protests of senior members of the Cognos Populi. Xenophobia ran deeper than the Sea of Storms in the Assembly, but few could argue that Pyros, clad in the black-and-gold *bianfu* of Primae Jiren, cropped scalp battle-scarred and tinted the color of death, didn't cut an imposing figure. He also had certain exploitable weaknesses.

"I have no evidence to investigate," Pyros said.

"I can provide all the evidence you need," Lucien said.

The Unum raised his hands. The gesture was meant to be calming. "My dearest Lucien, I took this meeting because you are as much of a friend as a colleague. But Mako's death is clouding your judgment. Nothing nefarious has—"

Lucien stormed away. His booming voice reverberated as he exited the chamber. "This crime will not stand!"

The Unum lowered his hands and plunked into his chair. So much for calming. "He can't be reasoned with."

"Could you if it was your son?" Pyros asked.

The Unum's gaze found Narses atop the divan.

The boy inhaled through his crescent-moon mouth. He fiddled with the grooll pouch clipped to his waist, investing more attention in its interwoven pattern than on the heavy events of the last few minutes.

The behavior was typical—and infuriating—but Pyros had a point. "Leave us, Narses."

Narses stirred, his trance broken. "But, Papa, I want to stay."

"And take Julinian with you!"

Narses pouted, lower lip thrust outward like a frustrated toddler. He and Julinian slinked out of the chamber.

The Unum raked his hands over his scalp the instant they were gone. "How many denizens died on the steps of the Center after the January S.A.T.?"

"Around five hundred," Pyros said. "My men detained double that number."

"And at the most recent test?"

"Another four hundred-fifty were culled after the February S.A.T. I'd need to verify the number of detainees, but it's in the thousands."

"From which Chengs do these dissenters hail?"

"Meiguo Cheng, Yindu Cheng, and Feizhou Cheng, mainly. A few hundred from Riben Cheng as well."

The Unum sighed for Pyros' benefit; he'd known the answer before he asked the question. "Fifty Chengs make up

Daqin Guojin. Why must the minority cause the most problems?"

"Raising the S.A.T.'s passing score may work in the short term to alleviate grooll shortages, but in the longer term it breeds more dissent. I shudder to think what might happen if the frequency of testing is also increased."

"Perhaps we need to send a stronger warning. Can't you round up the dissenters' families and send them to the Rig?"

"It's already operating beyond capacity."

The Unum leaned back. His chair protested the shift in weight. The unrest at the Center in the wake of the tests presented no concern. He'd only broached the subject as a prelude to what mattered.

What mattered was preventing exposure of the test-manipulation scheme. If Lucien had gained access to Julinian's prep-tests, it changed every calculation. He could use them to build a convincing case. A case that would prove S.A.T. scores were being altered. A case that would trace back to the seat of power in Daqin Guojin.

He cursed Gustar for switching Mako's score with his niece's, mindful to hide his ire from Pyros, then cursed himself for exercising poor oversight of the Librarian. The scheme had operated flawlessly for five years. He'd let its success lull him into complacency. His complacency had granted Gustar too much control over the selections.

Had he known beforehand, he would have vetoed Mako's selection. Not because Lucien was a decent man, but because he was a man who didn't let go of problems. By not letting go, he could undermine years of meticulous planning and threaten billions of pounds of grooll.

"What do you think Lucien will do?"

"He's a grieving father," Pyros said. "A grieving father is capable of anything."

"He'll press you to investigate."

"I serve at your command, Unum. If you want me to ignore his demands, I'll obey. But he can take another course to bring his concern to light."

"Such as?"

"He can raise it on the floor of the Assembly. Many members are still upset over your decision to raise the passing score without consultation or approval."

"I've always found a substantial infusion of grooll can soothe the most severe upsets."

"Not all members are open to such a remedy," Pyros said. "If Lucien gains enough support, an inquiry will have to be undertaken."

"The Asianoid faction would love that. They'd waste no time in leaking the inquiry's findings to the people."

"Undoubtedly."

The Unum made a show of wringing his hands. "It's one thing for the masses to suspect the S.A.T. can be manipulated for the benefit of the ruling caste. It's another thing for a respected member of the ruling caste to add his voice."

"His allegations would provoke wider unrest."

"Unrest your Jireni could address, I'm sure."

Pyros' eyelids tensed—the telltale sign of a pondering mind. "That depends. Our most recent reconnaissance indicates the mongrel colonies are facing a severe feeding crisis."

The Unum waved a dismissive hand at the ceiling's bas-relief panels. "They face one every other generation."

"The last crisis prompted an incursion and two million deaths. A resource war *and* an internal revolt would be more than my Jireni can handle."

The Unum celebrated the statement, careful to hide his joy. He never imagined it would be so easy to lead Pyros to this point. "So you agree Lucien's suspicion must be stilled."

Pyros frowned. "What are you suggesting?"

The Unum rose and beckoned Pyros to follow. He led him to a

chain of interlinked glass doors and out onto the adjoining balcony. The Unum reveled in its view.

Three hundred feet below, armed Jireni marched in lockstep across a massive square, dappled in brilliant sunlight. Five centuries ago, artisans had laid row upon row of ceramic tiles to create a majestic mosaic.

A red cupola with flared, golden eaves.

The epic representation of the Imperial Regalia evoked the colors of blood and sun in a format larger than life itself. It had humbled many an underling into compliance.

The Unum gripped the balcony railing. "I'm suggesting that with Mako's death still so raw, no one would question Lucien's decision to commit ritual suicide."

Pyros stuttered—a rarity for man not easily shocked. "Lucien al Braccus has faithfully served Daqin Guojin! I won't take his life for—"

"For the sake of Daqin Guojin's greater good? Then how about for a reason that strikes closer to home?"

Pyros' gaze flicked back and forth, no doubt searching the Unum's face for meaning.

The Unum selected his words with care. Manipulation demanded deft strokes, not careless lashings. "Your youngest daughter sits the S.A.T. next year?"

"You know she does."

"And how are Zola's prep-tests?"

Pyros' glower provided the answer.

"Narses' prep-tests are no better," the Unum said. "I'll do whatever it takes to prevent my son from becoming grooll. I can give that same protection to your daughter. Will you spill a few drops of blood to save her from the grooll mill?"

Pyros clutched the railing, gaze lowered to the square. He didn't voice an answer. He didn't have to. The answer was etched on his face.

The Unum allowed himself a satisfied smirk. He was as much

an artisan as the makers of the square below. They shaped ceramic tiles to achieve their breathculling designs; he shaped men's wills to achieve his necessary ends.

He let his expression harden to a more suitable solemnity. "Then for Zola's sake, *spill it*."

7

SONIC CHARGES

DAOREN AND HEQET arrived at Zhongguo Cheng's glass market thirty minutes after leaving the Hollows. It was the last place he'd expected to visit when she contacted him and asked to meet at the plinth.

Coming to the market brought them in the opposite direction of Meiguo Cheng and his abode, but he couldn't talk her out of the diversion. She wanted to find a gift for Cordelia and no amount of arguing would sway her. Some things never changed.

Despite his five-year absence, the market hadn't changed either. Mile upon mile of vendor stalls glittered amid the same thick columns supporting the same elevated transways. Shelves exhibited the same array of glass abodewares, ceramic jewelry, and crystalline sculptures. The only difference Daoren could sense was his companion.

Heqet strolled at arm's length, maintaining the uncomfortable silence that had marked their passage from the Hollows. Though he'd come close to crossing the conversational chasm, every topic that popped into his head seemed trivial. Every topic except for one, that is, but he couldn't gather the nerve to voice it;

Mako's death was still too raw. Instead, he buried it and let the buzz of commerce fill the space between them.

Of all the glass markets in Daqin Guojin, Zhongguo Cheng's was the largest. On a good day it attracted thousands of buyers. Today looked to be a good day.

Tubular levishuttles carrying buyers from throughout the district whisperglided to a stop on the market's perimeter. Parents strolled with their children, pointing at wares and haggling with vendors. Plump denizens in splendid shenyi threaded stalls on personal levidecks, using hand controls and shifts in body position to steer the hovering transports. Red-faced vendors called out to them the loudest; those who could afford personal levidecks had plenty of grooll to exchange.

On a good day tens of thousands of pounds of grooll would be exchanged. For buyers whose day-to-day lives held little vibrancy, the wares offered a colorful respite to an otherwise monochromatic existence. For vendors whose monthly rations left them calorie-deficient, the earnings meant survival. The ruling caste tolerated the market, but their acceptance came at a price. The Cognos Populi regularly dispatched Jireni squads to excise tithes, monitor gatherings, and confiscate items prohibited by the edicts.

Ceramic abodewares filled the first cluster of stalls on the western boundary. Vendors held up glossy plates and iridescent water jugs, angling the items to catch the sun's rays and the buyers' eyes.

"Do you know what you want to get her?"

"Not abodewares," Heqet said, scanning the stalls. "Something more personal."

He sighed. "I don't want to wander the market the rest of the day."

She lowered her chin and leveled a chilly glare. "Neither do I —especially if you're going to drag that attitude around with you."

He chambered a sharp reply. A crowded stall drew his attention before he could pull the trigger. "What's happening over there?"

"Let's go see."

They worked their way over to the stall. Its shelves brimmed with sculpted busts. Their sizes ranged from that of a fist to three times that of a human head. Their colors spanned the visible spectrum; frosted violets and blues, flushed yellows and oranges, fiery reds. Temperate, mid-spectrum greens freckled each shelf—a bold choice given the discussion within the Assembly of banning the color's display. For the sculptor, it was probably less a political statement than a sales ploy. The stall had attracted a sizable audience.

Daoren inched closer and craned his neck to see past the couple standing in front of him.

An Asianoid boy, all of six years old, sat before the stall. His thirtyish parents flanked him, clad in purple shenyi. The sculptor, a thin-set Africoid in his fifties, hunched opposite the boy. He guided a sonic chisel over a frosted-violet bust. The chisel's warbling pulses pulverized its glass, etching exquisite detail into a pair of inquisitive eyes.

The sculptor powered off the chisel and blew away a veneer of powdered silica. He held out the bust, comparing it to the flesh-and-blood template before him. He nodded and handed it to the boy. "Here's a handsome bust for the most handsome boy in Daqin Guojin."

The boy rotated the bust, examining it from assorted angles. "More handsome than your own son?"

"Alas, my S.A.T. score wasn't high enough to permit reproduction. So study hard, prospect. Mind your tutors and your parents." He glanced at the parents and winked. "Maybe one day you'll be the denizen who's clever enough to locate the lost seed vault."

"The lost seed vault?" the boy asked, face scrunched like a flexglass napkin.

The boy's father thrust a hand into his grooll pouch. "We don't fill his mind with ridiculous fables."

"That's a pity," the sculptor said. "It's still one of my favorite tales."

The father transferred a handful of grooll onto a glass tray next to a row of sonic chisels. He uttered a sanctimonious scoff. "We prefer our children to live in reality."

The sculptor shrugged. He peered at the grooll on the tray with equal indifference.

"Is that enough for the bust?"

The sculptor deflected the question. "What do you think, my handsome boy?"

The boy eyed the bust, clearly enthralled by its accuracy. He cast a less enthusiastic glance at the meager pile of grooll. "I think more, Papa."

Daoren grinned at the tactic. The sculptor may have dipped his S.A.T. score many years ago, but the man was no fid.

The father sighed. He deposited another handful onto the tray.

The sculptor stuffed the grooll into his own pouch, except for the piece he stuffed into his mouth. He worked his jaw from side to side. "Your kindness sustains me."

Daoren's stomach spasmed. Bile welled up his throat and filled his mouth. He swallowed the rancid liquid, grimacing.

"What's wrong?" Heqet asked.

"Nothing."

"You look like you're going to be sick."

It irked him that he hadn't better masked the nausea. It irked him more to have to explain it. "It's been a month since Mako was harvested, and the sight of grooll still bothers me."

"Give it time."

The casual statement slapped his ears. Give it time? Time for what? To forget that his brother's muscle, bone, and tendon had become part of the food chain? To forget that he'd been robbed of his future? To forget that Mako's mortal remains could be mixed among the grooll in his pouch? How much time would it take to—

"Excuse me, prospect."

Daoren pivoted to the phlegmy voice.

A Caucasoid woman extended a bony hand. Its translucent skin matched her baggy tunic's sepia hue. "Could you spare any grooll?"

Daoren emptied his pouch. "Take it all."

Her smile exposed a scattering of rotted teeth. "May Sha's sapience protect you, child."

The woman shuffled to the sculptor's stall and nodded at a blue bust, the size of a fist. She held out the grooll with both hands. "Is this enough?"

The sculptor answered by giving her the bust.

"That grooll was for eating," Daoren said, "not empty trinkets!"

The woman held up the crystal bust. It depicted a young man, a prospect judging by the twisted mound of hair. "Forgive my weakness, but it reminds me of my son." Her voice misted over. "He was harvested thirty years ago this month."

Daoren's cheeks grew warm. Who was he to determine the woman's choices? Who was he to define her grief? For some people, no amount of time could erase the pain of losing their kin. "My sorrow for your son."

He left the emaciated woman to commune with her dead son and wandered deeper into the market with Heqet. He ignored her persistent smirk as long as he could. "Did I do something to amuse you?"

"That was a kind act."

"What was?"

"Giving her your grooll," she said. "I had no idea you were so—"

"It had nothing to do with kindness. I have no stomach for grooll."

"Regardless, it was a decent thing to do."

"I did it for *me*. Does that still make it decent?"

Her smirk vanished. "You don't take compliments well, do you?"

"Save them for a more deserving recipient."

"Forgive me. I'm used to Mako's companionship."

"I'm not Mako."

Heqet rolled her eyes. "Don't state the obvious, Daoren. It insults your intelligence."

Daoren swallowed the bitter comment forming on his tongue. He didn't have the energy to argue further.

They neared a crowd gathered in the shade of an elevated transway. A dozen denizens surrounded a portly elder in a purple shenyi. A glass disk glowed under the elder's sandals.

The glowing disk betrayed the artifice of the otherwise flaw-less plasmonic projection. The unsubtle superiority of the elder's stance, the grandiose movement of its arms, and the pompous timbre of its vocal algorithm mimicked the Cognos Populi's bloated authority to perfection.

"It's your duty to report any suspicious activity to the Jireni," the elder intoned, wagging an ethereal finger. "Dissension is a threat to every Cheng in Daqin Guojin. Any information that leads to the culling of dissenters will be rewarded—and rewarded well."

Daoren glanced at Heqet. "More edicts on the Cognos Populi?"

She didn't respond. Her gaze fixed on something in the distance. He followed it to a smaller group, forty feet past the elder.

A Jiren restrained a prospect by her hair braids, sneering face inches from hers. A second Jiren gripped a glass phallus. A slight boy in a white pienfu stood between him and the girl, hands raised as if in mid-plea. The boy's eyes radiated fear, his words lost beneath the plasmonic elder's relentless blather. Both Asianoid prospects looked around eighteen years old.

"They're not going to test her *here*, are they?" Heqet asked.

"They've been cracking down on pre-denizenship coitus," Daoren said. "Who knows what the brutes will—"

The Jiren with the glass phallus backhanded the pleading prospect. The boy sprawled against a stand of crystal urns and crumpled to his knees. The other Jiren hip-tossed the girl, slamming her to the ground.

Daoren surged forward on instinct. Heqet caught his forearm and dug in her nails. "Don't! If you interfere they'll send you to the Rig!"

She was right. At best, challenges to Jireni authority led to immediate detainment. At worst, they ended in summary execution. He held back, rising gorge searing his throat.

The Jiren hiked up the girl's skirt and pried her legs apart. The other Jiren kneeled and thrust the phallus between her legs. The girl's pathetic squeals mixed with the grumblings from several brooding denizens among the stalls. They, too, held back.

The brutal violation lasted no more than five seconds. The Jiren slotted the phallus into a handheld quantum tile. Both men studied its screen, then resumed their foot patrol. Three other cackling Jireni joined the pair. The spectacle must have amused them.

Daoren stared at the aggrieved prospects. The boy wiped his bloodied lips, whimpering. The girl tugged her skirt back down, sobbing.

A harmony of hopelessness.

"She must have tested negative for penetration," Heqet said.

"We should go." Daoren took her arm. "They may be trolling for—"

An Indonoid man jostled between them. The inconsiderate

fid strode through the elder's projection and angled toward the
Jireni squad, quickening his pace.

Daoren primed his lungs to shout his annoyance. A spark of
recognition stilled his voice.

The man's sand-tone shenyi . . . its gold, corkscrew-shaped
columns. . . .

It was the father who'd held his dead daughter on the steps of
the Center, the day of Mako's S.A.T. The man's rapid, rigid gait
had a feverish quality. The back of his tunic appeared misshapen.

Daoren squinted.

Triangular lumps distended the tunic's fabric, deforming the
golden columns. The lumps were the same size and shape as—

A bolt of recognition culled Daoren's breath.

Sonic charges.

The Indonoid father broke into a run. He didn't stop until he
inserted himself in the midst of the Jireni. He wrapped his arms
around one of them. "In the name of free denizens, I pass judgment on your crimes!"

Daoren grabbed Heqet's arm and yanked. Her head snapped
to the side, prompting a squeal. He pulled her behind the transway's supporting column.

A deafening sound pulse walloped his ears. Instantaneous
overpressure condensed the air's water vapor to white mist. The
supersonic wavefront streaked past the column, dragging with it
the oxygen from his lungs.

Shards of bone and glass battered the opposite side of the
column, their furious peals a thousand jangling bells. Hissing
shrapnel shredded glass stalls and onlookers without distinction.

Daoren gripped Heqet, squeezing her to his chest, keeping
her out of the lethal slipstream. A blood-smeared chunk of blue
crystal clattered to a stop near the column's base.

The bust purchased by the emaciated woman.

Beyond the bust, the plasmonic elder held court atop his glass
disk, addressing no one. His audience had been swept away by

the blast. Dismembered denizens and prospects sprawled amid demolished stalls. Others lurched through the debris, faces blank with shock. They clutched gashed limbs and grisly wounds, bloody patches leaching through their splendid shenyi.

"What happened?" Heqet shouted.

The ringing in his ears all but muted her voice. "An attack on the Jireni!" He opened his mouth and stretched his jaw, trying to restore his hearing. "There may be another! We have to go!"

They dashed beneath the transway, hurdling bodies and collapsed stalls. The dying howled, crawling on their bellies, begging for help. Daoren ignored their pleas. Even if he could risk stopping, they were beyond saving.

In less than a minute they reached the multi-level structures lining the market's west end. Daoren sprinted into a laneway, dragging Heqet in his wake. Halfway down the laneway, a hand tugged on the back of his tunic.

"Stop! Stop!"

He stopped and scanned her body for wounds. "Are you hurt?"

Heqet massaged the back of her neck. "Just my neck from you yanking me."

The comment rekindled his ire. "Should I let you catch the full force of the sonic blasts next time?"

"You asked if I was hurt. I answered."

"So you did. My sorrow for your pain," he said with the utmost insincerity.

"My thanks for your sorrow," she said, the words slick with sarcasm. "Are *you* hurt?"

Daoren took inventory. His pienfu was free of blood. So were his arms and legs. He turned his hands, looking for cuts. They trembled—that was a wound of sorts.

"Trembling hands," she said. "So you're human after all."

He made fists. "It's adrenaline. I've seen death before."

"It's no sin to feel fear, Daoren."

"It's adrenaline!"

"So you said."

He shook his head. What was the use in arguing? "Come on."

After another two hundred feet, the laneway opened into a courtyard. Prospects filled it, seated cross-legged on cobbled sandstone before a dour Librarian on a bench.

Compared to the carnage in the market, the serenity was jarring. The concussive blasts of the sonic charges and cries of the wounded mustn't have penetrated the space. Either that or the Librarian had told his pupils to ignore the sounds.

The prospects were young, seven or eight years old at most. Pedagogical trips outside the Librarium's grounds were a rare occurrence. The children must have earned the reward through good behavior—if it could be called a reward. They labored over quantum tiles, screens laden with advanced integral-calculus equations.

Daoren grunted at the memories it dredged up. "The Libraria don't take long to indoctrinate them."

"They have to be ready to take on the responsibilities of denizenship," Heqet said.

"Has anyone stopped to weigh the price of denizenship?"

"The *price*? What do you—"

Two prospects squealed and scrambled to their feet. A Caucasoid girl chased after an Africoid boy. The pair charted an erratic circle around their cohorts.

"I'm going to get you, slag!"

"You're too slow to catch me, Jiren!" the boy replied, gigglesnicking.

The gigglesnicking spread to the seated audience. Prospects lowered their tiles and shouted encouragement, urging the slag to stay ahead of the Jiren.

The Librarian scowled from his bench-top perch. He rolled his own tile into a tube, then stretched the tube into a two-foot rod. He rapped the end of the rod into the firm sandstone.

Daoren's hands curled into fists. Shock-fusing the glass rod foreshadowed sinister repercussions. His suspicion was confirmed when the two prospects darted past the bench.

The Librarian jumped to his feet and seized the pursuer by the hair, jerking the girl to a stop. He thrashed her back with the rod. "I'll teach you to disrupt my class!"

Heqet gasped. "That's a bit harsh."

Daoren waded through the seated prospects and stole up behind the Librarian. He grabbed his arm, mid-beating. "That's enough!"

The Librarian whirled, eyes bulging. "How dare you lay your hand on me!"

Daoren twisted the man's arm. "Keep beating her and I'll lay more than my hand on you."

The Librarian winced. Pain dissolved his fury. He released the whimpering girl.

Daoren snatched the makeshift rod and rapped its end against the bench. The impact shock-separated the glass, transforming its crystalline atomic structure back to a malleable state. He bent the rod in half and tossed it to the Librarian. "Continue your indoctrination if you must, but don't abuse your pupils."

The Librarian caught the rod without making eye contact. He unrolled the tube and molded it back into a rectangular shape, hands trembling. "I . . . I won't."

Daoren picked his way over to Heqet. He ignored the stunned faces gawking up at him.

She greeted him with a smile that smacked of shock and admiration. "If it isn't Daoren, the Protector of Prospects. So tell me, oh wise one, what's the price of denizenship?"

He gaped at her. For the love of Sha, wasn't it obvious? "Our humanity, of course."

His blunt tone crushed her smile. For the second time today, he wished he'd softened it.

8

BLOOD SPILLED

PYROS STARED AT his quantum tile while he waited for the briefing to resume. If he angled its screen just right, he could see the chamber's decorative ceiling panels and still read the update displayed below the screen's glass. Ordinarily, he wouldn't devote a dot of attention to a trivial demonstration of light's simultaneous reflection and transmission—especially not in the shadow of such a serious incident—but he had little else to do.

Behind his desk, the Unum continued to fiddle with the Newton's Cradle like a child with a new toy. The rare device was a gift from an ally at the Librarium, he'd boasted when Pyros first arrived, and worth at least one thousand pounds of grooll.

Its six crystal orbs hung by gleamglass filaments beneath a ten-inch frame made from silver-infused crystalline. As the Unum had demonstrated eight times, drawing one orb back and releasing it set the cradle in motion. Its irksome clacking had filled the chamber for five of the six minutes Pyros had been here. He'd so far resisted the urge to hurl the device off the chamber's balcony.

He'd also resisted the urge to ask why a Librarian would give the Unum such an extravagant gift—or how the person could afford to do so. Libraria weren't known for their lavish grooll rations or for showering the Cognos Populi in largesse. He had his suspicions, but kept them to himself. He was here to discuss a more important issue.

His tile displayed the latest update from the on-scene commander at the glass market. Though details of the hour-old incident were still obscure, enough evidence had been gathered from survivors to piece together a preliminary conclusion.

"So you mentioned you had new information," the Unum said, at last muting his toy.

Pyros praised Sha for the silence. "It was a targeted attack. Three survivors saw the denizen approach the Jireni. They say he spoke before detonating the sonic charges."

The Unum lowered his hand from the cradle. "He spoke?"

"He made a statement about judging their crimes."

"Who was he?"

"It will take time to identify the body. There wasn't much left of him or the five Jireni he culled."

The Unum lifted his gaze to the ceiling—as was his habit when contemplating.

Or giving the appearance of contemplating, Pyros reminded himself. The Unum's moods defied rational analysis. They swung between warm regard and cold calculation so often, it was a wonder his mind didn't succumb to the temperature fluctuation.

"The attack serves to underscore my earlier point," the Unum said, staring at the ceiling. "How many more Jireni would die if word of Lucien's suspicion gets out? It must be done." He lowered his gaze. "And it must be done *today*."

Pyros studied the face on the other side of the desk, the finality in its deep-set eyes in particular. He'd seen it many times before. No words would sway the Unum from this path. One action might, however, delay the inevitable for an indefinite period.

"What if I intern Lucien at the Rig?" Pyros asked. "He may disclose information on who sent him Julinian's prep-tests. There could be considerable intelligence value in—"

"If you don't want to perform the task, then say so." The Unum shrugged. "I'm sure I can find another Jiren whose child risks failing the S.A.T. to carry it out. Of course, your daughter might pay a heavy price for your decision, but it's *your* decision."

Pyros tensed his eyelids and peered through the semi-veiled threat. The Unum may be capricious and manipulative, but he knew more about survival than any man in Daqin Guojin. He'd have no issue with revoking his promise to secure a passing S.A.T. score for Zola. If he didn't cull Lucien, another Jiren would do the deed at the Unum's behest before the swollen sun set.

He let the rationalization seep into his heart, hardening it. Twenty-five years of service in the Jireni and twenty-four years of union had proven one truth. When it came to kin, a person sometimes had to choose the lower path to gain the higher ground.

How could he return to his abode and tell Nailah he didn't choose the path that guaranteed their daughter's survival? What kind of husband could make such a decision? What kind of father?

He relaxed his eyes. His path was set.

The Unum set the cradle in motion again. Its loathsome clacking resumed.

Pyros raised his voice. "Where is he?"

TEN MINUTES LATER, Pyros plodded down a glass-lined hallway six levels below the Unum's chamber. Purple-tinted shadows flitted from chamber to chamber, scurrying from meeting to meeting. The Assembly members scarcely registered in his mind.

The task at hand devoured his focus. He'd culled many men

at close quarters—prospects, dissenters, mongrels—but this one would be different. This man was a respected colleague, a denizen with whom he'd taken grooll and grown to admire.

This culling would be intimate.

He rounded a corner, gaze downcast. He'd have to get behind him. Only from behind could he strike and make it look like ritual suicide. Any defensive wounds would cry out against that conclusion. Any calls for help would bring a rush of witnesses who'd see the truth in all its horrid—

"Bide a moment, sire?"

Pyros halted, steps before plowing into two Jireni.

Commander Cang's creased forehead and pursed lips hinted at concern. A young Asianoid Jiren shadowed her—an aide whose name Pyros could never remember.

The display of emotion surprised him. He'd known Cang alum Aridian for twenty years. They'd served together for three years on the Great Northern Border and executed countless reconnaissance missions in the mongrel colonies. Her ascent through the ranks owed as much to decisive leadership as incisive intellect, but her greatest pride was her Asianoid reticence. Emotions usually found no welcome on her visage. As district commander for Zhongguo Cheng, she and her reticence must have been disturbed by the day's events.

"What is it, commander?"

"The attack at the glass market," Cang said, selecting her words with typical care. "Its brashness worries me. The willingness to carry it out in daylight in such a public forum, to inflict so many casualties regardless of their social status."

"It marks a new trend among the dissenters."

"A dangerous trend. I wonder whether the edict to raise the S.A.T.'s passing score was adopted in haste."

"The edict came from the Unum himself."

"Be that as it may, the Unum isn't . . . infallible."

Pyros scowled at her aide. "Take five paces backward, Jiren."

The young Asianoid blinked, brow crumpled.

"Move, shadow."

The aide followed the order without hesitation.

"Radan isn't a threat," Cang said. "He's heard me question the Unum's edicts before."

Pyros inspected the hallway, gauging their isolation. Hearing his own thoughts echoed by Cang brought some relief, but the remark couldn't be overheard or go unchallenged. "We serve the ruling caste. The Unum represents the pinnacle of their interests."

"Without question, but he's temporary. Daqin Guojin isn't. A view that takes its stability into consideration may be needed."

Pyros didn't respond. He didn't trust what he might say.

"There's another issue that troubles me," Cang said. "I've received reports concerning the questionable activities of a prominent Librarian. I need to—"

"Can we discuss this later?"

The gruff interruption compelled her to step back. "Um . . . certainly. I'll forward you my preliminary and supplementary reports on the subject. Contact me to discuss it in depth whenever you have the time."

"Fine, fine."

Cang bowed her head. When she raised it again, puzzlement crimped her eyes. "Are you all right, sire? Is there another matter that weighs your mind?"

"Only today's attack," Pyros said. "Keep me informed of any findings."

He swept past her and her aide, eager to be done with the task at hand and dreading its completion at the same time.

PYROS ARRIVED AT the chamber's outer door fifty minutes later. It should have taken less than five minutes from the time he left Cang, but he'd come by a more indirect route. He'd diverted as far as the lower levels of the Assembly, hoping the delay would free enough mind-space to determine a plan of attack.

It hadn't. He could wander the hallways for the rest of the day and come no closer to an answer. He needed to see the chamber, get the lay of the land, and discover its ground truth. Once inside, a plan would present itself—with any luck.

Fortuitous timing had delivered him unseen to the outer door. He rapped its clear glass and entered without waiting for an invitation.

The inner chamber was much smaller than the Unum's and far less ornate. Its ceiling hosted no scenic panels, its glass walls no geometric patterns. A ceramic water fountain gurgled ten feet beyond the door—the space's sole piece of sculpture. Ten feet beyond it, Lucien sat behind a simple transparent desk, his gaze lowered to its surface.

Pyros cursed the man's humility. It made the task no easier.

Lucien lifted his head. His face brightened. "Pyros, welcome."

He stalked over and paced before the desk, still no closer to a plan of attack. Constant movement tended to sharpen his thoughts, but not today. Visions of his daughter being processed into grooll kept bubbling up like pools of slag on molten glass.

"You look as though your mind's being stretched in opposite directions," Lucien said, an undertone of wariness coloring the statement.

The wariness in Lucien's voice was the beacon Pyros needed. He saw his path.

Keep him off-balance. Make him draw me in.

He kept up his pacing. "The more paranoid denizens of Daqin Guojin have long suspected that senior members of the Cognos Populi are manipulating the S.A.T. for the benefit of their kin." He halted and leveled a bloodless stare. "I've dealt with these threats as they arise."

Lucien's brightness dimmed. "You think me a threat?"

"That depends. You have Julinian's prep-tests?"

"I received them earlier this afternoon."

"From whom?"

"An anonymous source." Lucien beckoned him to come around the desk. "A datakeeper at the Librarium, I assume."

Pyros rounded the desk and positioned himself behind Lucien's seat, heartbeat throbbing in his fingertips. He glanced at the glass walls enveloping the chamber. They left him far too exposed. "I'd prefer this visit to be anonymous," he said. "The Unum doesn't know I'm here."

Lucien tapped the desktop; the chamber's walls tinted black. He manipulated the desk's embedded tile. A multitude of documents opened, under-lighting his chin and amplifying the creases around his mouth. His fingers swiped and pinched, arranging the documents in five rows.

"Are those her prep-tests?"

"For the past five years."

"Have you shown them to anyone else?"

"You're the first," Lucien said. "You won't be the last."

"What do you mean?"

"I'm going to present them to the Assembly."

He placed a hand on Lucien's shoulder. "Is that the wisest course of action?"

"It's the *right* course of action. Not because it involves my son, but because it involves the sanctity of the S.A.T."

The statement confirmed his suspicion; Lucien wouldn't be swayed. "Is the evidence strong enough to warrant an inquiry?"

"Judge for yourself." Lucien pointed at the documents arrayed on the desktop. "There. See Julinian's average score over twenty prep-tests? She earned less than ten thousand points."

Pyros leaned over. He slipped his hand inside his tunic and felt for its shoulder sheath. "Less than ten thousand, you say?"

"Yet she receives a score high enough to gain unrestricted

entry to the Cognos Populi when it truly matters. Does that make sense to you?"

Pyros grasped the dagger's handle with an overhand grip. He drew the weapon into the open, keeping it out of Lucien's sightline. Its ceramic blade glimmered in the desk's glow.

It wasn't the straight, double-edged blade preferred by the Jireni. It was a smaller, curved blade with a single, serrated edge. The kind that anyone could obtain in a glass market. The kind that was difficult to extract once driven home.

Pyros steadied his breathing. He raised the dagger, higher and higher. "No, my friend. It doesn't make sense."

Lucien's head shook from side to side. "Mako's prep-tests averaged twenty-nine thousand points. Is that supposed to be a coincidence? There's no way he could have—"

Pyros clamped his free hand over Lucien's mouth and swung the dagger downward. It plunged hilt-deep into Lucien's pelvis.

Lucien's body arched and stiffened. He clawed at the dagger's handle, trying to draw it out. His muffled screams pumped moist air against Pyros' fingers.

Pyros closed his eyes and rip-sawed upward, hacking through gleamglass, skin, and entrails. He didn't stop until the blade rasped on bone. He pressed his lips to Lucien's ear. "Forgive me, Lucien. *Forgive me.*"

Lucien's body went limp. His muffled cries grew fainter and fainter. When Pyros felt no more breath against his fingers, he opened his eyes.

Blood drenched his knife hand. Red rivulets streamed off Lucien's shenyi and dribbled onto the opaque floor.

Pyros blinked, summoning the clarity he needed to complete the task. He folded Lucien's blood-soaked hands around the dagger's handle. He used his own unbloodied hand to expunge Julinian's prep-tests and open a cache of quantum images.

One by one, Mako's likeness resolved, filling the desk's

surface. Red droplets spattered the boy's smiling face like bloody tears.

Pyros rounded the desk and surveyed the scene for signs of his presence. None jumped out, but ample evidence of another kind leapt to the forefront.

He'd culled an innocent man.

He'd culled a man who was a credit to Daqin Guojin.

He'd culled a man who but for a quirk of lineage and a decent heart would have been a great Unum.

Only now, seeing the aftermath of his decision, did he recognize it.

He'd made the wrong choice.

Pyros trudged to the fountain. He thrust his hand into its cool stream and rinsed away the blood. His shoulders slumped.

His path was set.

9

SEA OF STORMS

TWO HOURS AFTER leaving the abusive Librarian in the courtyard, Heqet arrived at the southern habitation complex in Meiguo Cheng with Daoren at her side.

She was last here just over a month ago. The pediwalks hemming the transways bristled with the same mix of Caucasoids. The yellow, blue, and purple abodes still resembled haphazardly stacked children's blocks. Groups of prospects, no more than twelve at a time in keeping with the restriction on associations, played *Jireni and Slags* or *Mongrel Incursions* in the open spaces around the complex. The familiar landmarks offered no comfort thanks to the foreign entity walking beside her.

He was so unlike his brother. Mako couldn't walk five paces without saying ten words. Daoren could walk ten thousand paces without saying five words. Mako tread lightly in both his physical movements and his personal interactions. Daoren had a swagger that never went away, even when he was standing still, and a personality as abrasive as a mouthful of sand. Yes, he was smart—Mako had told her many times how Daoren was receiving stellar results on his prep-tests despite leaving the Librarium—but did that give him the right to be such a *glasshole*?

She stole another glance at him as they walked. Sure enough, his expression hadn't changed. The same disheveled bangs curtained the same disaffected brow. The same impervious cheekbones crowned the same imperious jawline.

He turned his head and skewered her with an impenetrable gaze. He didn't smile nor frown. He didn't cross his eyes nor stick out his tongue. He simply granted a different view of his face.

She looked away, too quickly. She cursed herself, again.

"We'll be there soon," he said.

"I'm not a distant relative from another district. I could close my eyes from here and still find my way to your abode."

"Oh . . . right."

Heqet sighed. Maybe she should do just that. At least with her eyes closed, she wouldn't get caught stealing glances at him.

Daoren possessed uncanny intuition, a sixth-sense so incisive it smacked of second-sight. He'd displayed the gift in the market when he pulled her behind the transway column. If he'd delayed as much as a second, she'd be dead.

Mako wouldn't have reacted that way. He'd have been too busy pointing out the wares in the stalls to notice the man with the sonic charges, let alone the sonic charges. He wouldn't have responded to the comment about her sore neck with indignation either; he'd have laughed at the irony. And challenge a Librarian's authority to protect a prospect? Never.

The incident in the courtyard made Daoren more of a puzzle. What prompted him to race over and stop the beating? Was it compassion? Was it anger? Did he feel sorry for the prospect or did he despise the Libraria that much?

True to form, he'd ruined the moment by snapping at her. Humanity was the price of denizenship? Daoren al Lucien was one to talk of humanity. She'd known him thirteen years, and he'd divulged few human traits other than intelligence. Yet she couldn't shake the feeling that much more lay trapped below his sterile surface, buried like the artifact caches her grandfather so loved to examine.

They walked another ten minutes in deliberate silence before reaching the abode's door. Daoren opened it.

She snatched his sleeve. "Are you sure she'll want to see me?"

"Why wouldn't she?"

"I might remind her of Mako. I don't want to upset her."

"This is the only abode we've ever lived in. You think it isn't full of reminders already?"

Heqet dammed her tongue with her teeth, barricading a biting retort. It wasn't just his words; it was the way he said them —like his excrement didn't stink. "I suppose you're right . . . as always."

His barbed glance bit into her.

She queued a sharp comment, ready to deflate *his* sharp comment, but he entered the abode without another word. She followed him, disappointed by his restraint.

The entry nave radiated an eerie familiarity. Lucien and Cordelia had simple tastes and precious little grooll to exchange for decorative wares, but their abode always gave off a vibrant and welcoming atmosphere. Now an oppressive aura dampened it.

A crystal urn filled with grooll perched on a side table near the door as was the custom of Western Caucasoids. She took a piece and placed it onto her tongue. Its macronutrients embittered her mouth, provoking a shudder.

Daoren walked past the urn, foregoing the offering. Three hallways lined with tan-tinted glass tiles branched off from the nave to the parlor, the pantry, and the sleeping chambers.

Another shudder swept through her body. The cramped abode felt more confining for Mako's absence. Did it feel the same way for Daoren? Was he capable of experiencing loss on his island of isolation? She declined to ask him. If the last few hours were any indication, he wouldn't deign her with a reply.

"Cordelia?" he called out. "Heqet is here."

Heqet bunched her shoulders. His insistence on calling his parents by their first names grated her sensibility. She wouldn't have dared address her parents in such an informal manner. In truth, she'd gladly forsake her future to address them in any manner.

The clink of glass-on-glass wafted down the hallway leading to the sleeping chambers. Mako's chamber was at the end, sixteen paces away, on the right-hand side. Two feet from its doorway, a loose floor tile would squeak in protest if trod upon. She'd learned as a child how to be quiet in this abode.

"Don't mention the market or what we discussed at the Hollows," Daoren said. "I don't want to worry her."

Heqet would sooner forget the events herself, and none quicker than his hunch about Mako's score being switched with a prospect related to the Unum. Now that they were here, she wished she hadn't met him at the Hollows and agreed to come. A month may have passed since the January S.A.T., but standing in the abode conjured up a miserable tangle of emotions, the worst of which was angst at seeing Cordelia again.

She trailed him down the hallway. Her heart raced faster with each step—faster than any time she'd stolen late-night visits with Mako. It skipped a beat when Daoren's foot landed on the loose tile. He didn't react to its squeak, nor did he slow before entering the chamber. She stepped over the tile out of habit and crossed the door's threshold.

Cordelia stood next to Mako's bed with her back to the door. Sheer, gray fabric bereft of embroidery and adornments draped her body. A mourning shroud.

That was odd. Heqet had worn one for seven days while she fasted for Mako, in keeping with the custom. Seven days and no more. Cordelia's shroud hung loose, its hemline skimming the floor. Its sleeves swallowed her arms. Hadn't she broken her fast?

Cordelia plucked sculptglass models from the nooks recessed into the walls between the bed and desk. Cantilevered bridges.

Terraced water fountains. Twisting spans of elevated transways. Angular structures with breathculling geometries.

Mako had dreamed of constructing epic public works after his S.A.T. *I'll build us a glinty life as I build the people a better Daqin Guojin*, he'd say, voice plump with mock authority.

Seeing his models again tore at her heart. Seeing Cordelia set them in a glass crate, as if to be packed away in an unlit space, rent it in two.

Cordelia spotted them when she turned to clear another nook. Her disposition morphed from blankness to surprise to joy in a single breath. She whisked over. "Heqet!"

Heqet felt genuine love in the embrace. She rested her chin on Cordelia's bony collar and squeezed back. Her tears fell as silently as the footfalls that had brought her to this chamber on so many nights—then she noticed the quantum images.

Four images glowed, embedded in the glass face of the recessed nook above the desk; Mako and Lucien in his father's chamber at the Assembly, Mako and Cordelia in the abode's rear courtyard, Mako and her grandfather in the Spires of the Librarium. The fourth image in the nook captured Mako and her, arm-in-arm in the abode's parlor, less than a year ago.

Cracks ringed the glass overlying the fourth image. The impact looked severe enough to have fractured Mako's knuckles.

Heqet couldn't rip her gaze from the shattered image. He'd struck it the night before his S.A.T., moments before she fled the chamber in tears. He'd rambled for hours beforehand about their imminent union and glinty future together. She'd ended their relationship because she couldn't keep lying to him . . . or to herself.

The fifth image was missing from the nook; the one of Mako and Daoren, taken at the Hollows. He'd spent five minutes cajoling Daoren to pose for it. She'd been forced to dawdle, stomach growling and patience thinning, while they argued. She'd rendered the image on Mako's quantum tile three months ago on a humid November afternoon. It was the last time the three of them were together.

She glanced over Cordelia's shoulder at Daoren. Had he noticed the cracked and missing images?

He stared at the pile of models set in the crate. Grief moistened his eyes and weighted his cheeks. The emotional cues vanished in a single breath, but they answered her question on whether he could feel loss.

"It's been too long, child," Cordelia said, releasing her.

"A month."

"You needn't have waited all this time before coming by. You know you're always welcome here."

Heqet also knew why she'd waited. She hadn't come by because she thought she was responsible for Mako's failure. She'd convinced herself that ending the relationship had wrecked his ability to concentrate on the S.A.T. She'd also convinced herself that Cordelia knew and would blame her for his harvesting. Yet here she was without a hint of blame on her face, as loving as ever.

The emotional burden's lifting lightened Heqet's tone. "How are you?" She cringed at the inane question the moment it passed her lips.

Cordelia shrugged it off with a tentative smile. "I'm surviving, child. And you?"

"I'm taking it day by day."

"How's your grandfather?" Cordelia asked. "On the day of the S.A.T., he seemed to take Mako's failure personally. I hope he's forgiven himself."

"I've hardly seen him. He's been working on some project."

"I'd wager he's seeking solace in his artifacts. Tell him you're both to come over at your earliest convenience. Lucien and I would—"

Heavy footfalls resounded in the hallway.

Cordelia's smile faded. "Lucien? Is that you?"

The footfalls grew louder. Daoren inched toward the door. His hands clenched and unclenched by his side.

A pang of sorrow pricked Heqet; Mako used to exhibit the same unconscious tic when anxious. It was one of the few traits the brothers shared.

Daoren stopped at the door's threshold. Beyond it, the telltale tile squeaked. . . .

The Unum brushed past him and swept into the chamber.

Heqet gasped. His appearance was so sudden and so unexpected, she forgot to bow. A hulking Africoid with a scarred scalp and joyless eyes entered a second later. The gold piping on his black bianfu identified him; Pyros, the Primae Jiren.

The Unum halted before Cordelia. She managed an awkward semi-bow and clasped her hands before her chest. "Unum, what brings you here?"

The Unum rubbed his blotchy scalp, averting his gaze. Pyros stared at Daoren, thumb hooked on his waist belt. He slid the hand closer to his dagger's opaque sheath.

Heqet's throat tightened as her gaze flicked between Pyros and the Unum. Their stilted movements had a mechanical air, more rehearsed than natural. Her instinct told her the behavior foreshadowed ill tidings.

Cordelia must have sensed it, too. "Unum, please. If you have news for me, speak it."

"Cordelia," the Unum said, voice a mere whisper. "I don't know how to say this. There's been a horrible . . ." His searching gaze shifted to Pyros, like he needed help in finding the words.

The hairs on the back of Heqet's neck stood. From her vantage point, she gleaned more than a loss for words in the glance. The Unum had looked at Pyros to confirm that his Primae Jiren was positioned between him and Daoren. *For protection.*

"I'm afraid I have terrible news," the Unum continued. "An hour ago, Lucien's body was found in his chamber at the Assembly. He committed ritual suicide."

Cordelia's piercing cry reverberated off the chamber's glass walls, rising in pitch until it bordered on inaudible. She collapsed onto the edge of the bed and rocked back and forth. Her body shrank with each ragged wheeze of despair.

Daoren bared his teeth and lunged at the Unum. "His blood is on your hands!"

The Unum retreated from the attack. He stumbled over the crate of models and nearly went to the floor. He would have gone to the floor had Pyros not intercepted Daoren.

"Calm yourself, boy!" he said, struggling to hold him back. "Don't make this worse than it is! Attend to your mother!"

The command penetrated Daoren's fury. He pulled away and joined Cordelia on the bed. She buried her face against his chest, bawling.

The Unum gave them a wide berth and rejoined Pyros near the door. "You're upset, Daoren. I'll forgive that outburst . . . this time." He straightened his bestudded zhaoshan and puffed his chest, no doubt eager to reclaim a portion of dignity. "You have my deepest sorrow for your loss, Cordelia. Lucien was a credit to Daqin Guojin. I promise he'll have a funeral worthy of his status."

He swept into the hallway with Pyros. Their footfalls faded away.

Heqet folded her arms across her chest. Under her shell of skin, a numb cavity resonated like a memorial tube in the Hollows. She squeezed, needing the counter-pressure of her body to prove she was still here, still whole, still breathing.

Memories of her parents' death resurfaced, crisp and unbidden. She pictured her grandfather sitting her down in the parlor of their old abode, his wringing, wrinkled hands so coarse it might have taken place this morning. She felt his grief-mangled words bludgeoning her heart. She heard her sobs blustering in wretched squalls that raged for hours . . . for days.

Heqet blinked back tears. After five years, the memories retained their clarity, as detailed as the models set in the crate before her. They would never be packed away in an unlit space. For some, no amount of time could erase the pain of losing their kin.

She glanced at Daoren, expecting to see the same pain inscribed on his face, ready to go to him to help erase it.

It wasn't there. He sat beside Cordelia on the bed, eyes as dry as the Great Saharan Desert, body as inert as a sculptglass statue.

"I'm so sorry, Daoren," Heqet said. "What can I do?"

He didn't move. He didn't make a sound. He stared across Mako's sleeping chamber, within arm's reach of his last living family member.

Heqet inched closer, half-expecting him to go off like the sonic charges in the glass market. "What do you need?"

He looked up at her. He looked through her. "There's only one thing I need."

He didn't voice the need. His eyes communicated it without ambiguity. Their cold finality sent a shiver down her spine. "You can't," she said. "He's too powerful, too—"

"You can't stop me." Daoren's frozen gaze lowered to the crate of models. "No one can stop me."

SEVEN DAYS LATER, Daoren stood next to Cordelia in the center of the funeral aerostat's passenger gondola. Banks of convex blister-windows provided a panoramic view of the wind-tossed waves one hundred feet below. They'd cleared the coastline ten minutes ago.

Beyond the forward windows, the aerostat's gray nose pointed toward a dense field of wind turbines sixty miles distant. White columns erupted from the Sea of Storms, spanning the horizon. They supported the whirling, one thousand-foot blades of the Southern Turbine Complex. At this range, the blades glinted like tiny daggers.

Daoren fingered his mourning shroud—the second he'd worn in a month—picking at a loose burrglass thread. Around him, hundreds of mourners from all castes filled the gondola. Members of the Cognos Populi. Notable Libraria. Silica engineers his father had worked with in his youth. Ordinary denizens. A sprinkling of prospects. The morose field of gray was gathered to honor Lucien's passing.

His father's shrouded body lay ten feet before him on a low pedestal. In his head, Daoren knew he was seeing the outline of Lucien's face, torso, and limbs beneath the purple fabric. In his heart, they were anonymous contours on an unknowable landscape.

He hadn't talked to his father much over the past ten years. What few words they'd shared were charged with scorn and tainted with hostility. There were so many questions Daoren hadn't asked him. One question burned to be answered now.

Whose hand was holding the knife?

He may not have known his father well, but he knew one aspect of his character with sandstone certainty. Lucien would never have committed ritual suicide. Not while Cordelia still drew breath. Not while she still mourned Mako's harvesting. Not while he promised to talk later.

Across the gondola, the Unum, Julinian, and Narses huddled, clad in creaseless mourning shrouds that flirted with opulence. Julinian's eyes drooped like she was on the verge of falling asleep. Daoren hadn't seen Narses in over a year or spoken to him in three, but his shroud did little to sharpen his dull expression. The misaligned forehead studs and mouth-breathing didn't help; they gave the impression of someone in mid-yawn.

The Unum lumbered forward and kneeled beside Lucien's body. He played the part of a mourner well. His pyramidal studs complemented his ashen pallor. He shook his head in apparent disbelief and placed a hand on Lucien's shrouded chest.

Daoren shuddered. It was like witnessing an indignity to the body.

"Today we grieve the loss of Lucien al Braccus," the Unum said, venting a soliloquy more somnolent than solemn, "a man whose love for family equaled his love for Daqin Guojin. From the day he was conferred denizenship, he lived to serve the people, holding key positions in silica sourcing and grooll distribution."

He rose, grunting from the effort, and scrutinized the mourners. His pseudo-somber gaze landed on Daoren and Cordelia. "He leaves behind a beautiful wife and two promising sons."

Whispers of shock coursed through the gondola.

The Unum's face flushed. "Forgive me—*one* promising son."

Cordelia released a lacerated moan. She staggered over to the body and fell to the deck beside it, wailing.

Women in the crowd added their own laments, compounding the grief. Men wept, shoulders heaving in time with the disturbed waters below.

Daoren willed himself not to react. He needed to stay focused on the bloated ruler of Daqin Guojin. He needed to remain receptive to the signals on his brittle Slavvic face. His attention was rewarded when the Unum flicked a glance at Julinian and Narses. It surrendered one fleeting clue.

Smugness.

Daoren curled his hands into fists. Acidic words boiled up from his gut and etched through his teeth. "Your funeral aerostat will soon take flight, Unum," he whispered.

"Brave words, but far too foolish for such a clever boy."

Daoren wheeled to the hushed voice.

Laoshi grasped his shoulders. He leaned in to touch foreheads.

Daoren stayed rigid and upright, leaving him hanging. He cared as much for the gesture of greeting and farewell as he did for crowds, especially when it came to the Libraria.

"Still rejecting custom and authority at every opportunity, hmm?" Laoshi said, straightening. "Even as a child you were your own man."

"I'm not a child anymore."

"Yet you're seen as one in the eyes of the edicts. Until you pass the S.A.T., you hold no rights, no privileges." He swept a wrinkled hand to the forward windows. "What do you see out there?"

"The Southern Turbine Complex."

"And what does it represent to you?"

"Sixty percent of Daqin Guojin's power," Daoren said, unable to filter the sullenness from his voice.

"Don't give me snide answers, boy."

"Seventy percent?"

Laoshi tightened his grip and shook him. "That's the southern border of Daqin Guojin, the southern limit of your world." He pinched Daoren's earlobe. "The nanocharges so thoughtfully implanted in your skull by the Cognos Populi aren't deactivated until you sit the S.A.T. They—"

"They prevent prospects from venturing beyond the border," Daoren said, pulling his head back from the grasping Librarian. "I know, Laoshi. Just because I've studied on my own doesn't mean I'm—"

Cordelia's wails tore into a wracking climax. Daoren tried to turn to her, but Laoshi prevented him. He was strong for an old man.

"Bide a moment longer."

"I must attend to my mother."

"You must attend to your final test preparation under my tutelage."

Daoren snorted. "I don't need your tutelage to survive the S.A.T."

Laoshi yanked him into an embrace. "I know, boy," he whispered in Daoren's ear. "You need it to survive the forces aligned against you." He relaxed his grip. "Look now to your mother. But later, look to me."

Daoren wandered to the pedestal. Laoshi's words gnawed at his mind, but his mother's grief demanded his immediate attention. "Momma, come."

He helped her to her feet. She clutched his arm, swaying and trembling. The rest of the mourners gathered around them.

The pedestal canted sideways, revealing a breach in the gondola's lower hull. Lucien's shrouded body slid along the pedestal's smooth crystalline surface and dropped into the open air.

It tumbled one hundred feet into the Sea of Storms.

10

INTER LIBRARIUM

JID 736390-112489-ZC
PRIMAE JIREN'S EYES ONLY
SUBJECT: LAOSHI AL EUCLIDIUS

1. Sixty-six scrolls authored by the subject have been forwarded to my office by Gustar al Vlodisar, a senior Librarian assigned to datakeeping within the Spires. (See accompanying Jireni Investigative Decree 736390-112253-ZC for more details.)

2. Based on the seditious nature of the writings, sufficient cause exists to open an investigation into the subject's activities and associations over the last five years.

3. Immediate detention and questioning in the Rig is problematic given the subject's prominent position and widespread support among the Libraria and denizens at large.

4. If evidence of dissension is found, my office will be forced to apply the harshest punitive penalty.

*Preparations will have to be made to quell the
social unrest this action would prompt.*
5. *Supplementary reports will follow for your eyes only.*

Survival Through Sapience.
Cang alum Aridian
District Commander, Zhongguo Cheng

A HUVVATRAIN LADEN with ceramic pillars inched past Daoren.

One hundred feet in length and ten feet in diameter, the pillars were bound for the new administrative structures being raised in Zhongguo Cheng's western boroughs—their glossy mauve veneer was a dead giveaway. The construction project had razed seven habitation complexes and displaced four thousand families to make room, but those costs carried no significance. The Cognos Populi needed more meeting space in which to conduct their murky affairs.

Thirty-eight linked carriers had crawled by so far, with two left to go. That made the huvvatrain nearly a mile long and Sha-knows-how-many tons. Whatever its mass, its bulk blocked the pediwalk and his progress, holding him captive within striking distance of the Librarium's entrance.

He muttered under his breath. The only act more annoying than returning to the Librarium was languishing under the mid-day sun for the privilege to do so. Scorching rays drilled into the top of his head; they'd soon tap the vast pain reservoir behind his eyes. The loads of pillars had delayed him twenty minutes *and* set him on the path toward a splitting headache.

The last carrier cleared the pediwalk, revealing the Librarium's southern perimeter. Ninety feet away, a twelve-foot wall topped with crystal spikes encircled the grounds. A crystalline archway served as the sole access point. Its prismatic sunglow blocks bore an ancient inscription, letters darkened by shadow.

Survival Through Sapience.

Daoren tramped across the transway, comparing the sights to a storechamber of mental images from ten years ago. The wall and archway seemed smaller and less imposing now, the inscription's letters duller and less accurate. Otherwise, time hadn't changed their appearance. The same couldn't be said of him—or anyone else in his life.

Since his father's funeral, Cordelia had spent her days and nights in the abode's parlor, sifting through cache after cache of quantum images. She no longer wept when she viewed the renditions of Lucien and Mako—not even when she converted them to plasmonic projections whose haptic feedback made them substantive enough to touch—but she no longer ate either. No amount of his pleading could persuade her to take grooll. His mother was intent on shriveling out of existence.

Heqet had vanished altogether. She didn't attend Lucien's funeral. Daoren had searched for her on the passage back to the southern aerodrome, combing through the aerostat's gondola, straining for a glimpse of her twin braids and sparkling microstuds. A casual onlooker might have assumed he was thanking the mourners for their attendance; out of character, but understandable given the circumstances.

In reality, he'd *ached* to see her. That was also out of character. Heqet's presence had affected him for good and ill over the past thirteen years, but he couldn't recall a time when her absence had caused physical pain. It felt as though he'd lost a vital organ —without the benefit of anesthetic. Why it felt that way he couldn't say, but her disappearance irked him. That much he could put a finger on.

In the days after the funeral, his hunch that the Unum played a part in Mako and Lucien's deaths had solidified to a near certainty. Mako's S.A.T. score couldn't have been swapped with

Julinian's score without the authorization of the ruler of Daqin Guojin. No sane member of the Cognos Populi or the Libraria would risk exposing the Unum to charges of S.A.T. manipulation without his foreknowledge. And no sane man would accuse the Unum of tampering with S.A.T. scores without some measure of proof.

The prep-test results Lucien received in his chamber at the Assembly during Daoren's visit had triggered a reaction best described as shock—had they implicated the Unum in some kind of scheme? Had his father paid for receiving them with his life? The more Daoren pondered the question, the more the answer pointed to yes.

Like every inhabitant of Daqin Guojin, Lucien suffered from blind-spots. Guileless to a fault, he had no appetite for cunning or intrigue. Whereas another man might have used evidence of test manipulation as leverage to advance his own interests, Lucien would have spared no effort to bring it to light. As straightforward as his father was, however, Daoren couldn't see him confronting the Unum—at least not directly. He must have shared his suspicion—and the prep-test results—with the wrong person in the Assembly.

Who that person might be remained a mystery, but Daoren was convinced the answers lay within the Librarium. Not in the fictions and propaganda embedded in its glass scrolls, but in its Primae Librarian. *The forces aligned against you,* Laoshi had said at the funeral. It was time to discover what those forces looked like.

He reached the far side of the transway and angled for the archway. Ten feet from its overhanging inscription, a shrill hiss washed over him. A guttural voice cut through the din. "Hold fast, prospect!"

A levideck whisked to a halt before him, blocking the entrance. Transparent armor panels curled around the craft's leading edges, forming the shape of a raised shield. Cylindrical airpacks nestled in banded stacks behind the panels. Screens glowed in a wraparound dash above a pair of handgrips.

Its Jireni rider twisted a handgrip. Varinozzles mounted below the horizontal deck powered off. The hiss of compressed air faded and the craft settled onto the ground. "What's your business in the Librarium, slag?"

"S.A.T. prep."

"Who's your tutor?"

"I've been studying on my own."

"One of *those* prospects, hmm?" The Jiren plucked a thin glass probe from the craft's dash and waved him closer. "Come then, lend me your ear."

Daoren eyed the archway. A few more paces and he'd have been on the Librarium's grounds, beyond the brute's authority. He cursed the huvvatrain for delaying him and stepped forward, raking his hair back.

The probe's cold tip entered his ear canal. Colder chirps announced its air-query.

The levideck's dash screens flickered. Daoren's fingerprint scans, genetic sequence, patterns of movement, and other information replicated on them. They broadcasted a lifetime's worth of biometric data, captured and stored in the spintronic diodes injected behind his eardrums nineteen years earlier.

"What kind of name is Daoren?"

"The kind my parents gave me."

The Jiren harrumphed. He studied a screen. "Just thirty days till your S.A.T., I see. Decided to sit it earlier rather than later, hmm?"

"Good to know you can read," Daoren said. "I've heard tales of Jireni who had difficulty with basic comprehension."

The Jiren sneered. "Clever, slag. Very clever." He extracted the probe and stowed it. A twist of a handgrip activated the varinozzles. "But I'm guessing I'll be the one munching on *your* marrow in a month's time."

The levideck rose atop an expanding cloud of compressed air. It leveled off a few inches above the ground. The Jiren leaned forward, cacklebracking, and whisked away.

Daoren shook his head as the brute receded. "What a glasshole."

THIRTY MINUTES LATER, Daoren followed a wide tiled pathway through the central part of the Librarium, each step a labor thanks to the throbbing behind his eyes.

The impersonal grounds touched him in a strangely intimate way. Every few hundred feet, narrower pediwalks branched off from the pathway. They led to hexagonal habitation complexes, geodesic messing facilities capable of feeding thousands per sitting, domed infirmaries, and the myriad functional buildings he'd called home as a child. The Librarium was a city within the city-state, as self-sufficient as it was self-contained. A prospect could spend years on its grounds and never want for anything—except an education.

He'd encountered countless prospects so far. Four-year-olds gathered in the hundreds before their habitation complexes—the edict restricting associations didn't apply within the Librarium—gripping quantum tiles as big as their tunics. They were recent arrivals, judging by the glut of tutors accompanying them, learning the intricacies of their new tiles and the rules of their new environment.

Older prospects scurried from structure to structure in smaller groups, noses pressed to their tiles, eyes blinded to the world. Libraria strolled at a more dignified pace, alone and in pairs. A half-dozen had breezed past on personal levidecks, yellow lanshan flapping in the airstream. Seeing Libraria on levidecks represented a change from his time here as a child, one that struck him as comical.

Daoren plodded on for another fifteen minutes, his headache's fiery tendrils spreading to his temples, before rounding a curve in the pathway. Thirty feet ahead, four Libraria occupied an open quad.

Three reclined on low benches, chucklebucking to themselves. The fourth strutted before them, flailing his arms while he talked. He was thickset for a Librarian—as hefty as the wealthier members of the ruling caste. A grizzled beard mottled his Slavvic features. The implants in his scalp revealed different facets of a fractal pentagram and sparkled like a five-pointed crown. His grating voice drifted over, scuffing his regal airs and graces. "No no no! I have a more elegant solution!"

"Do you?" one of the reclining Libraria asked. "Then tell us, Gustar. What's this elegant solution of yours?"

The strutting Librarian—Gustar—waved his hands. "Pah! It's far too elegant for a dense lot like you to assimilate. I wouldn't know where to begin."

Rasplaughter exploded from the others. "I knew it," one of them said. "Your boasts are as empty as a mongrel's stomach!"

"Are they? *Are they*?" Gustar spread his arms as if poised to reveal the secret to life everlasting. "The solution is quantum resonance."

The statement snuffed their glee.

Gustar launched into his explanation. "Quantum resonance will—"

"Where can I find Laoshi al Euclidius?" Daoren asked, not waiting for a break in the conversation.

Gustar scowled. "The Spires, boy. Where else?"

"Could you be more specific?"

"In the B Stacks if the last few years are any indication. Now march on so I can educate these fids." He turned to his colleagues. "Quantum resonance holds the best potential for transmitting an encrypted signal in a crystalline matrix. But only if—"

"Only if the resonance is bounded," Daoren interjected. "Unbounded resonance will cause harmonic oscillations at the covalent level and dampen the signal."

Gustar's jaw dropped. "How did you know that?"

He shrugged and stepped around him. "Any fid knows that."

Gustar seized his arm. "What's your name, prospect?"

Daoren examined the Librarian's swollen face, trying to decipher the emotional foundation beneath its scrim of sweat. Shock resided at its core, certainly, but it also exhibited a clasping hunger he couldn't quite put a finger on. Anticipation? Appetite? Avarice?

"It isn't a request, boy. Tell me your name!"

"Daoren."

"Your family name!"

"Daoren al Lucien."

Gustar's puffy eyes reduced to impacted slits. "Have you applied to sit the S.A.T.?"

"Sha's silica teeth, Gustar," one of the other Libraria said. "Let the boy get on his way."

"Why do you want to know?" Daoren asked.

Gustar tightened his grip. "What harm can come from it?" He smiled, exposing needlelike eyeteeth. "Tell me and I'll let you go."

"I sit the May S.A.T." Daoren yanked his arm free. "And I'll let myself go, thank you."

He resumed his march along the pathway, cursing the clutching Librarian and his cronies.

———

DAOREN HEAVED A sigh of relief when he arrived at the Spires forty minutes later. He'd forgotten how vast the Librarium's grounds were; no wonder the Libraria had starting using levidecks. He paused at the base of the steps to let his headache fade before ascending.

The steps led to a vaulted entrance finished in thousands of sunglow tiles, each no bigger than his hand. Cut at precise angles, the prismatic tiles absorbed every wavelength of light except the deepest oranges and yellows. As the name suggested, their brilliance rivaled the sun. The steps, in contrast, were formed from one hundred slabs of frosted glass. He'd counted them once when he was five. At this time of day they basked in shade, praise be to Sha.

The Spires was the tallest structure in the Librarium and the largest in Daqin Guojin in terms of internal volume. Its white-crystalline façade lofted five hundred feet above the grounds. Recessed trefoils, quatrefoils, and other aesthetic accents pock-marked the windowless face. Two conical towers climbed another two hundred feet higher along its major axis, their parapets supported by muscular corbels. The towers bracketed a central spire that soared two hundred feet higher still, not counting its crowning Imperial Regalia.

Less than a week after Daoren arrived here fifteen years ago, a tutor had told his intake group a cautionary tale. It featured a despondent prospect who, on the eve of his S.A.T., had thrown himself off the tallest spire rather than face certain failure in the Center. *From such a height*, the tutor had gushed in a foreboding whisper, *he took a full minute to hit the steps. His body shattered like whisperglass.*

Daoren's fellow prospects had blanched, mortified by the graphic description. He'd taken a few seconds to calculate the fall time according to the body's estimated mass, acceleration due to gravity, and height of the spire. He knew at once the story wasn't true; the data didn't support it. The distrust it instilled hardened into outright disdain in four short years.

Daoren climbed the steps, counting them to verify his child-hood memory. Sure enough, he hit one hundred when he reached the entrance's double-doors.

Bas-relief figures decorated each door—the likenesses of

famous Libraria dating back to Daqin Guojin's founding in 98 A.C.E. He'd been forced to memorize their names as part of his indoctrination. In the years since they'd been overwritten by more useful information. He straight-armed a door and entered the nave.

He strode past the crystal columns buttressing the high glass ceiling, accompanied by the hollow echo of his footfalls. Two grand staircases wound upward to a mezzanine spanning the nave's generous width. Colorful frescoes graced the mezzanine's towering walls. They depicted Libraria and prospects engaged in a variety of pedagogical pursuits. Each fresco's perspective elevated the Libraria to the most dominant position. Prospects were rendered with looks of adulation that smacked of worship.

The left-hand staircase led to the A Stacks and their five billion scrolls on technological subjects. The right-hand staircase led to the B Stacks and over three billion scrolls on cultural history. The divine dialectic, as it was known to the Libraria, encompassed the collective knowledge of the human species.

Daqin Guojin's founders—the remnants of humanity that survived the displacements and deprivations of the Cycle of Extinctions—had done their best to collect and catalog the knowledge of the ancient societies. The city-state owed its advances in silica chemistry, glass production, nano-engineering, hydrogen infusion, quantum computing, and other technologies to those efforts, but most Libraria agreed it represented a fraction of the technological know-how that once existed.

The cultural records were even more fragmented. Little beyond the imperial habits of Mother China had been preserved. The few surviving political and social constructs of societies that dwelled beyond the empire's control had undergone centuries of reevaluation and reinterpretation by the Libraria, molding them to suit the needs of the Cognos Populi.

How a repository of half-truths, manifestos, and outright lies could be called divine, Daoren could never quite fathom. He climbed the staircase leading to the B stacks and its library of cultural fiction.

AN HOUR LATER, Daoren still threaded rows of stacks on the first level, one of ten levels in the Spires. At this rate, he might spend the rest of the day and most of the night finding Laoshi.

Fifty feet high and two hundred feet long, each stack held two hundred-thousand glass scrolls in individual nooks. Readouts below each nook identified the scroll's repository number, the digits highlighted in blue or red. Blue indicated an unlocked scroll, free for prospects to remove and examine. Red meant the scroll was locked and forbidden to access. Red digits outnumbered blue by a factor of ten to one, the same depressing ratio he'd encountered during his four years of tutelage under the Libraria.

Despite the abject censorship and general disinterest in cultural history, the stacks teemed with prospects. They perched on slender huvvadisks, ascending and traversing the looming faces, plucking scrolls for closer study. Using their quantum tiles, prospects could air-query the Spires' repositories by number, topic, historical period, and a host of other metrics. Huvvadisks would then take them to the desired scrolls, eliminating the need for aimless wandering in the city-state's most voluminous structure.

Daoren emerged from the stacks and entered a yawning amphitheater. Hundreds of seated prospects gazed upon a stage finished in black lumenglass.

An Asianoid Librarian paced the stage amid a plasmonic map. A three-dimensional representation of continents and oceans lapped at her knees, the expanses labeled with the names assigned by the ancients. A red swath tinted *Eurasia*. It spanned the supercontinent from the *East China Sea* to the *English Channel*.

The Librarian halted. She motioned to the swath. "See the bounds of Mother China before the Cycle of Extinctions? It was the most powerful empire the world had ever known."

An Africoid prospect stood, a ten-year-old girl with inquisitive eyes. "What's its size today?"

The Librarian aimed her reply at the map. "Advance time."

The red swath retreated westward upon the command, then shrank southward toward the *Italian Peninsula*. A sandy-brown stain advanced in its place. When the motion ceased, the red swath tinted no more than three-quarters of the peninsula.

"Our empire may be smaller," the Librarian said, "but it's still the most powerful. Mother China lives on in Daqin Guojin."

"What caused the sands to grow?" the Africoid prospect asked.

"The death of all things living and millennia of erosion, child. Our best technological minds couldn't stop its advance."

"Is it true the closest mongrel colony lies two hundred miles to the north?" another prospect asked.

"One hundred and ninety miles, boy. Beyond the Great Northern Border."

The plasmonic map complemented the Librarian's reply by tracing a raised line that bisected the peninsula from west to east, three-quarters of the way up its length. A dagger-shaped outline resolved north of the border wall. Its southernmost tip pointed at the heart of Daqin Guojin. A single word appeared beside the outline.

Havoc.

"The mongrel colony Havoc will render our civilization extinct if we let down our guard," the Librarian said. "We must be ever wary of its incursions."

Daoren rolled his eyes. Her tone reminded him of the tutor who'd spun the fiction about the despondent, spire-diving prospect. He skirted the amphitheater's perimeter, searching for Laoshi among the glass stalls surrounding it.

Prospects huddled in the stalls, unrolling scrolls and scanning the embedded data using their handheld tiles. Others debated with tutors. Their hushed voices created a sleepy layer of white noise.

Twenty feet away, one tutor stroked his wispy gray beard. He leaned over a female prospect whose twin hair braids streamed down the back of her tunic. The tutor glanced to the side. Silver-gray studs swept up and over his temple from his eyebrow.

Laoshi beamed. "Daoren! Welcome to the Spires!"

Daoren gave him a hesitant nod. The female prospect spun in her seat.

Heqet locked her eyes onto his.

Daoren spotted a flicker of joy in them—or was it confusion? Whatever it was, looking upon her radiance matched staring into the swollen sun. He averted his gaze, then cursed himself for showing weakness.

Laoshi must have mistaken the reaction for irritation. "You don't object to Heqet accompanying us, do you?"

"Why should I? She's free to choose how she spends her time."

"How noble of you," Heqet said under her breath, but loud enough for him to hear.

"Good, good." Laoshi slung an opaque satchel over his shoulder. "Come then. We've much to do before you sit for your S.A.T."

Heqet rose from her seat and paced away with her grandfather.

"We aren't staying here?"

"No, boy," Laoshi said without turning. "The tools needed for your education lie beyond these walls."

Daoren sighed. Why couldn't the Libraria ever give straightforward answers? He trailed the pair past the amphitheater and back into the stacks. Apparently, the forces aligned against him would remain a mystery a while longer.

11

INTO THE VOID

JID 736390-112489-ZC-SUP
PRIMAE JIREN'S EYES ONLY
SUBJECT: LAOSHI AL EUCLIDIUS

1. *The subject has occupied the position of Primae Librarian for twelve years. He is renowned for his expertise in silica chemistry and is an ardent collector of ancient artifacts.*
2. *The subject gained denizenship in 655 A.C.E. and fought with distinction in the resource war of 656 A.C.E. Wounded during the Second Stand on the Great Northern Border, he spent two years convalescing before taking up the vocation of Librarian.*
3. *The subject's wife bore him a son, Fengsei al Laoshi, in 659 A.C.E. (She died two years later while pregnant with their second child.) Indications of radicalized thought do not appear until after the death of the subject's son in 695 A.C.E.*
4. *A secondary investigation into the levitran accident*

that claimed Fengsei al Laoshi and his wife, Danica
alum Atum, has been opened. It may yield clues
into the changes in the subject's political and social
views.

> *Survival Through Sapience.*
> *Cang alum Aridian*
> *District Commander, Zhongguo Cheng*

———————

DAOREN TRAILED HEQET and Laoshi on the ceramic-tile pathway. His headache had flared up again, sparked by the volatile sunlight and his abrasive unease. Wandering the grounds of the Librarium had upset his internal equilibrium.

Twenty paces ahead, Heqet gripped the crook of Laoshi's elbow, lending support while they talked. What words passed between them, Daoren couldn't say. If asked for an opinion, he'd have to admit he couldn't muster enough concern to care. The longer he walked behind the pair, however, the more he realized that the physical environment wasn't causing his imbalance.

It stemmed from being near Heqet again.

She possessed an attribute that Mako had failed to list. The unnameable quality made it impossible to concentrate whenever she was around. It made speaking to her an exercise in futility. No matter how hard he tried, he couldn't force the right words past his knotted tongue. No matter how hard he tried, he couldn't stop the wrong words from spewing out of his mouth.

The maddening ailment frustrated him to no end. More often than not, his frustration spilled out onto her and fueled endless, unintended slights. Rather than risk another, he'd let her drift ahead with Laoshi, envying their easy banter.

They'd ambled well beyond the shadow of the Spires and into an area bristling with habitation complexes. Cylindrical towers supported numerous hexagonal levels, resembling stacks of locking nuts on threaded bolts. Circular windows dotted the six faces of every level. Each window represented a living chamber. Most were tinted black against the swollen sun.

Daoren had lived in a similar complex in the northern part of the grounds for three years. In those days, the youngest prospects resided ten per living chamber. Forgetting to tint the window before leaving for the day's tutelage in the Spires meant coming back to a stifling chamber and an uncomfortable night's sleep. Judging by the number of clear windows above him, hundreds of prospects would be tossing and turning tonight.

Oppressive heat.

Repressive tutors.

Flawed curriculum.

False knowledge.

Those were the clearest memories of his time here. Now he was back, plodding the pathways he swore he'd never touch again. If it wasn't for Laoshi's disturbing words in the funeral aerostat, he'd be—

"Does our pace trouble you, boy?"

Ahead, Laoshi and Heqet had stopped while his mind wandered. They stared at him like he was a lost child.

"Or is another problem weighing on you?" Laoshi asked.

"In the funeral aerostat," Daoren said, coming to a halt. "What did you mean by the forces aligned against me?"

"We'll discuss that in good time," Laoshi said, "and in a more private venue. Heqet tells me you've been writing your prep-tests every quarter."

"I have."

"But not here in the Librarium."

"No. Via my quantum tile."

"Odd that a prospect who opted for self-study should still write the prep-tests sanctioned by the Libraria."

Daoren shrugged. "So it's odd. What of it?"

"Why did you choose self-study over tutelage with the Libraria?" Heqet asked.

Daoren stared at her like *she* was the lost child. "You might ask me why I choose truth over fiction."

"Ah," Laoshi said. "You think we while away our time spinning falsehoods for the Cognos Populi?"

"I think when it comes to educating the people, you go a finger deep. I wanted to go deeper."

Laoshi's smile hinted at amusement. "A finger deep," he said to Heqet, eyebrows arching. "Faint praise indeed, wouldn't you say, my dear?"

Heqet's smile hinted at surprise. "At least you're able to pull words from his mouth. For me he reserves silence—unless he wants to argue, that is."

Daoren ignored her prodding. "Here's a hard fact for you, Laoshi. If the Libraria started teaching unpopular truths, the Cognos Populi would start writing edicts that weren't so respectful of your independence."

"That's faint praise of your father's chosen vocation," Laoshi said, smile waning. "He did far more than write self-serving edicts, boy. Do you know how many denizens wanted to attend his funeral? Do you know how many had to be turned away because the aerostat couldn't accommodate them? After what he did for Daqin Guojin and its people, I'd have thought you'd show more respect."

The comment sliced into Daoren's heart, as sharp as shrapnel. In his head, he knew it had merit.

Lucien had been a proud member of the Cognos Populi. Wearing the purple shenyi fulfilled his life's dream of serving the people. Over the past few days, Daoren's pain over his father's death had clashed with his contempt for the Cognos Populi. The noxious aftereffect of that conflict ate away at his gut and might be contributing to his sense of unbalance.

He groped for the right words. They still sounded wrong leaving his mouth. "My father was a good man."

"You say that as if I didn't know," Laoshi said. "What you don't know is just how good a man he was."

He limped away with Heqet at his side. Daoren watched them recede, inch by inch and foot by foot, until a nagging thought burned through his headache. "What am I doing here?"

The question hung in the air no more than a second before his attention fell on Heqet.

In contrast to Laoshi's hobbled gait, her strides struck an elegant mechanical harmony with every swing of her arms. Her twin braids swayed like lustrous pendulums, sweeping across her back and hips. Her toned calves flexed with each footfall. She was just as glinty from behind as from—

She glanced over her shoulder. Her curious eyes met his.

Daoren averted his gaze. He cursed himself for getting caught looking.

While he bathed in his embarrassment, Heqet and Laoshi veered onto a tiled pathway leading to a single-level structure. Five tapered steps led to an unassuming door bracketed by mirrored windows. Faded yellow tiles dressed the flared eaves of a triple-tiered red roof.

Daoren recognized the structure from his days as a young prospect. It was the chamber of the Primae Librarian, more commonly known as the Temple.

———

THE TEMPLE LACKED an entry nave. Its solitary door led into an open parlor with a sparse collection of abodewares; two divans, a simple desk, and not one piece of sculpture.

Daoren surveyed the space. Its lone concession to aesthetics was the floor-to-ceiling windows spanning the walls on either side of the door. They provided an unimpeded view of the Librarium's grounds, including the Spires a few miles to the southwest.

Thirty feet away, on the opposite side of the parlor, Laoshi and Heqet lingered before a set of gloss-black double-doors.

"You have simple tastes," Daoren said.

"You may think otherwise when you see where I spend most of my time," Laoshi said. The double-doors swished open. He led Heqet into an antechamber. "Come, boy. Don't tarry."

Daoren eyed the stunted compartment. Its footprint couldn't be more than forty square-feet, made smaller by its occupants. His palms grew moist. "In there? Why?"

"You'll see in due course."

"It looks . . . cramped."

"You have an issue with small spaces?" Laoshi asked.

Try as he might, Daoren couldn't stop another flush of embarrassment from warming his cheeks. He'd sooner go to a watery grave than admit to the psychological shortcoming.

"It's all right," Heqet said. "We won't be in here long. There's plenty of air."

Daoren gulped two lungfuls of air. He crossed the parlor and entered the antechamber.

It felt even smaller on the inside. Recessed lights shone in its paneled ceiling, dappling three bare walls. The rear wall boasted a waist-high handrail.

Laoshi and Heqet gripped the handrail. Daoren's heart rate doubled, compounding his headache's molten throbs. Icy needles pricked his hands and feet in an unnerving thermal counterpoint. He inhaled through his nose and exhaled through his mouth.

"Better take a handhold," Laoshi said, "if you want to maintain your footing."

He eyed the handrail. Gripping it meant moving closer to Laoshi and Heqet. He needed space more than stability.

"Do as he says." Heqet's eyes gleamed. "Trust me."

The double-doors closed behind Daoren. "I trust no one but myself."

Heqet snorted. "Then blame no one but yourself for what happens."

The antechamber shuddered. Daoren detected its descent in his stomach—a quavering hollowness that ballooned up his throat and into his head. His sandals broke contact with the floor.

He shot his arms out to the side, legs pinwheeling for purchase. He rotated, floating free, and locked his panicky gaze onto Heqet.

Her twin braids stood straight up. Her smirk hinted at glee.

Laoshi whistled beside her, fingers curled around the handrail. He was still whistling when the elevating chamber's free-fall descent slowed ten seconds later.

Daoren sank to the floor and settled onto his hands and knees. He glared up at Laoshi once the motion stopped.

Laoshi's smile hiked his beard off his tunic's lapels. "You said you wanted to go deeper."

The double-doors swished open before Daoren. A blackness more total than any he'd ever seen lay beyond them.

He rose onto wobbly legs and edged to the doors' threshold. For all he knew, another step would send him to the center of the Earth. He glanced at Laoshi, looking for confirmation it was safe to exit.

"This is as deep as it gets, Daoren. Welcome to the Void."

Daoren stepped into the blackness.

Lights flared, illuminating a cavernous void that rivaled the size of the Center. From nothingness, jagged rock walls resolved. They enveloped row upon row of glass tables. Hundreds, maybe thousands of objects covered the tables, each spotlit from beneath.

The sensory overload assailed him from all points of the compass. He stumbled forward, trying and failing to fix his gaze on a single object, then he noticed the arches.

Crumbling stone arches traced a partial oval along the southernmost wall. They extended at least six hundred feet, encompassing a third of the void's perimeter. In several sections, the decrepit arches stood three-levels high and topped one hundred-fifty feet. The ruin's shape implied it had once formed part of a larger, continuous structure, but what was it doing so far below the surface? When was it built? Who had built it?

Daoren tried to impose order onto the swirling questions, but he couldn't still his mind. He could only gape at Laoshi in a bewildered daze.

"This site was once known as the Roman Colosseum," Laoshi said. "Untold millennia before Daqin Guojin became the western capital of Mother China, it served as the capital of another great empire." He motioned to the arches. "An echolocation survey discovered these arches two hundred years ago during the Librarium's construction. They're the remnants of a grand stadium built for epic contests—a stadium that the ancients would have called ancient."

"And what is it now?"

"A vault for artifacts discovered during silica-sourcing expeditions around the world. And a place I can study, work, and write without the prying eyes of the ruling caste peering in."

Daoren gaped at Heqet. "How long have you known about this place?"

"Since I came to live with Grandfather."

"Did you ever bring Mako down here?"

"He had no interest in artifacts," she said. "And he refused to enter the elevating chamber on the few occasions I invited him."

Daoren nodded. Mako's discomfort with small spaces was more . . . *had been* more severe than his own. He wouldn't have set foot in the elevating chamber, at least not without heavy sedation. Still, his brother had known about the Void while he'd been blissfully ignorant. What other secrets may lay buried, beyond his knowing?

He crept to the closest table. On its transparent surface, three round podiums supported three artifacts. Each steeped in its own well of light.

The first artifact reminded him of a quantum tile. Its canted glass screen attached to a flat, silver base studded with six rows of black keys. Eroded letters and faded numbers flecked the keys.

The object next to it was the length of his arm. A slender black neck attached to an hourglass body that shone like polished sandstone. The slimmest part of the hollow body featured two S-shaped slots, suggesting an acoustic purpose. Four knobs jutted from the end of the neck, two per side. Closer inspection revealed a notched plate standing between the S-shaped slots. Four knobs; four notches. Could they have held four connective threads?

"That's a Stradivarius violin," Laoshi said.

"A what?"

"A musical instrument. It was discovered seventy-five years ago in a cryocache buried near the city-state once known as Paris. Unfortunately, the strings weren't preserved, so its voice is forever silenced."

Daoren shifted focus to the third artifact, overcome with burning curiosity.

It, too, was a foreign entity. Thick, squat, and rectangular, the object's cracked, brown covering encased a sheath of yellowed material.

He ran his fingers over the covering's raised letters.

Biblio Sacra Latina.

A shiver dimpled his skin. He drew his hand back. "This isn't made of glass."

"It's a book," Laoshi said. "One of the earliest ever produced. The covering comes from the hide of a bovine species that once roamed the planet. The interior pages were fashioned from a type of vegetation that could be harvested, replanted, and re-harvested again and again." He pointed at the acoustic instrument. "The same vegetation from which that was made."

Daoren blinked. Laoshi's words were as foreign as the artifacts. "I don't understand."

"That's because your eyes have been closed to the world that once existed, Daoren. Every prospect's eyes have been closed thanks to the edicts of the Cognos Populi." He motioned to the cram of tables. "As you can see, our ancestors had an abundance of materials from which to construct their world. We have sand, and from sand we've fashioned our city-state, our clothing, our weapons and aeroshrikes, *everything*."

"If life gives you sand, make glass."

"Mako used to say that," Heqet said.

"It was our father's favorite expression." Daoren peered at Laoshi. "Is this why you brought me here? To see these artifacts?"

Laoshi rummaged in his satchel. "I brought you here to talk about this."

He lobbed a small object to Daoren.

Daoren one-handed the piece of grooll. He snorted. "You want *me*, a lowly prospect, to discuss grooll with *you*, Daqin Guojin's Primae Librarian."

"There's a method to my madness."

Daoren eyed the torus-shaped grooll in his palm. What in Sha's name did the old man expect him to say?

"Come, boy. Indulge an old man."

Daoren rolled his eyes. He'd play Laoshi's game if it meant taking a step closer to learning the truth about his brother and father. "It was invented four hundred years ago. Some call it Sha's Mercy for saving humanity from extinction." He tossed the piece back to Laoshi. "You know as well as I do that it's a synthetic, silica-based food."

Laoshi caught the grooll. "Is that all you have to say? I thought you were the smarter brother."

The barb stung Daoren. "It's nano-engineered to maximize

the surface area of the harvested protein, carbon hydrate, and triglyceride chains, and to minimize the energy required to break their chemical bonds."

Laoshi fingered the grooll like he was seeing it for the first time. "Why maximize the surface area of the macronutrient chains?"

"Caloric equivalence. Maximizing the surface area at the molecular level provides a caloric equivalence that's thousands of times greater than the caloric content of the unprocessed macronutrients."

"And why minimize the energy needed to break their chemical bonds?"

Daoren tossed Heqet a pleading glance. She shrugged, displaying similar confusion over her grandfather's inquisition.

"Don't stop now, boy. Impress me with the depth of your independent study."

"To increase metabolic efficiency in the body after it's ingested," Daoren said, irked by the prompt.

Laoshi raised the grooll to his nose and sniffed it. "Shelf life?"

Daoren released a despairing laugh. How many questions was this damned Librarian going to throw at him? "It's indefinite," he said. "The silica substrate is inorganic, and the precursor is bio-stabilized using sixty enzymes derived from living tissue."

"*Living tissue?*"

"Tissue harvested from living donors," Daoren said, unable to temper his irritation.

"*Donors?*"

"Prospects who fail the S.A.T.!" He took a deep breath to tamp down his anger. "Is there a point to this method of yours?"

"Besides proving that you can speak fictions with as much conviction as the Libraria?" Laoshi deposited the grooll into his mouth and chewed. "The ugly truth of Daqin Guojin is that we eat our young. We've been doing it for so long, few question the practice anymore. But there's an uglier truth about grooll that no one ever questions."

"We also use it as our currency," Daoren said.

"Clever boy." Laoshi pulled a quantum tile from his satchel. "Come, both of you."

He led them past rows of tables to a lumenglass stage standing amid a clearing in the center of the Void. Its black panels shimmered.

Laoshi mounted the stage with a grunt. He manipulated the tile's screen as he spoke. "You asked about the forces aligned against you, Daoren. Let me show you what they look like."

He tapped the tile and disappeared behind a loom of brilliant white light.

12

GROSS MANIPULATION

JID 736390-112489-ZC-SUP
PRIMAE JIREN'S EYES ONLY
SUBJECT: LAOSHI AL EUCLIDIUS

1. *According to Gustar al Vlodisar, the subject spends the majority of his time in a site located beneath the Temple (as the chamber of the Primae Librarian is known).*
2. *The subterranean site is part of an archeological preserve that pre-dates the Librarium's founding. The purpose for the subject's frequent visits is unknown and raises troubling questions.*
3. *Gustar believes the tunnels used to excavate material from the site may be intact. He is investigating their possible locations, all of which lie within the Librarium's grounds.*
4. *While Jireni would be prohibited from using the tunnels and gaining access to the site, Gustar would likely be amenable to investigating the*

subject's activities on our behalf if offered a sizable reward.

Survival Through Sapience.
Cang alum Aridian
District Commander, Zhongguo Cheng

———

THE UNUM SPRAWLED on a low bench in his chamber, seeking distraction in the ceiling's bas-relief panels. It was an old habit.

He'd picked it up a year after gaining power, around the time his father succumbed to a mental illness. Despite offers of lavish reward and threats of appalling punishment, the city-state's best medical practitioners couldn't determine the cause behind the rapid deterioration of cognitive functions in a man for whom the most labyrinthine political calculations had been as effortless as breathing.

The Unum suspected—then and now—that a neurotoxin was to blame. One derived from the few heavy metals still available to those with the right contacts and sufficient grooll. Mercury, perhaps, or lead. Delivered in trace doses over months or years, the toxin would have gone undetected. The question of who delivered it had also defied diagnosis, but he wagered the Asianoid members of the Assembly could shed light on the mystery.

At the time of his father's death, the Unum was no more than a spindly youth, ill-fitted for the demands and responsibilities of rule. During his first year of reign, he'd directed the sum of his political calculus toward retaining power. In those days, the chamber had felt like a gilded tomb, and a vicious whisper-campaign among senior Asianoid members of the Cognos Populi had sought to bury him inside it. He'd spent untold hours staring at the panels, wondering if they'd be the final images he'd process after an assassin's dagger found him, while he and his younger brother plotted to crush the mutinous factions within the Assembly.

The Unum heaved a sigh, but only in part from nostalgia. A tomb-like atmosphere had again descended on the chamber. This time he faced it alone. His brother had joined their father in the Great After eighteen months ago under eerily similar circumstances. Mysterious mental illnesses, it seemed, ran in the family.

After another minute of disquiet, he had to accept that the stirring scenes from the *Siege of Havoc* weren't up to the task. The revelation still weighed on his mind. Only one distraction would suffice.

He loosened his tunic and unbuttoned eight layers of gleamglass undergarments. He ran his hand across his bare chest.

His skin tingled at his touch. He guided his hand lower . . . and lower still.

There.

He worked his hand up and down and closed his eyes.

Oh, yes. Right there.

He rubbed his belly, kneading its pillowy flesh, squeezing its prodigious skin folds. It had taken decades of concentrated effort to gain such solidity. He enjoyed the feel of its girth as much as he enjoyed the awe it inspired among the malnourished masses. His chamber, his palace, and his heft spoke of power, prestige, and wealth. No man in Daqin Guojin had more.

No man in Daqin Guojin wanted more, his wife used to say. She had a way of saying it that tread the line between admiration and disdain. That used to bother him, but no longer. She was dead, he was Unum, and he'd amassed more grooll than anyone in the history of the city-state . . . at least for now.

Daoren al Lucien could take it all away.

The Unum stilled his hand and opened his eyes.

Yes, why couldn't he?

The Unum's father had secured his son's position as ruler thirty-one years ago through a—what had he called it?—*an unparalleled investment in the Cognos Populi.* He bought his son's place as Unum Potentate, to put an indecorous spin on the transaction. In so doing, he ended three hundred-fifty unbroken years of Asianoid rule. His father hadn't secured his legacy though; that task rested on his own broad, Slavvic shoulders.

He abandoned his belly and reached for the quantum tile beside the bench. He skimmed the prep-tests displayed on its screen for the third time. Gustar had relayed them through an intermediary proxy an hour ago. It wasn't the first time he'd forwarded prep-tests, but it was the first time the Unum had demanded their verification. Gustar had done so. *Twice.*

Daoren had achieved perfect results on his last eight prep-tests.

Sha damn the boy's eyes! Of all the prospects who could write a perfect S.A.T., why did it have to be Daoren al Lucien? And of all the edicts the old rulers of Daqin Guojin could have declared inviolate, why did it have to be the one guaranteeing any prospect who attained a perfect S.A.T. score the irrefutable right to become Unum Potentate?

Sha could damn their eyes, too.

The Unum sat up and swung his legs off the bench. The crystalline floor kissed the bare soles of his feet. A chill coursed up his legs and caressed his spine.

Perfect results.

Daoren had written his prep-tests remotely, Gustar relayed in his message. The data repository he used to identify suitable prospects for the test-manipulation scheme hadn't captured the scores. The Librarian typically needed two months of preparation to switch S.A.T. scores between specific prospects. In this case he'd have thirty days. The Unum wasn't sure how Gustar had learned of the boy's unprecedented scores or whether he could complete the preparations in time, but he knew this; if Daoren wrote a perfect S.A.T. and earned the right of Unum Potentate, he'd strip every ounce of grooll from—

Shrill gigglesnicks filled the chamber.

Ten feet away, Narses and Julinian whispered like conspirators on a divan. Julinian tugged at Narses' hair, teasing him. Narses protested with a pathetic screech.

The Unum spent a minute studying the pair. He hoped his son and niece weren't engaging in improper behavior during their idle time. Interfamilial coitus wasn't an unforgivable social taboo—the ever-draining pool of humanity made it impossible to avoid in some Chengs—but it wasn't embraced either.

Julinian's frequent disappearances from the Assembly gave him solace. She'd vanish for hours at a time and usually returned with a flushed glow. He wagered she was stealing time with a romantic partner in a sleeping chamber somewhere in Zhongguo Cheng. Narses never joined her, ruling him out as a lover.

Another flurry of screeches drifted over from the divan. The Unum's tolerance breached its limit. "Must you speak in whispers and carry on like little girls?" He pinned Narses with a needling stare. "I'd be far more comfortable with you becoming Unum if you exhibited one of the requisite qualities."

The comment drew a classic pout, but the boy knew better than to argue. Julinian perked up at the rebuke.

His niece would make a far better ruler than his son, but she had the misfortune to be born to the wrong sibling. Still, the Unum had granted his younger brother's dying wish and ensured his daughter didn't perish in the grooll mill. In fact, he'd gone a step further, guaranteeing Julinian's place in the Cognos Populi by arranging for her test results to be switched with another prospect whose prep-tests showed great promise. What Gustar al Vlodisar failed to divulge was the promising prospect's name.

Sha could damn Gustar's eyes as well! Thanks to his grievous oversight, a decent boy had been harvested and a decent man culled. For that there would be a reckoning.

The Unum scooped grooll from the urn beside the bench. He needed sustenance to soothe his stomach and energy to ponder the way forward. He foresaw two possible paths.

If he issued a cull order against Daoren *before* the S.A.T., he could mitigate the threat with one dagger stroke. Quick. Simple. Certain.

If he let the boy sit the test and had his score assigned to Narses, he could guarantee his son's ascent to Unum Potentate. That would forego the need to buy his place and forever protect billions of pounds of grooll. Not so quick. Not so simple. Not so certain.

Which path to take depended on two unknowns; Daoren's potential to write a perfect test, and Gustar's ability to make the necessary preparations. The Unum loathed unknowns.

Pyros entered through the door leading from the outer chamber, interrupting the rumination. He crossed the floor with his back hunched, a man burdened.

The Unum munched grooll and studied his Primae Jiren's demeanor. Pyros had been more sullen than usual since culling Lucien and slower to respond to summons. Behavioral changes were never a welcome sign, and never more unwelcome than in men who held influential positions. He'd have to monitor him more closely.

Pyros halted before the bench and bowed from the neck.

"Well?" the Unum asked, picking his teeth with his thumbnail. "Did you locate him?"

"Yes. Daoren was bio-scanned entering the Librarium."

The Unum stuffed another handful of grooll into his mouth. "When?"

"Four hours ago. There's no evidence he's left the grounds yet."

"He has no tutor," the Unum said, chewing. "Why would he go there?"

The last time he'd seen Daoren, the boy was tending to his

mother at Lucien's funeral. But before that, wasn't he talking to Laoshi? The Primae Librarian was a friend of the family. The two might have been exchanging vapid condolences. Then again, Daoren shunned social niceties and they'd spoken at length. If it was any other prospect, he might have dismissed the interaction out of hand. Daoren, however, wasn't like any other prospect.

The Unum swallowed. "I want him locked in your sights until he sits his S.A.T."

"Jireni can't enter the Librarium, Unum. By edict."

Full-throated laughter triggered undulating waves across the Unum's exposed belly. Pyros' skills as a tactician far outstripped his skills as a political strategist. "Then divest a few Jireni of their titles before you send them onto the grounds. Dress them as Libraria."

He glanced at the divan to make sure Narses had glommed the deft maneuver. Of course, the boy hadn't, but Julinian appeared keen and attentive. The girl didn't miss a trick.

The Unum snatched another handful of grooll and flung the pieces at his son. "Pay attention, boy! Do you see the qualities needed in an Unum?"

Narses nodded, more startled than engaged.

The Unum couldn't be certain he understood. Pyros proved easier to read. He stiffened, as he was wont to do whenever he disagreed with the Unum's decisions. And what of it? He could be as stiff as ceramic armor for all the Unum cared. He wouldn't dare disobey the order, not with his daughter's S.A.T. approaching and her prep-tests so dismal.

"Another couple awaits in your outer chamber for an audience," Pyros said. "Shall I bring them in?"

The Unum folded his tunic closed, leaving his undergarments unbuttoned, and slipped his feet into his sandals. "In five minutes," he said with a dismissive wave.

Pyros trudged toward the door, rounded spine bearing the ills of the sterile world. Hushed gigglesnicks ebbed over from the divan. Narses' emasculating screeches punctuated them.

The squabbling boiled the Unum's blood. He hurled his tile.

It whizzed past Narses' head and smashed into an urn. Shards of ceramic and pieces of grooll cascaded across the floor.

———

IN THE VOID, Daoren and Heqet stood upon the lumenglass panels, transfixed by a rotating plasmonic projection as large as the Temple. Laoshi tarried near the edge of the stage and let them gape. They'd need time to process what they were seeing.

What they were seeing transcended any frame of reference they possessed. The projection rendered a structure of irreducible complexity in exhaustive detail, but at a scale orders of magnitude smaller than its real-world counterpart. Two-hundred narrow platforms nestled in parallel, resembling the river-spanning suspension bridges of antiquity. Each was crowned with two-hundred ovoid pods that reminded Laoshi of the eggs of an extinct bird species; *Turdus migratorius*. A maze of transparent pipes undergirded the platforms, terminating in a series of open tanks at their base. Support cables criss-crossed the structure. Some cables tracked at shallow angles from the platforms to the floor beyond the tanks.

When Daoren and Heqet ripped their focus from the projection, Laoshi knew they were ready to hear the truth. "This marks a historic first," he said. "No prospects have ever seen the grooll mill. Not even those unfortunate enough to fail the S.A.T. and end up in there see it with their own eyes."

"Why's that, Grandfather?"

"Because they're stunned by electric shock before harvesting."

Heqet's eyes widened. Daoren's gaze returned to the projection. He glowered, perhaps thinking of his brother's fate.

"It's better that way," Laoshi said, hoping to ease Daoren's mind. "In fact, it's a kindness compared to the feeding method used by the mongrel colonies beyond our border."

"What do you know of their methods?" Daoren asked.

Laoshi drew a weighty breath. "I fought in Havoc during the resource war, well before you were born."

"*You* fought in the resource war?"

"I wasn't always a Librarian, boy. And while I was in Havoc, I saw the breeding farms."

"Breeding farms?" Heqet asked.

"Low structures framed in blackened nullglass that stretched to infinity," he said, "in which women younger than you underwent artificial insemination to induce multiple births. Women whose gestation periods were genetically shortened to maximize production, who spent their miserable lives in cramped pens as they bred brood after brood." He shuddered at the memory. "We called it Hope's Graveyard. I'll never forget the sound of tens of thousands of wailing infants destined for the slaughterchamber, not if I live another sixty-five years."

Heqet paled. Her hands shot up to her mouth.

It pained him to illuminate this dark matter for her, but she deserved to know. Every prospect deserved to know what lay beyond the border . . . and within it. He motioned to the projection. "But in Daqin Guojin, our brightest minds spent generations perfecting the grooll-making process. A more humane, civilized process that initially relied on those who died of natural causes to feed the population, that is until—"

"Until it couldn't keep pace with population growth," Daoren said.

The boy's candor impressed Laoshi. "That's correct. And in time, those lacking—"

"Those lacking technological ability came to be viewed as a drain on society," Daoren interjected, "consuming a precious resource while contributing nothing in return. So the Cognos

Populi came up with a solution two hundred years ago. They called it the S.A.T."

Laoshi couldn't contain his surprise. The roots of the S.A.T. had long been buried. Scrolls that discussed the subject, even in passing, had been locked to prospect access for close to thirty years. Daoren must have deduced the facts on his own.

"And in their infinite wisdom," Daoren continued, "the Cognos Populi have kept raising the S.A.T.'s frequency and passing score in the centuries since."

"All the more prospects to harvest," Heqet said.

"Which means all the more currency to acquire and hoard." Daoren leveled an accusing glare at Laoshi. "That's the true cause of the grooll shortage, isn't it?"

Laoshi marveled at Daoren's insight. He was hearing his own thoughts, channeled through the mouth of a nineteen-year-old boy who didn't even know the roots of his own existence. "The truth of the grooll shortage is that there should be no shortage," he said. "The dietary requirements of Daqin Guojin's inhabitants can be met with a ration of one pound per person per day. For a population of fifteen million, that works out to five-and-a-half billion pounds of grooll per year."

"Five billion, four hundred seventy-five million pounds."

Laoshi raised his eyebrows. Either Daoren had worked out the sum in advance or he performed the calculation in his head. Whichever was the case, it made another impression. "And do you know how much grooll is produced every year?"

Daoren shook his head.

"Five hundred-thousand prospects sit the test annually," Laoshi said. "Half are harvested and processed into grooll precursor. On average, eighty pounds of precursor is derived from each failing prospect, which is then mixed with the silica substrate at a one-to-five-hundred ratio. How much does that yield?"

Daoren lifted his gaze to the rocky ceiling. He lowered it again after a few seconds. "Ten billion pounds."

Laoshi smiled. The boy's response clarified whether he'd calculated the previous sum on the spot. "Which means if we rationed grooll in equal measure to every inhabitant, we'd enjoy a surplus of more than four billion pounds every year."

"But we don't ration it equally," Heqet said.

"No, child. The ruling caste accounts for eight percent of the population, but over fifty percent of the grooll ration. But taking unequal distribution into account, we should still have an annual surplus of two billion pounds."

"Then why don't we?" she asked. "Millions are starving throughout the city-state!"

"Because the surplus—and more—is being concentrated in the hands of a few wealthy elites," Daoren said. "You don't teach that in the Librarium, do you, Laoshi?"

"No, Daoren. In the Librarium, we teach that grooll is the answer to our petitions. We teach that the S.A.T. is a fair process because all prospects, regardless of wealth or lineage, must sit it. We teach that it's a necessary adaptation for ensuring the survival of our species."

Heqet's brow crimped. "You don't believe it anymore."

Laoshi drew another weighty breath. He stopped believing it when her mother and father were taken from her, but she didn't need to know that . . . not yet. "When grooll was just a food source, it may have been true. But now?"

"A minority amasses a fortune while the majority starves," Daoren said.

"Sapient Sha," Laoshi said. "If you only knew."

13

A STAGGERING SUM

JID 736390-112489-ZC-SUP
PRIMAE JIREN'S EYES ONLY
SUBJECT: LAOSHI AL EUCLIDIUS

1. Gustar al Vlodisar has located two excavation
   tunnels leading into the void beneath the Temple.
   Both tunnels are intact and may allow undetected
   ingress into the site.
2. Gustar has indicated his willingness to investigate
   the subject's subterranean activities. He is
   demanding 40,000 pounds of grooll in exchange for
   this service.
3. Though considerable, the sum reflects the intelligence
   value the investigation could provide. With your
   permission, I will authorize the reward and task
   him to perform this service.

   Survival Through Sapience.
   Cang alum Aridian
   District Commander, Zhongguo Cheng

THE UNUM SAT behind his desk, undergarments and tunic cinched and regal once again. Over by the divan, Pyros conversed with Narses and Julinian. That was unusual; the Primae Jiren always excused himself from these meetings and rarely deigned to speak to the pair. The Unum pricked up his ears, hoping to catch pieces of their conversation, but the trio was out of earshot. He made a mental note to ask his son and niece about the topic.

"As I was saying, Unum, he's a hardworking boy . . ."

The Unum brought his focus back to the Indonoid husband and wife—the couple seeking an audience—groveling before his desk. Their purple shenyi marked them as members of the ruling caste. The fabric's cheap quality marked them as less-affluent members.

". . . but our son doesn't have the cognitive ability needed to pass the S.A.T.," the husband continued. "Medical practitioners say it's an attention deficit, but he's smart. He could contribute to the city-state in many positive ways." He cast a fretting glance at his wife. "We hoped we might come to an agreement."

The wife clasped her hands before her chest. "Please, Unum, we beg of you."

"No need to beg." The Unum hoisted a crystal orb dangling from the Newton's Cradle atop his desk. He let the orb drop, setting off its clacking pendulum motion. "A passing score will cost a minimum of five thousand pounds, but that's all it is. It may not be high enough to confer any other rights or privileges. For ten thousand pounds, however, your son can secure a score that will also guarantee union, reproduction rights, a fulfilling vocation, and a private abode."

"But, Unum," the husband said, voice raised to compete with the cradle. "Daqin Guojin allots each of us one thousand pounds of grooll a year!"

"One thousand pounds each, hmm? You're nano-engineers?"

They answered with one voice. "Yes, Unum."

"From Yindu Cheng?"

"Yes, Unum."

The cradle's clacking filled the dead air while the Unum pondered. The pondering was for show; he'd known what needed to be said before the couple entered the chamber. "Then I wager you'll be *childless* nano-engineers from Yindu Cheng come the December S.A.T."

The husband and wife traded agonizing looks, drifting toward an all-but-foregone conclusion. "We'll get ten thousand pounds," the husband said. "I don't know how, but we'll get it. On our honor."

"Be certain you do." The Unum palmed the orbs, stopping the cradle. The silence that followed was as foreboding as he'd intended. "And be certain to keep this arrangement to yourselves or your son will enjoy your company in the grooll mill."

The husband and wife bowed at the waist and scurried out of the chamber. Narses and Julinian shuffled to the desk. "You drive a hard bargain, Uncle," Julinian said, admiration coloring the observation.

"A pittance compared to what my father paid for my place as Unum." He peered at Narses. The boy's vacant expression told him one thing. It would cost infinitely more in bribes to the Cognos Populi to elevate him to Unum Potentate—unless his claim to the title was undisputed. Only one path could deliver that result. "But I think securing your place will cost me far, far less."

Pyros cleared his throat. "May I be excused? I have some issues to attend."

The Unum noted the chafed posture and black sheen of disapproval behind Pyros' eyes. He'd voiced his revulsion of the test-manipulation scheme upon assuming the mantle of Primae Jiren, yet he now relied on it to save his daughter's life. His belief in the Unum's promise to keep Zola out of the grooll mill ought to be enough to keep him in line, but one had to be careful not to place too much faith in other people's faith . . . or promises. He dismissed Pyros with a finger-flick. "By all means, go attend to your issues."

Pyros exited the chamber. The Unum addressed Narses the instant the door to the outer chamber closed. "You need to submit your application to sit the May S.A.T., and you need to do it today."

"I thought I was going to sit it later in the year."

"You'll sit it next month."

"Why, Papa?"

"There's a prospect who may achieve a perfect score on the test."

Narses' mouth widened. "That would mean I—"

"I know what it means, boy! Just make sure you get your application submitted!"

"Who's the prospect?" Narses asked.

"You don't need to know."

"It's Daoren al Lucien, isn't it?"

The Unum glared at this niece. At times, her cunning was too sharp for her own good. "It doesn't matter! Neither of you are to discuss this with anyone. Is that understood?"

They both agreed. With that concluded, one more matter needed attention. "Do you know where Commander Cang's district office is located?"

Narses' nasally haws accompanied an ever-more vacant expression. Julinian sniggered into her hand. "I know where it is."

"Good. Later today I want you to go there. Speak to Cang, and Cang alone. Tell her to come see me at her earliest convenience. Use those words exactly."

"Is there a reason for the summons?" Julinian asked. "She'll want to know."

"Say it's a matter of urgency and delicacy. And she's to inform no one. Not even Pyros."

Julinian nodded, eyes aglow.

The Unum couldn't be certain, but his niece might be cunning enough to know the true reason for the summons.

PYROS STALKED THE bowels of the Assembly, struggling to contain the outrage churning within him. He'd sought out the lower, less populated level due to its lack of witnesses.

He'd known about the test-manipulation scheme for years. A month into his tenure as Primae Jiren, he'd asked the Unum why so many parents requested audiences with him. The answer confirmed a long-simmering suspicion; the dim progeny of the ruling caste could buy its way out of harvesting. Until now, he hadn't fully appreciated the cost to the city-state.

Ten thousand pounds of grooll.

It was a staggering sum—enough to feed ten thousand for one day. The scheme deprived far more than ten-thousand denizens of their daily sustenance though. The Unum's arrangement with the Indonoid couple signified a drop in the sea. He made hundreds of similar arrangements before each monthly S.A.T., snatching millions of pounds of grooll from the peoples' mouths every year.

Pyros grasped the handle of his crystal dagger as he marched. He didn't draw the blade from its belt-sheath. He just needed something to squeeze.

The truest measure of the Unum's excess might be its consequences. Faced with starvation, the people he deprived might decide they had nothing left to lose. A people with nothing to lose often chose courses of action that led to the greatest loss of life. The Unum's greed could very well trigger the extinction of every man, woman, and child in Daqin Guojin.

He tightened his grip on the dagger's handle. A few weeks ago, the Unum had asked him to cull Lucien for the greater good of Daqin Guojin. He'd done it for the greater good of his daughter instead, but what use was saving Zola from the grooll mill if she was destined to perish in a bloody insurrection? Did the greater good of the city-state now demand the removal of another man?

He rounded a corner and slowed his pace. While the hallway was vacant, prying eyes still lurked behind every glass wall. The faintest glimmer of anger or dissent would be noticed.

As usual, the continuous movement honed his thoughts. They cut through his fears and doubts, clearing a path to an inescapable conclusion. The greater good of Daqin Guojin demanded the Unum's removal. As he strode past closed chamber doors and empty alcoves, his thoughts carved up more questions that proved just as unsettling.

Could he trust Commander Cang to aid in the plan? Her questioning of the edict to raise the S.A.T.'s passing score suggested she might be an ally, but what if she was a tool of the Unum, feigning dissent to entrap others? Her investigation of Laoshi al Euclidius suggested she was marching in lock-step with the Cognos Populi. Could *that* be a ruse to disguise her discontent with the ruling caste?

Pyros navigated the maze of potential angles, dizzy from the murky calculations. Two questions above all others kept him centered.

If he revealed his hand to Cang, would he be condemning himself? If he didn't, would he be condemning humanity?

He stalked the hallways for another five minutes, wrestling with the questions, before recognizing their false dichotomy. The stakes demanded one answer.

He had to trust Cang. He'd have to meet with her, but not here in the Assembly. It would have to take place in a less-populated locale. And soon.

Pyros pulled his quantum tile from his tunic and raised its screen to his mouth. "Contact Commander Cang."

* * *

DAOREN STALKED THE Void's lumenglass stage. He passed through the grooll mill's rotating plasmonic projection, struggling to digest the words Laoshi had fed him. He had to repeat them to ensure he'd heard him right. "You're saying the Unum has been manipulating S.A.T. scores for *years*?"

"Mako's prep-tests were stellar," Laoshi said from the side of the stage. "His failure made no sense, so in the months following his test I conducted my own discreet investigation. In the past year alone, nineteen hundred prospects with failing prep-test results received higher-than-average S.A.T. scores. That number falls well outside the statistical norm . . . and all were children of the ruling caste. Only one man in Daqin Guojin has the placement and power to make that happen."

"Is he doing it in exchange for grooll?"

"I found no direct evidence of that, but the Unum isn't known for his altruistic tendencies."

"How is this possible?" Heqet asked, twisting her hair braids beside the projection. "Aren't there safeguards in place to prevent it?"

"Quantum encryption protects individual scores from being altered," Laoshi said. "Each S.A.T. is encoded using the prospect's unique biometric data. Scores could only be switched between prospects by someone who has access to the datasets, but it would require tremendous effort and considerable foresight to avoid detection."

"And that's what happened to Mako?" Daoren asked.

"His score was switched with the Unum's niece." Laoshi wrung his hands. "In my haste to spark an inquiry, I broke a sacred edict and sent Julinian's prep-tests to your father. I fear he used them instead to confront the Unum and paid for it with his life."

Hearing his own suspicions echoed in Laoshi's words proved too much to bear. Daoren's jaw clenched so tight, he thought his teeth might shatter. "I'll cull the Unum! I swear it!"

"That, dear boy, is exactly what he intends to do to *you*."

Daoren's jaw slackened. "What?"

Laoshi shook his head. "I uncovered air-link transactions that prove prep-test results have been sent by one or more of my Librarians to an entity outside the Librarium. If I'm right, the Unum is the recipient. He'll know that your results are the highest ever recorded. He'll know that you may become the first prospect in history to write a perfect S.A.T."

Heqet gasped. "You'd earn the incontestable right to become Unum Potentate."

"I'd sooner be harvested for grooll!"

"And so you will be," Laoshi said. "It's a right the Unum covets for his son."

Daoren gulped a spine-bracing breath. At last the truth was out. The forces aligned against him included the most powerful man in Daqin Guojin—and the security apparatus of the city-state under his control. One solution existed for such a problem. "All the more reason to cull the Unum!"

"Brave words, Daoren, but even if you could get close enough to strike him down, you'd have precious little lifespan afterward in which to savor the triumph." Laoshi stroked his beard. "Besides, there's a more intelligent way to defeat him."

"I'm listening."

"We'll get to that in good time. First, I need your help with a problem of my own."

"What problem?"

Laoshi limped closer. "I need your help to save Heqet's life."

Daoren rattled his head, sure he'd misheard. Laoshi's words

often skirted the point by such a wide margin, they missed it alto-gether. "Did you say *Heqet's* life?"

Laoshi leveled an adoring gaze at her. "She's as bright as cold-rolled crystal, but a reading disability means she won't be able to complete the S.A.T. in the allotted time. I need your help to save her."

"How in Sha's name can I help save her if I'm going to be harvested as well?"

Laoshi limped closer still. "Do you know who you remind me of?"

Daoren scowled. Damn this Librarian and his endless ques-tions! "I haven't the faintest idea."

"Dominus, your mother's father. We were friends in our youth."

Daoren scrutinized Laoshi's face, trying to read his intent in its folds and creases. His grandfather had died young, but his mother had never mentioned how he met his fate. "So I remind you of my grandfather. What of it?"

"Did you know he died defending Daqin Guojin from Havoc when your mother was an infant? That he took hundreds of mongrels with him before he departed for the Great After?"

"No."

Laoshi grasped Daoren's shoulders. "I watched you save your mother on the day of Mako's S.A.T. Seeing you charge up the northern stairway into the teeth of that storm brought back so many memories. It proved what I'd always suspected. Dominus' strength and courage, his determination to protect the innocent from harm—all these qualities inhabit *you*."

Daoren blinked, struggling to believe him, struggling to over-come years of distrust in his kind. For reasons he couldn't articu-late, he needed to see Heqet's reaction.

The glint in her eyes conveyed her thoughts with absolute clarity. *She believed.*

Laoshi lowered his voice to a hushed, almost reverent volume.

"I can't prevent you or Heqet from failing the S.A.T. I can't spirit you out of the city-state without activating your sonic nanocharges. But I can—"

"Why not hide us in here?" Daoren's gaze panned the immense Void. "The Jireni can't touch us and it would buy time to—"

"It would buy time, but nothing more. The Cognos Populi likes to make examples of prospects who flout the test. Once they discovered your failure to sit the S.A.T., you'd be hunted. If the two of you remained at large after a month, they'd—"

"Remotely activate the nanocharges." Daoren grimaced. "I'd forgotten about that capability."

"It has to be this way," Laoshi said. "All I can do is arrange for you and Heqet to sit together in the same row in the Center." He pointed at the grooll mill's plasmonic projection. "And before you do, we must figure out a way to survive *that*."

Daoren gazed upon the mill's infinite complexity. Daqin Guojin's brightest minds had designed it to convert prospects into grooll with brutal efficiency. The process had operated, uninterrupted and without failure, for two hundred years.

Maybe they could survive it, but he hadn't the faintest idea how.

14

PLAN OF ATTACK

P YROS GUIDED THE Hexalite levicart around a sharp curve near Meiguo Cheng's grooll-distribution center. In this part of the district, the drab structures lining the transway topped a few hundred feet above ground-level. They stayed in permanent shadow thanks to the loftier structures gracing the wealthier surrounding boroughs of Zhongguo Cheng.

He gripped the steering yoke with both hands and counter-steered. Compressed air jetted from varinozzles in the port nacelles, nudging the levicart's front end to the right and aligning its snubbed nose with the transway. Despite the additional hydro-gen-infusion cells, the hullform's armor cladding made the vehicle top-heavy, calling for a light touch on the control inputs. A push of the throttle-control activated the aft varinozzles—their abrasive hiss resonated in the empty troop compartment.

The levicart accelerated down the straightaway. Seated in the cabin's forward passenger seat, Cang resumed the conversation after the hiss faded. "How much grooll do you think he's acquired?"

"Sha knows. The Unum demanded ten thousand pounds from the couple. He's had audiences with hundreds of parents over the past few months in his chamber. He may see the richest parents at his palace and demand even larger sums for his service."

Pyros glanced over to gauge her reaction.

Cang tugged at the collar of her tunic, loosening it. She stared out the passenger window, brooding in silence.

They'd left her district office in Zhongguo Cheng forty minutes ago. She hadn't questioned the reason for the sudden meeting, nor why her aide couldn't attend, nor why they were holding it in a levicart in the middle of Meiguo Cheng. She'd absorbed the details of the Indonoid couple's audience without comment. He'd tried to take her emotional pulse a dozen times, but Cang was a difficult woman to read.

The pulse of Meiguo Cheng was easier to measure. Beyond the levicart's armored glass, Caucasoids massed on the pediwalks lining the transway. They carried urns, jars, and other containers. Today was a ration day. Entire families had ventured from their abodes to collect their monthly grooll allotments. Their shriveled cheeks and lank limbs attested to the paltry amounts they received from the distribution center.

"How long has he been running the scheme?" Cang asked.

"At least four years."

"Do other members of the Assembly know about it?"

"Some, but he's bribing them to blind their eyes."

"While the people starve," she said, still gazing out the passenger window. "We can't allow this to . . ."

Pyros sensed a tremor of fear in her voice before it faded. Was she afraid to reveal her hand, just as he'd been to reveal his? It was time set a new path, and that started with setting her mind at ease.

"You needn't fear me, Cang. I believe the Unum's greed will spell the end of Daqin Guojin." He steadied his breathing; the next statement would seal his fate for good or ill. "And I believe we must take action to stop that from happening."

She turned from the window. Relief rinsed her face. "Then we're of the same mind," she said, offering her hand.

He grasped it. They shook; one palm up, one palm down. The gesture was symbolic, but significant. It represented their bond, in words and deeds. "Now for the hard question," he said. "How do we address the problem?"

If Cang had the answer, she kept it to herself.

"What of your investigation into Laoshi al Euclidius? Are there any indications of him inciting dissent? He could be a useful ally."

"None yet," she said, "but I think he—"

Four dense thuds rippled through the cabin.

Pyros flinched at the impacts. Four oblong craters marred the windshield, etching a diagonal line inches from his face. They came from one source. "Dart gun!"

Cang shifted forward in her seat, neck craned to scan the tops of the adjacent structures. "High-angle trajectory!"

Three more thuds rang out. Three more craters gouged Cang's side of the windshield. She recoiled from the din, but recovered in short order.

Pyros shoved the throttle-control forward. Compressed air shrieked; the levicart accelerated. He scanned the pediwalk.

Denizens scattered, dropping urns and jars. Parents scooped up their children and ran hunchbacked, using their own bodies as shields. None carried weapons.

A tattoo of clangorous thuds signaled more dart strikes against the aft hullform.

"Where are the dissenters firing from?"

"An elevated position," Cang said, still scanning the rooftops. "I think they're trying to draw us forward!"

Pyros peered through the cratered windshield.

Two hundred feet ahead, the pediwalks ended. They gave way to vertical glass façades that hugged the transway.

A natural bottleneck.

A choke point.

An ideal spot for an—

He reefed the throttle backward. Compressed air blasted from the forward grill, creating a billowy wall of mist. The levicart bucked, bleeding off speed.

Fifty feet ahead, through the dissolving mist, the transway deformed and blistered. A split-second later, the ear-popping roar of sonic charges hammered the vehicle.

Crystalline hail showered the windshield, its ferocious ticks veiling Cang's savage profanities. The concussive blasts decelerated the levicart from fifty miles an hour to a dead stop in the space of twelve inches.

Pyros pitched forward. His shock belt alone spared him from the lethal arrest. He yanked back on the steering yoke, cranking it to the right until he hit the limiter stops.

The sweeping reverse turn yawed the vehicle. It canted forty degrees and a hair's breadth from tipping. Its nose dug into a guardrail, splintering a series of stanchions before breaking loose.

He stopped the turn and slammed the throttle forward, heart skip-beating in his throat. Beside him, Cang's arm flexed as if she was pushing her own imaginary throttle, urging the levicart to accelerate.

Within seconds, they streaked past one hundred miles per hour. He didn't back off the throttle until they'd doubled the speed and cleared the cull zone.

Cang released a whooshing breath. "You have good instincts, sire. Dissenters don't often place sonic charges beneath transways."

Pyros wiped sweat from his brow. "My instincts tell me that if the Unum stays on his present course, we'll be seeing more of these attacks in the days to come." He glanced at Cang. "I need a favor from you."

"You only have to ask."

"It will be risky."

She nodded at the cracked and cratered windshield. "What isn't nowadays?"

"I need you to meet with the district commanders. Gauge where their loyalties lie."

"To what end?"

"We can't turn all the Jireni against the ruling caste, but we have to find enough support to remove the Unum from power."

"And who'll take his place?"

Pyros squeezed the steering yoke. He didn't have an answer for that question. Not yet. "I'd best get you back before your absence is noted."

"How soon do you need to know the loyalties of the other commanders?"

"Could you complete the task before the May S.A.T.?"

Cang mulled the question. "Yes, but I'll need an innocent way to frame the inquiry. One that won't arouse the suspicions of those allied with the Unum."

"You're a courageous woman. I won't forget this."

She didn't acknowledge the compliment.

Pyros allowed himself a smile; the years hadn't changed her disposition toward flattery. He slowed the levicart and descended the next ramp onto a northbound transway. It would take them back into the heart of Zhongguo Cheng's administrative district, back into the heart of the Unum's reign.

With any luck that heart would soon beat no more.

⁂

IN THE VOID, Laoshi, Daoren, and Heqet gathered atop the lumenglass stage. The grooll mill's plasmonic projection dwarfed them.

Laoshi manipulated his quantum tile, calling up a variety of renderings. Each presented a new perspective on the mill's structure, displaying its intricacies from different angles and at multiple scales. "We'll spend the next few weeks reviewing the grooll-making process," he said. "You'll study the mill's design until you know every component, every system, and every step in the process by heart."

Daoren and Heqet nodded, engaged and attentive.

Laoshi was relieved to see interest rather than anxiety in their eyes. They'd need all their faculties to survive the coming challenge. "The key to your survival is timing," he continued. "The grooll-making process is fully automated and begins inside the Center. Failing prospects are stunned while they're still restrained in their seats. Two minutes later, the seats rotate beneath the floor." He tapped his tile.

The projection's perspective zoomed in, highlighting a single platform. Blue, egg-shaped pods dotted its surface, arrayed in an evenly spaced line.

"The Center's rows and seats are aligned with the mill's platforms and pods," Laoshi said. "The seat restraints unlock after another minute, dropping the stunned prospects into their individual pods."

Another tap of the tile reduced the perspective to that of a single life-sized pod.

Daoren and Heqet paced around the plasmonic pod, inspecting it from various angles. An opening measuring seven feet long and two feet wide middled its upper surface. Below the opening, a reclining seat mounted to its base. Twelve half-dome lenses protruded from the curved interior walls positioned around the seat. At the rear, twelve cables sprouted from the pod's exterior surface. Six hoses connected to the base, each three inches in diameter.

Laoshi circled the pod while his charges examined its components. "Once you're in the pod, you'd best get out right away."

He tapped the tile—a transparent panel sealed the pod's opening.

Heqet flinched at the panel's blinding speed. "It's self-sealing?"

"And airtight. It can't be reopened by hand."

Daoren passed his hand through the dozen cables connected to the pod's rear surface. "What are these?"

"Power cables." Laoshi swiped the tile. "For the photonic cutters."

A ruddy matrix of hair-thin, monochromatic beams emanated from the half-dome lenses. They intersected an inch below the transparent panel, forming a horizontal grid. After ten seconds, the beams angled downward, sweeping back and forth over the seat's longitudinal and lateral axes.

Daoren gazed at the dancing, cross-hatched light pattern. He shuddered, perhaps imagining Mako's fate at the January S.A.T.

Laoshi drew a breath. This wouldn't be easy for the boy to hear, but it had to be said. "The cutters pre-slice the prospect's pienfu and skin to ease their removal."

Daoren squeezed his eyes shut. Heqet's hands shot up to her mouth.

"I know this is difficult," he said, "but you need to focus. You must know what to expect if you're to survive."

Daoren opened his eyes. Heqet lowered her hands. They were back in the moment.

"After pre-slicing, hoses in the pod's base evacuate the air, creating a high vacuum. The vacuum de-gloves the skin and removes the entrails." Laoshi paused to make sure they were still with him. "And here's the most important point to remember. Each pod uses ultrasonic energy to liquify its occupant. You must be clear of the platform before the process starts."

Daoren and Heqet spoke with one wary voice. "Or else?"

Laoshi wished he had a gentler answer, but no words could soften this hard truth. "Or else you'll be converted into slurry."

THE UNUM CROSSED the chamber floor, returning to his desk from his afternoon ablutions. It was another old habit—though less mature than his panel-gazing.

His gang of medical practitioners constantly berated him about the need for exercise. To still their concerns, he'd taken to using the waste chamber on the south side of the Assembly to empty his bladder and bowels. Every afternoon for the past three years, he walked ten minutes out and ten minutes back to render his effluent unto Daqin Guojin. He'd grown to enjoy the brief respite—to look forward to it, in fact. As much as he appreciated his chamber's opulence, it could take on the suffocating feel of a prison after a half-day of inertia.

He eased into his chair. A knock issued from the door to the outer chamber the moment his posterior took his weight. He sighed—so much for the respite. "Come in if you must."

The door swung open and Cang entered. She marched over, sandals clipping an assertive beat on the crystalline floor.

"Ah, commander," he said. "Thank you for coming on such short notice."

Cang halted before the desk and bowed. She straightened and clasped her hands behind her back, adopting a rigid posture that still looked relaxed. Her unblinking gaze fixed straight forward, tracking a foot above the Unum's head.

He waited for her to speak. Most district commanders couldn't stop chatterwailing in his presence; a byproduct of nerves, he presumed, or a desire to steer the conversation toward topics they knew to be safe. Cang, in contrast, was a monument to reticence, and an unadorned one at that. She wore no glass implants, at least none visible to the naked eye. Beneath her black bianfu, however, her svelte body might boast the most alluring patterns.

After ten wordless seconds, the Unum realized he'd have to take the lead lest they bide the rest of the afternoon in awkward quiet. "I must tell you," he said, "your handling of the investigation into the attack at the glass market was exemplary. I read your reports with keen interest."

"My thanks."

After a lengthy pause, it became clear that Cang had finished speaking. Evidently, she was a woman of few words. "I'm also told that since your appointment as district commander, acts of dissent in Zhongguo Cheng have declined by forty percent."

"I have many good men under my command," she said. "They're responsible for the success."

The Unum scanned for signs of insincerity on her unadorned face. He found none. Sapient Sha—she actually meant it. "You're too modest. Good men are forged by great leaders."

"Forgive me, Unum, but is there a specific reason you wanted to see me today? Your niece wasn't able to provide one."

"There is," he said, appreciating her directness—a rare trait among senior Jireni. "How many open investigations do you have in your district?"

"Hundreds. I'd have to check my records to be sure."

"Could you add one more?"

"Of course. Who's the subject?"

"Pyros."

He'd spent the better part of an hour pondering how to deliver the name. Should he creep up on it, planting hints as he went, to avoid alarming her? Or should he blurt it out and strive for the greatest impact? He decided the latter approach would be most revealing, but it proved disappointing.

If hearing the name shocked Cang, she hid it well. He couldn't detect any changes to her expression, not even to the size of her pupils, that indicated concern. She remained a monument to reticence.

"Primae Jiren Pyros?"

"Yes. *That* Pyros."

"It would help if I knew what you . . . what *was* suspected."

"Nothing specific," he said, tucking away the verbal slip for future reference. "It's as much for his own protection as for that of the city-state. It would put some minds at ease."

Cang's brow granted the slightest wrinkle before smoothing. He wagered she ached to ask whose minds were uneasy. It spoke well of her political intelligence that she wasn't willing to voice the question.

"I want you to observe him," he said, rising from his chair. "And report to me on a weekly basis regarding any behavior that seems out of character for a Primae Jiren. Can you do that?"

"I can, Unum."

"Excellent! It goes without saying that this investigation is for no one's eyes but my own. I'm trusting your discretion."

Cang bowed. "You will have it."

She marched back to the door, sandals clipping another assertive beat.

The Unum studied her departure. Reticent, humble, direct, and unflappable—Commander Cang harbored many admirable qualities.

If only more of his district commanders could be the same.

———

CANG EMERGED FROM the Unum's chamber and proceeded down the hallway at a measured pace. She passed a dozen members of the Cognos Populi, nodding her usual terse greeting, before entering the waste chamber.

Inside, ten stalls lined a wall opposite a row of hand basins and a mirror. She crouched to check the stalls for occupants.

They were vacant.

Cang entered the first stall and locked its door. The nausea that had welled before she entered the Unum's chamber crested a second later. She leaned over and retched into the waste basin. She braced her hands against her knees and retched again . . . and again.

A minute later, she spat out the remnants of bile and grooll and flushed the evidence away. She exited the stall and crossed to the hand basins.

Cang gargled water and checked the mirror to make sure she'd left no evidence on her tunic. There was none, but the redness of her scalp and bulging veins over her temples spoke of her exertion. She'd have to wait until both subsided before leaving the chamber. It would give her time to sort through the last few minutes.

She'd walked into the Unum's chamber thinking she'd been betrayed.

Julinian had arrived at the district office with the Unum's summons an hour after the meeting with Pyros. The timing made it appear that she'd been set up by the Primae Jiren, enticed by him to voice her dissent toward the ruling caste. Even the attack on the levicart became suspicious; Pyros could have arranged it to strengthen their bond of trust.

She'd walked into the Unum's chamber thinking she'd never walk out again.

Cang didn't know what to make of the Unum's request, but she'd wager ten years of grooll rations that *he* was the one with an uneasy mind. If he wanted Pyros investigated, it had to mean he viewed him as a threat. It had to mean Pyros was her ally, did it not?

She leaned on the hand basin, trying to get a grip on the situation. After a minute, she straightened her back.

The Unum's request must be authentic. It wouldn't make sense to ask her to monitor Pyros as a test of her loyalty if she'd already proven her loyalty to be lacking. The very fact that she was standing in a waste chamber with the acrid aftertaste of vomit in her mouth instead of facing a firing line of Jireni with a gag in her mouth was proof enough.

The question now was whether to inform Pyros. If he knew he was being investigated on the Unum's orders, would it affect his behavior and decision-making, making an ill situation worse? She'd have to think it over.

She wouldn't have to think over how to frame her inquiry into the loyalty of the district commanders. A sanctioned investigation into Pyros' behavior gave her the perfect excuse to take their pulse. The realization brought a smile to her lips.

The Unum had handed her an ideal cover story.

The chamber's door swung open. An Africoid elder in a purple shenyi entered.

"Afternoon, Jiren," the elder said, hobbling toward the stalls.

Cang gave him a terse nod and checked her reflection. Her skin tone and veins had returned to normal.

She exited the chamber before the door swung closed.

D AOREN AND HEQET occupied the center of the lumenglass stage in the Void. The grooll mill's plasmonic projection loomed high above them.

Daoren craned his neck, taking in the expanse of glass piping. It glinted beneath a single platform, every bend and twist rendered with pinpoint accuracy. He'd been staring up at the glutted snarls for nearly an hour.

Heqet pointed at another section. "What about that route?"

Daoren squinted, but he couldn't make out what she was pointing at. "Could you reduce the scale, Laoshi?"

Laoshi lingered on the side of the stage. He'd stayed silent the entire time, seemingly content to let them chart the best path from the top of the platform to the floor of the grooll mill. He manipulated his quantum tile—the projection shrank to a more reasonable size. "How's that?"

"Perfect," Daoren said, rubbing his stiff neck. The wall of piping now rose only ten feet above the stage, but retained its fidelity. "But I still don't see a workable route."

"There," Heqet said, arm still extended, finger still pointing. "That one has good handholds all the way along."

He eyed the horizontal length of pipe. "And no footholds for about forty feet."

"So?"

He glanced at her—his neck protested the sudden rotational movement. "So you'd have to support your weight with your hands alone."

"So?" she asked, heated tone matching her reddening cheeks.

"So you'd have to work your way hand-over-hand until we got to there." He pointed at an area where the sections of piping grew more concentrated. "You're telling me you have the grip strength to do that?"

She dipped her chin and glared. "Give me something to squeeze and I'll prove it to you."

He snorted. "That's a constructive input."

She snorted back. "More of a threat, actually."

"Why don't you take your threats and stick them up your—"

"Enough!" Laoshi shouted from the stage's margin. "You two, honestly."

Heqet spun to her grandfather. "Is it my fault he thinks I'm weak?"

"For the love of Sha," Daoren said. "*I'm* not strong enough to make that transit!"

She spun back to him. "How would you know?"

"I used to climb Rhyger's Cliffs on the Western Mound."

"*You* climbed Rhyger's Cliffs."

"It was one of my favorite haunts."

"That explains so much . . ."

"What do you mean?"

"I always wondered if you'd fallen on your head as a child."

Daoren bit his tongue until his ire subsided. "All I'm saying is that I know what it takes to traverse a difficult section." He pointed at the route Heqet favored. "I'd have problems making that work without solid footholds."

"Then which route would you suggest?" she asked.

He scanned the piping. In truth, he couldn't see any workable route that spanned its entire height and width. Not without mechanical aids of some kind. "I don't know."

Laoshi limped closer. "Let's leave the problem of climbing down from the platform for another day. There are plenty of others left to solve."

Daoren sighed—the old Librarian was right. The grooll mill was replete with problems, each more deadly than the last.

"What should we focus on next?" Heqet asked.

Laoshi cleared his throat. His somber gaze dropped to the stage's lumenglass panels. "I think we need to discuss the problem of sympathetic liquidation."

Daoren swallowed his dread. In the pit of his stomach, he suspected the term was even worse than it sounded.

* * *

CANG WAITED IN the chamber of Riben Cheng's district commander. She'd arrived ten minutes ago, electing to stand rather than sit. She wanted to remain on her feet for the meeting —the better to evade a swinging fist or thrusting dagger. So far neither had come in her direction; Commander Hyro had already been called away twice.

The interruptions left her with little to do. Radan had remained in Zhongguo Cheng despite his desire to accompany her on the whirlwind tour of all fifty Chengs. She would have enjoyed his company, but she needed to engage the district commanders one-on-one. It offered the best chance for honest exchanges.

The downtime gave her another chance to examine the chamber and, by extension, the mind of Commander Hyro. Riben Cheng was Daqin Guojin's easternmost district. It occupied thirteen square-miles of territory on the Eastern Sea and was home to over a million denizens and prospects. Some of the city-state's wealthiest families resided here, but Cang saw no evidence of conspicuous affluence inside the chamber.

The forty-by-forty space afforded ample room for expensive artisanal wares. Commander Hyro instead chose to display a single sculpture. The spiraling crystalline vase glinted atop a glass pedestal on the corner of her desk. The piece was remarkable only for its rudimentary design and simple aesthetic. Beyond it, a bank of windows looked out onto the Eastern Sea. Curling wave-crests broke on a narrow strip of sand, scouring the shoreline. No denizens wandered the beachfront.

"My apologies for the delays, Commander Cang."

Commander Hyro alum Takeda entered clutching a quantum tile before her. At five feet, three inches tall, she held the distinction of being the shortest serving Jireni. Unlike other diminutive Jireni, she didn't offset the shortfall with an oversized personality. In fact, Hyro ranked as one of the more self-effacing members of the security force.

Hyro didn't look up from the tile's screen as she crossed the floor. "We have three operations underway to detain three cells of dissenters."

"I understand," Cang said. "It's given me time to admire your chamber. It has a simple serenity."

Hyro settled behind the desk and set the quantum tile on its surface. "I'll take my serenity wherever I can find it."

Cang motioned to the spiral vase. "That's an interesting piece. From a local artisan?"

"In a manner of speaking. My daughter made it for me."

"How old is she?"

"Thirteen," Hyro said. "A very difficult thirteen. Kimye thinks she knows more than me."

Cang nodded. Part of her had always wondered what it must be like to have children. How strange it must be for parents to see their living, breathing self-caricatures discovering the world anew, displaying familiar character traits once thought unique.

How powerful the desire must be to protect that precious creation, to do anything to safeguard its future. She dismissed the idle musing. "Let's get down to the business of why I'm here." She nodded at the quantum tile on the desk. "Before you're called away again."

"I know why you're here."

"You do?"

"You've visited a dozen district commanders over the past week. Word travels."

"Allow me to state the reason plainly so there's no ambiguity," she said. "I'm here at the Unum's request. He asked me investigate the Primae Jiren's loyalty."

"I understand," Hyro said, seemingly unfazed. "Though I don't understand why the Unum would question Pyros' loyalty."

"You don't?"

"I've known Pyros for fifteen years. He cares as much for power as I do for the trappings of wealth."

"So you've never seen any indications of dissent from him?"

Hyro leaned forward and chucklebucked. "No, for Sha's sake! Have you?"

The frank response caught her off guard. The dozen district commanders she'd visited so far had been evasive in their responses to the question, not wishing to tip their hand in any direction. A handful had thought she was trying to foster dissent against the ruling caste. The district commander from Nansilafu Cheng had drawn his crystal dagger from his belt-sheath and lunged at her before she'd convinced him she was acting on the Unum's orders.

"You don't have to talk around the issue with me," Hyro said. "I can see from the look on your face that you don't believe Pyros is disloyal."

"You're saying the Unum is wrong."

"I'm saying the Unum is like any other Unum. They all tend to grow paranoid after a certain time in power."

Cang sensed an opening. With the previous commanders, she'd broached the subject with much greater delicacy. With Commander Hyro, she abandoned delicacy in favor of expediency. "Did you know he plans to install his son as Unum Potentate?"

Hyro squeezed her eyes shut. "There's a terrifying thought."

Cang blinked. She'd come into the meeting suspecting that Hyro would support the plan to remove the Unum from power. But she never imagined she'd be so . . . forthright. "Forgive me, but I didn't expect this level of . . ."

"Honesty?"

"Yes."

Hyro sighed. "At least fifty cells of dissenters are operating in my district. Forty percent of the denizens in Riben Cheng are calorie-deficient." She swiveled in her chair and faced the windows overlooking the sea. "Every week, at least ten families wade into the Eastern Sea rather than starve to death." She shuddered. "That sea is acidic. Imagine the hopelessness that must occupy a denizen's mind if drowning in acid is preferable to living another day."

"What if I told you there was hope?"

Hyro swiveled back. "Then I would embrace you as I would embrace my own sister." The quantum tile on her desk chirped. She glanced at its screen. "It's my aide in the operations center. I swear that girl needs to ask my permission to use the waste chamber."

"Do you need to leave again?"

"No." Hyro looked up from the screen. "I'd wager we have more important matters to discuss, don't we?"

Cang allowed herself a cautious smile. "Yes, we do."

THE UNUM SKULKED up the pathway and stopped before the

abode's purple door. A single potlight burned above the door-frame, warding off the gloom. He paused to catch his breath.

The regal fleet had delivered him to the southern habitation complex in Meiguo Cheng ten minutes earlier. He'd ordered the fleet to stop well away from the abode so as not to draw undue attention to the visit—or to alert the abode's inhabitants. He'd walked the rest of the way.

The commander of his personal guard had protested the break in security protocol, insisting he accompany the Unum to the abode. The Jiren needn't have worried. The few shadows the Unum had passed on the pediwalks paid him no attention. From their perspective, he was just another denizen. Larger than most, perhaps, but nothing to warrant undue curiosity.

The Unum swiped his forehead. The absence of studs triggered a fleeting moment of cognitive disconnect. He wiped his hand across a blue pienfu, already darkened with sweat. He'd worn the simple pienfu for the same reason he'd removed his studs and ordered the fleet to stand off despite the late hour.

The visit needed to remain anonymous.

He knocked on the door and counted off the seconds. After half a minute, he knocked again. Harder this time.

Fifteen seconds later, the door opened. He suppressed a gasp.

Cordelia stood in the nave, as haggard as he'd ever seen her. A crumpled mourning robe clung to her pallid skin as if it hadn't been removed in days. Her eyes reflected hollowed fatigue—like they hadn't been closed in weeks. She displayed no signs of surprise or alarm. For a moment, he assumed she hadn't recognized him in his plain garments.

"Unum," she said. "What brings you here at this hour?"

"Forgive the intrusion, Cordelia," he said, "but may I come in?"

Her eyes narrowed as though she was pondering a refusal. She opened the door wider. "If you must."

He stepped into the nave. The abode reeked of grief and

resonated with an oppressing quietude that begged to be filled, but no words came to him. Instead, he took a piece of grooll from the urn on the side table and placed it on his tongue. He gazed at her while he chewed, hoping his silence might prompt her into speaking first.

"Why are you here?" she asked, voice slurred and diluted.

"To make sure you're all right," he said after he swallowed. "Might we talk for a minute?"

Cordelia shrugged. She led him into the parlor, placing one foot in front of the other like an automaton. She reached a divan and slumped onto its glass surface.

The Unum settled onto the divan along the opposite wall. He eyed the square table near the windows. It still had four place settings on its surface—double the necessary number. Dust coated the wares.

"So talk," she said.

He brought his gaze back to her and adopted a well-practiced look of concern. "I'm worried about you."

"My thanks for your worry," she said, "but you needn't be."

"You're obviously not eating." He motioned to the courtyard beyond the windows. "And when's the last time you stepped outside?"

"I don't remember."

The Unum glanced at the parlor door. "Is Daoren here?"

Cordelia shook her head.

"How is he taking Lucien's . . . the most recent loss?"

She fingered her mourning robe's sleeve. "You'll have to ask him."

He masked his irritation. He'd come here seeking specific answers, not vague generalities. He tried another tack. "How's the boy been spending his time?"

Cordelia's brow creased. "Why?"

"I know how . . . difficult he can be. I imagine these heavy events haven't helped in that regard."

Her darkened gaze fell upon the floor's tan-colored tiles. Whatever thoughts had prompted the expression, she kept to herself.

"Has Pyros come by to visit?"

She raised her head. The creases on her forehead deepened. "Why would the Primae Jiren visit me?"

"I asked him to stop by. Just to check on you."

"He hasn't."

"He must have been too busy," the Unum said, recognizing the futility of further discussion. Cordelia had no answers; the proof was inscribed on her face. He rose from the divan with a grunt. "I want you to know that I'm here for you. If you need anything—anything at all—you only have to ask."

She remained seated. Her upper body swayed before finding its center. "If I needed anything, I already would have."

The Unum forced a smile onto his lips. "I'll let myself out then."

He swept out of the parlor and into the nave. He exited the front door and paced down the tiled pathway. By the time he reached the pediwalk, he was cursing the time wasted. Cordelia had no more insights into Daoren's activity than Pyros and his useless Jireni.

Only one useful fact had surfaced during the visit—she'd shown genuine confusion when asked if Pyros had stopped by to see her. In truth, he hadn't asked Pyros to do so. Deep down, he suspected his Primae Jiren might be in contact with the family, seeking to strike up an alliance. Cordelia's reaction told him that wasn't the case. It told him that—

The Unum halted. Why was he walking back to the regal fleet? He pulled his quantum tile from his pienfu and raised it to his mouth. "I'm finished here. Come pick me up." He terminated the call without waiting for an acknowledgement and took in the surroundings.

Across the transway, clutches of Caucasoid denizens plied the pediwalk. None gave him a second glance.

The behavior struck him as strange. Take away his splendid regal mianfu, his edicts, and his personal guard and he was just another denizen. Invisible. Inaudible. Expendable.

He shuddered—there was a horrid thought. He lowered his gaze to the tile. Another question ached to be asked, but he dare not ask it over the insecure device. Instead, he confined the question to the relative safety of his mind, not even risking to whisper it aloud.

How was Gustar progressing with the test preparations?

GUSTAR SHIVERED AND swore. He drew a flexglass quilt up over his shoulders and rubbed his hands together.

The alcove's temperature tended to reach its lowest point in the middle of the night. Since forwarding Daoren al Lucien's prep-test scores to the Unum, he'd spent every night trapped in its confines. The decision might prove to be one of the most regrettable he'd ever made.

In alerting the Unum to Daoren's perfect results, Gustar had set himself upon an impossible task. Switching Daoren's score with Narses' score in the upcoming S.A.T. required the deft manipulation of countless qubits of biometric data—the most heavily encrypted data in the city-state. A tunneling algorithm was necessary for bypassing and sub-linking the encrypted data fields, but its multivariate computations proved horrendously complex.

So far, he'd devoted every iota of attention to the task, forgoing sleeping, eating, and all but the most basal biological functions. It wasn't enough. The intermittent chatter from Indonoid brothers in the adjacent alcove didn't help matters.

"Don't forget you need to go to the Center tonight," the older brother said.

The younger brother sucked his teeth. "I hate going there alone."

"It's not haunted. How many times do I have to tell you?"

"I can feel them watching me. Do you have any idea how many prospects have died in there?"

"No, but I could pull the data in a few seconds and tell you."

"I'll pull the data. You go test the tabulator."

The older brother sighed. "Sha's silica teeth! It's your turn to calibrate it!"

Gustar flinched and rocked back in his seat. The flexglass quilt slipped from his shoulders and dropped to the floor.

The tabulator!

The Center's tabulator summed every test and displayed the scores based on the unique row and seat number assigned to each prospect. The encryption protocol protecting the assigned information was much less robust than the layered protocols protecting biometric data. Switching scores based on seat assignments would be a relatively simple matter.

His elation dimmed as quickly as it had flared. Switching scores based on seat assignments would also be detectable. The rigorous post-S.A.T. examination conducted by his fellow datakeepers would easily spot the anomaly. At best, Narses' claim to Unum Potentate would be suspect. At worst, his claim would be denied. Neither result would sit well with the Unum.

Gustar cursed the wretched dilemma. The switch could either be undetectable and too late, or detectable and in time. The first option would certainly lead to his demise, but would the second?

He rubbed his hands together to revive their circulation and center his thoughts. It took less than ten seconds to reach a decision. He had to risk it. What other choice did he have?

The younger Indonoid passed by the alcove. Gustar snatched

his quantum tile off the desk and hustled after him. He caught up with the boy mid-way down a row of quantum cradles.

"Tarry, friend!" Gustar would have used the brother's name if he'd known it. "Did I hear you mention you're going to the Center?"

The Indonoid frowned, no doubt puzzled by the sudden interest. "I am."

"Care for some company? I have some tests of my own I've been meaning to conduct there."

The boy's mood brightened. "I'd welcome it. That place gives me the creeps at night."

Gustar feigned an empathetic smile. "Me, too."

16

TREAD CAREFULLY

DAOREN TIPTOED DOWN the gloomy hallway leading from his sleeping chamber, guided by the anemic yellow glow seeping from the parlor door. The stillness amplified every footfall, however lightly placed. His apprehension intensified every breath, however lightly drawn.

Cordelia had been asleep in the parlor when he crept into the abode late last night. He'd watched her for five minutes. Were it not for her chest rising and falling in fitful respirations, he could have mistaken her for a corpse.

He'd used all his restraint not to rush over and hold her, as any decent son might do, but the show of affection wouldn't have done either of them any good. With any luck, he'd be on his way back to the Librarium before she awoke.

He edged by the parlor door and risked a glance inside.

Cordelia lay on the same divan, curled up on her right side. A single wall tile glowed near her head. Diluted yellow light spilled over the mourning shroud serving as a makeshift bedsheet.

Blunt pangs mauled Daoren's heart. Cordelia had lost Mako and Lucien. Now his prolonged absences during the past few weeks had robbed her of him. Grief had drawn her into ever-murkier waters. She might never find her way back unless someone reached out to her.

He couldn't be the one to reach out—not with one week left to go before his S.A.T. Any contact with her would lead to questions he couldn't answer. The less his mother knew of his activities in the Void, the better.

Daoren slinked into the entry nave, keeping his movements slow and silent. He scooped grooll from the crystal urn, stuffing his waist pouch until its seams stretched.

Laoshi kept little grooll in the Temple and never ate. How he'd preserved his strength over these past weeks was a mystery. Rather than ebb, his vitality had increased by the day, and his intellect proved as keen as it was vast. The old Librarian's knowledge of the grooll mill was encyclopedic; his tutelage clear, concise, and lightened with unexpected flashes of humor.

Heqet's resolve had also surprised Daoren. Not once had she expressed worry or fear over the coming S.A.T. She possessed an inner strength that he'd never fully appreciated when she was seeing Mako, as well as a boundless capacity for absorbing technological knowledge and problem-solving. Laoshi hadn't lied; she *was* as bright as cold-rolled crystal.

Daoren had spoken more with her over the last few weeks than over the last few years, though the conversations were still as likely to lead to argument as agreement. Many of their quarrels stemmed from his continued inability to say the right thing in her presence, but she brought her own brand of friction to the mix; the unflinching desire to get in the final word. If one word described Heqet, it was *challenging*.

He managed to cram one more handful into his grooll pouch and pivoted to the door.

Cordelia blocked it, skin wane in the subdued light. Her cheekbones had sharpened to a dagger's edge since Lucien's funeral. They matched her eyes.

He masked his surprise. "I didn't know you were awake."

She folded her arms and nodded at the bulging grooll pouch. "You must be working up quite an appetite . . . doing whatever you've been doing these past weeks."

He shifted to the side to step around her. She mirrored his movement. Her brow pinched, rumpling the skin between her eyebrows. "What have you been doing, Daoren?"

"Nothing to warrant your worry."

"You must tread carefully."

"What makes you think I'm not?"

"Nineteen years of being your mother." She cupped his chin. "And with Sha's sapience you'll be my son for many more."

Her finger tracked up his cheek and crossed his forehead.

Daoren closed his eyes and regressed to his childhood, to the last time she'd touched his face. He wasn't certain, but it may have been in this very spot.

He would have frozen the present moment, stretched it to infinity if he could, but her finger reached his nose. An outlying memory told him it would descend from the bridge to the tip, then retract . . . and it did. He opened his eyes.

"You've seen what happened to your brother and father." She moved aside, unblocking the door. "You never know who's watching, so promise me you'll tread carefully."

He stepped past her, squeezing her forearm to affirm his promise. The limb's thinness unnerved him. "I'll tread carefully if you'll take some grooll."

Her fragile smile channeled the understated beauty not seen since Mako's test. He nodded at the urn. "Now."

Cordelia extracted a piece and held it in her palm. She stared at the grooll, reddened eyes fixed and unblinking—the same way she looked upon Mako's quantum images. With agonizing lethargy, she raised the piece to her mouth.

Daoren cupped her hand, assisting.

She placed the grooll onto her tongue. Her eyes closed.

"Chew and swallow."

Tears traced the sidewalls of her nose. She chewed and swallowed.

"The first piece is the hardest," he said. "Now promise me you'll eat."

"I will."

He exited the abode.

PYROS ENTERED THE chamber and embarked on the long march across the crystalline floor to the Unum's desk. On average, it took seventy-six paces to cover the distance. He'd taken to counting them a few weeks ago.

Why he'd taken to counting his paces, he couldn't say. It might be a subconscious tactical imperative bubbling to the surface, or a superstitious reflex manifesting from the genetic sequence handed down by his ancestors. Perhaps he needed a final, mindless distraction before responding to the Unum's frequent summons. This latest summons centered on his obsession with Daoren al Lucien.

Over the past few weeks, it had become clear that the Unum planned to have Daoren's score switched with Narses' score in the upcoming S.A.T. The Unum wasn't so brazen that he admitted it. Narses had let the information slip during an idle conversation a week earlier. He'd boasted about it, in fact, and more.

A source at the Librarium had sent Daoren's prep-tests to the Unum, in direct violation of one of Daqin Guojin's most sacred edicts. The results apparently showed the potential for a perfect S.A.T., which made Daoren a dire threat or a stellar opportunity. Pyros had little interest in the machinations of power; he couldn't be sure how the Unum viewed the boy. Nor could he be sure whether Narses' tale was true. The odds of a prospect writing a perfect S.A.T. were so low they were all but nonexistent.

He was sure of one truth though. In the unlikely event that

Daoren lived up to his potential and the plan to switch scores succeeded, Narses would be named Unum Potentate. The consequences for the city-state would be more disastrous than a mongrel incursion.

Commander Cang's work was all the more vital as a result. She'd been busy, traveling to all fifty Chengs to meet with the district commanders, using her investigation into the Primae Jiren as a guise to gain their trust. He appreciated the irony.

She'd described her ominous afternoon meeting with the Unum. He could relate to the dread she must have felt walking into the chamber. As Primae Jiren, he'd always assumed he was under one covert investigation or another. The Cognos Populi lived in an echo-chamber of self-reinforcing paranoia. The tremolo of whisper-campaigns and mutterings of covert inquests forever filled the Assembly's hallways. That Cang was conducting the latest probe eased his concerns.

So did the results of her meetings. One-third of the district commanders had pledged to back the plan to remove the Unum from power. Another third promised not to oppose it if rewarded for their apathy. The rest were bedded in the Unum's camp—including the personal guard responsible for his close protection—and refused to be roused. A meeting with the sympathetic commanders was scheduled for after the May S.A.T. to discuss the path forward.

Another of Cang's probes had raised fresh concerns. The investigation into Laoshi al Euclidius had uncovered disturbing evidence related to a silica-sourcing expedition led by Laoshi's son, Fengsei. Five years ago, fifteen denizens had embarked on the expedition, including Fengsei's wife. Within a month of their return, all were dead. The causes included levitran accidents, falls from structures, and mysterious illnesses. Despite this, no subsequent investigations were carried out. No reports on the expedition's destination or findings could be located.

On the surface, the evidence was as sinister as it was sparse. It showed the hallmarks of a purge. Why someone would want to erase a silica-sourcing expedition from existence defied understanding; dozens of them occurred in a given year. *Who* could erase it presented less of a puzzle; the number of people in Daqin Guojin wielding sufficient power wouldn't fill a levitran. One of them occupied this very chamber.

Seated behind the desk ten paces away, the Unum raked his hands over his blotchy scalp. Those were never good signs, and they were becoming more and more common of late.

"I shouldn't have to chase you for these reports on Daoren," the Unum said.

Pyros halted before the desk. He chose his words with care. "You wanted him locked in our sights. My men have done that." He consulted his quantum tile—a convenient way to break eye contact. "Daoren has met with Laoshi daily for the past three weeks."

The Unum thumped the desk with his fist. "Every day you come in here and tell me the what. I'm interested in the *why*. It's seven days until the May S.A.T. and I still don't know why he's meeting with Laoshi!"

"My men can't access the Temple undetected. Perhaps he's receiving one-on-one tutelage for the upcoming test."

The Unum leaned back and lifted his gaze to the ceiling as though seeking an answer in its carvings. He must have found one. "Detain the boy."

"Detain him?"

"In the Rig. And do it immediately."

"On what charge?"

The Unum's head flushed, skin turning sour purple. His lower lip bulged and quivered. For a hopeful moment, Pyros suspected the man might be experiencing a terminal cerebral violation.

"He's a prospect! Does it matter?"

The thunderous shout verified that an easy resolution to the problem of the Unum's reign wouldn't be forthcoming. Pyros came to attention, masking his disgust. "As you command."

He spun on his heels, happy to show the Unum his back. He made it five paces from the desk.

"Bide a moment, Pyros."

He halted and turned around.

The Unum leaned forward, elbows propped on the desktop. His skin's sour hue receded. "I heard that a Hexalite levicart came under attack," he said, the words cold and colorless. "Three weeks ago. In Meiguo Cheng."

Pyros expended every ounce of willpower to censor his shock. "That's correct."

"Why wasn't I informed?"

Pyros tried to read the intent behind the question, but he faced a master of inscrutability. If the Unum knew Pyros and Cang were the sole occupants of the levicart and failed to report the attack, they'd face extensive questioning in the Rig. If the Unum was testing whether his Primae Jiren would lie to his face, Pyros would face summary execution before the day was out.

He had no choice but to lie; his path was set. He petitioned Sha that it wouldn't lead to a premature plunge into the Sea of Storms. "My men suffered no casualties," he said, "so I didn't think it warranted your worry."

"Then you have a full report on the incident?"

"Yes, though there wasn't much to report."

"Regardless, I want to see it."

"You'll have it before the end of the day."

"Excellent." The Unum flicked his fingers. "That is all."

Pyros bowed and resumed his long march to the chamber door. He petitioned Sha that he wouldn't throw up before he got there.

17

THE RIG

L AOSHI GRIPPED THE handrail, whistling. During his twelve years as Primae Librarian, he'd never grown tired of the elevating chamber's free-fall sensation. It reminded him of the night his section of Jireni assault troops performed an aerial insertion into Havoc during the resource war. The numbing howl of buffeting airstream and malevolent hiss of hostile projectiles were the only sensory elements missing.

The memory conjured a wistful smile—as terrifying recollections tended to do when viewed through the long lens of time. His days of aerial insertions may be over, but he could still save Daqin Guojin from a new enemy. To do that, he first had to save Heqet and Daoren. He glanced at his granddaughter.

Her twin braids stood at attention, their tips tickling the paneled ceiling. Her sparkling eyes and giddy grin hinted that she, too, relished weightlessness.

Beside her, Daoren gripped the handrail with both hands. He'd needed no additional prompting after his first descent into the Void. White knuckles and a clenched jaw signaled he didn't savor free-fall as much as Heqet, but he seemed to have grown accustomed to it.

Laoshi had enjoyed watching the two of them work together over the past three weeks, solving the puzzles of the grooll mill and developing the techniques to circumvent its host of deadly threats. Working toward a common goal of survival had helped sooth their more antagonistic tendencies, at least some of the time. They still fought like the fiercest rivals—as evidenced by their feuding in the Temple minutes earlier—but it was obvious they cared for one another, from his perspective if not their own.

The elevating chamber slowed and stopped. Its double-doors swished open. They stepped into the Void and proceeded to the work area Laoshi had set up last week.

Glass decanters, pressure vessels, coiled tubing, and thermal isopads spanned several tables, resembling a haphazard model of the human digestive system. The distillation of stable liquid glass was a labor-intensive process at the best of times, but this batch also required precise insulating qualities. The lives of his grand-daughter and Daoren depended on it.

Laoshi grabbed a beaker from the isopad beneath the output coil. He held it up to the light and swirled its contents. No air bubbles clouded the viscous glass. That was crucial. "Good. It's set properly."

"What now?" Heqet asked.

"We test it. Or rather, one of you tests it. Who wants to volunteer?"

Daoren and Heqet exchanged dubious glances. Heqet spoke first. "I will."

Daoren scowled. "No, I'll do it."

"Are you deaf? I said I would!"

Laoshi inserted himself between the pair. "Now, now. It doesn't matter who—"

"You shouldn't be the one to test it!" Daoren said, ignoring the attempted mediation.

"Why? Because I'm female?"

"That isn't—"

"Would it emasculate you?" She lowered her voice and adopted a mocking cadence that matched Daoren's timbre. "I'm the great Daoren al Lucien, capable of felling scores of Jireni with a single brooding glance, and I won't let a mere girl show more courage than me."

"For the love of Sha! You're such a pain in the—"

"Enough!" Laoshi said. "Try not to cull each other before you sit the S.A.T., hmm? Heqet will test it. You can apply the voltage, Daoren."

The pair fell silent and let their brooding glances do the talking. Laoshi tipped the beaker and poured a drizzle into his cupped palm. The liquid glass warmed his skin like a sunbeam. It was a good portent, and another indication it had set properly.

He coated a fingertip and smeared the glass onto Heqet's palm, rubbing it in expanding circles, careful to apply an even coverage. The material glistened before disappearing.

Heqet positioned her palm below an optical lens on the next table. Laoshi peered through the lens' polarized eyepiece.

The glass' birefringent property showed up well against the fine lines in her skin. It shifted them toward the red and violet ends of the spectrum, refracting the colors along different optical paths and doubling each line. No discontinuities tainted the film.

"Flex your hand, child."

She flexed her hand.

Laoshi adjusted the magnification. "Again."

She flexed it again.

"No cracks or delamination. Good."

"That's important?"

"Critical. The film must be continuous to impart the proper insulation against the stun shock. Our preparations will be for naught if you lose consciousness before the grooll-making process begins."

"Will the insulation be adequate?" Daoren asked.

"Let's find out." Laoshi handed him a clear wire. "Hold the end an inch above her palm."

Daoren complied. Laoshi hooked the other end of the wire to a discharge box and checked the voltage setting on its readout.

"How high are you setting the voltage?" Heqet asked, voice weighted with concern.

"High enough to cause pain, but low enough to avoid permanent damage."

Daoren's brow rumpled. "How much pain?"

"With any luck, none," Laoshi said. "Ready, Heqet?"

She swallowed and nodded.

"Ready, Daoren?"

He swallowed and nodded.

"On three. One . . . two . . . three!"

Laoshi pressed a button on the discharge box. A crackling spark jumped from the end of the wire to Heqet's palm.

She tensed, then raised her head and smiled.

Laoshi clapped. It was precisely the reaction he'd hoped for. "Excellent!"

Heqet eyed her palm. She flexed her hand. "May I try it on Daoren?"

"Certainly." Laoshi picked up the beaker. "Just let me apply the—"

"*Without* the insulation," she said, leveling a defiant grin at her rival.

HOURS LATER, DAOREN and Heqet passed through the southern archway, leaving the Librarium. They stepped onto the deserted transway. Its blue surface shimmered. Stars speckled the sky.

Daoren dug his hand into his grooll pouch. He had no idea what time it was—maybe a few hours from sunrise. The cool night air condensed his breath to a frail cloud, but the day's work left him with a warm afterglow. Finding a solution for the stun shock represented significant progress.

Heqet walked beside him, gaze fixed on the transway's sparkling sheen. The micro-studs in her cheeks twinkled. They put the patchwork of stars to shame.

He extended his hand and offered her a piece. She stared at the grooll like it was an ill premonition. "What odds do we have of surviving the grooll mill?"

He'd spent most of the evening pondering the same question. The insulating glass film would absorb the stun shock, so long as they heeded Laoshi's warning and weren't so absentminded to rub the fragile coating off their temples during the test. They'd memorized each step of the grooll mill's sequence down to the split-second. They knew the best ways to exit the mill and the best routes to get from the Center to the Librarium afterward. The single problem left to solve was getting off the platform before the ultrasonic-liquifying process began.

"Getting off the platform in time is paramount," he said. "Unless we find a way to do that, I'd say the odds are dismal." He turned to her without breaking stride. "Sliding down a support cable might work, but the friction burns to our hands would be—"

Heqet twisted one of her hair braids while she listened. He eyed the braid's thickness and length. A trill of excitement vibrated deep in his chest.

"Would be what?" she asked.

He grabbed the braid and squeezed it between his thumb and forefinger. Its density confirmed his hunch. It would work; he was sure of it. He looked up.

A blush tinted Heqet's cheeks.

Daoren sensed a flush in his own cheeks; touching the braid without her consent was an unspeakably forward act. He let go and drew his hand back. "My sorrow for that, but I think the odds of survival will swing in our favor if I can smuggle a dagger into the Center."

"Why would you need a—"

A chorus of shrill hisses cut her off. Five Jireni on armored levidecks streaked across the transway. They whisked to a stop, encircling Daoren and Heqet.

Daoren snatched Heqet's arm, halting her.

One Jiren powered off his levideck's varinozzles and dismounted. He swaggered closer, hand hidden behind his back. "Aren't these two a glinty couple, comrades?"

"Glinty indeed," a Jiren said atop his hovering craft. "If he isn't warming his jackstaff in her tasty pocket, he deserves to be harvested."

The others cacklebracked in agreement. The dismounted Jiren's hand appeared. It waggled a phallic glass device. "One sure way to find out if he is."

Daoren stepped in front of Heqet, heart thudding in his throat. He tugged his quantum tile from his tunic's inner pocket. Without taking his eyes off the dismounted Jiren, he stretched and rolled it into a three-foot rod.

The Jiren rasplaughed. "This boy's a cocky one, isn't he? Thinks his pathetic rod can stop me from testing his playmate."

Daoren thumped one end of the rod into the ground, shock-fusing the glass, giving it solidity. "I'd think twice about that if I were you."

"Your glass rod isn't combat-hardened, slag," the Jiren said.

Daoren steadied his breathing, keeping his intent hidden from his eyes. "Funny . . . neither is your jaw."

He swung the rod with both hands. It sliced the air and struck the Jiren's jaw with a withering crack.

Broken teeth and bloody spittle sprayed from the brute's mouth. He yelped and sagged to his knees.

Still astride his levideck, another Jiren swung a combat-hardened staff at Daoren's skull.

Daoren ducked the staff and thrust his glass rod under the craft's hovering deck. He levered the rod upward and drove his shoulder into levideck's armored panel.

The levideck heeled, tipping the Jiren. Man and craft crunched into the adjacent levideck, knocking its rider off his feet.

Both craft lurched sideways, out of control and gaining speed. They veered across the transway and smashed into the Librarium's fence. The impact hurled the riders into the fence's unyielding crystalline blocks.

Daoren whirled and faced the two Jireni left standing.

One held a crystal dagger to Heqet's throat. "Drop it or she dies!"

Heqet whimpered, eyes bulbed with terror. Daoren hesitated, his mind scrambling for a solution . . . *any* solution.

"Drop it now!"

He had no choice. His makeshift rod clattered onto the transway.

The dagger-wielding Jiren sneered. "You've earned a stay at the Rig, Daoren. I hope you enjoy pain."

The other Jiren fired a ceramic twitchgun. Micro-darts spat from its muzzle.

They thudded into Daoren's chest. He glanced down at the twin darts, sensing no pain. He raised his hands to yank them out.

The darts emitted a sizzling zap.

Daoren's muscles seized and relaxed at sixteen cycles per second. His jaw clenched and unclenched so rapidly, he thought his teeth might shatter.

Heqet and the Jireni melted behind a loom of brilliant white light.

THE UNUM STRODE the main concourse of the Rig's seventy-fifth floor the next morning. Like most denizens, he held a morbid fascination for the city-state's detention facility. Unlike most denizens, he didn't have to break an edict to see inside its black-crystalline walls.

He'd first visited the facility as a child, when he was nine. His father's unique position within the Cognos Populi had secured the privilege—either that or he'd given a sizable bribe to the Rig's regent. Truth is, the Unum didn't know how his father had arranged the visit, but he knew why.

He'd wanted his son to see with his own eyes what became of dissent in Daqin Guojin.

It left a lasting impression. As he made his way along the concourse, grainy memories of that first visit swept through his mind like a mid-winter sandstorm. Much to his delight, the facility hadn't changed.

The Rig took its name from the rigs bracketing the concourse. The devices consisted of a seven-by-three-foot glass slab encased by tubular framework. Ceramic disks, two feet in diameter and half as thick, hung from the framework at the head of each slab. At the foot of each slab, sand-filled funnels the size of wash tubs counterbalanced the disks via intermediary cables and pulleys. Thinner cables with load-bearing ringlets led to the wrists and ankles of the dissenters splayed upon the slabs.

The design made it possible to apply any amount of strain to any limb in any direction. By allowing sand to drain from the funnels, the strain could be increased over time if so desired. In most cases, it was highly desirable; it proved an effective method for extracting information and contrition.

Hundreds of men and women—dissenters from the Chengs —lay spreadeagled upon the rigs, arms and legs yanked in opposing directions. Their contorted faces implied incalculable pain, their yawning mouths protracted screams.

The Unum halted. He had to hear it again. He plucked the glass plugs from his ears and was rewarded by—

A cacophony of wails, groans, pleads, and petitions to Sha.

He smiled. The awesome chorus sang in perfect harmony with his memory from four decades earlier—and that was just the dissenters on this level. Beneath his feet, dissenters filled another seventy-four levels to capacity. If only the city-state's acoustic engineers could harness the sonic energy of the agony; Daqin Guojin would never want for power again.

The Unum reinserted the ear plugs. He continued along the concourse toward his destination, which was conveniently land-marked by Pyros and another Jiren.

Pyros bowed upon his arrival. He removed a plug from his right ear. The Unum did the same. He raised his voice to be heard above the din. "Has he spoken about his activity with Laoshi?"

"No," Pyros said. "He hasn't said a word since he arrived."

The Unum gazed at the rig's slab.

Daoren lay on his back, arms and legs reefed in opposite directions. Purple bruises dappled his cheekbones and jaw. Sand drained from the funnels at the foot of his slab, shedding mass, but the boy's face betrayed no emotion.

"So you assault three Jireni, then refuse to answer questions," the Unum said. "Perhaps you aren't as smart as your prep-tests imply."

Daoren remained an impenetrable cipher.

"Did you know there was a dissenter who survived eighteen days while subject to ninety percent strain from his rig?" The Unum checked the funnels; they were half full. "You're experiencing fifty percent strain. Not to be taken lightly, to be sure, but not severe enough to cause permanent damage." He grabbed a cable and leaned back. "Ninety percent strain would feel more like this."

The cable hummed, protesting the added tension. Daoren's mouth warped. He bared his teeth.

The Unum put the full measure of his heft into the effort. The cable hummed and twanged. . . .

Daoren's face blanched as white as sun-bleached sand, but he didn't say a word.

"Imagine eighteen days of *this*," the Unum said, still pulling. "Remarkable, don't you think? The dissenter was a fellow Slavv. Part of me takes pride in that."

He released the cable. The strain eased.

Daoren gulped shallow breaths, recovering.

The Unum walked to the head of the rig. "Why do I get the feeling you could survive even longer?"

The boy's burning, unblinking eyes communicated a clear message. He wouldn't be broken.

"How lucky for you that your skills are needed elsewhere in six days time," the Unum said. "You'll be held here with the other dissenters until Jireni escort you to the Center."

He leaned closer to make certain Daoren heard him. "And lest you think you can maintain this veil of unresponsiveness during the S.A.T., *know this*. Should you score one point less than thirty thousand, your lovely mother will be mounted in her own rig before you receive your stun shot."

Daoren's expression stayed disturbingly stoic, as if etched in sculptglass. The Unum grabbed a handful of hair and lifted his head from the slab. The boy needed to see this with his own eyes.

Across the concourse, the other Jiren stood at the foot of another rig. A skeletal Asianoid boy with festering knee wounds lay upon its slab. He'd been interned on the day of the January S.A.T. for trying to breach the Great Northern Border. The two dissenters with him had succumbed to their sonic nanocharges before they could be detained. They'd got off lightly.

"Watch, Daoren," he said. "Watch and see what dissent begets."

The Jiren detached the funnels at the foot of the slab. They thumped to the floor.

Without the counterweight, the full force of the ceramic disks transferred to the cables attached to the dissenter's arms and legs. Its rapid onset lifted his body off the slab.

The Asianoid boy bellowed in agony, suspended two feet in the air, until his legs parted at the knees with a grisly crack. His body thudded onto the slab. Blood geysered from the twitching stumps, pulsing in sync with his heartbeat. The torrent slowed and ceased within thirty seconds.

The Unum released Daoren's head. "Dissent begets death." He turned away. An afterthought made him turn back. "I almost forgot," he said. "You'll be pleased to know that Heqet tested negative for penetration. It seems she and Mako were respectful of our edicts. You'd do well to follow their example."

He hoped to see a reaction to the affront, a sign of contrition on Daoren's face. The boy conceded none; he'd apparently retreated to a place where he couldn't be touched. The Unum concealed his disappointment and glanced at Pyros.

His sullen aspect broadcasted his disapproval without distortion. No matter. It wasn't his place to approve. "He's to be kept in the rig until the S.A.T.," the Unum said, "but be sure no more than fifty percent strain is applied. I don't want him incapacitated for the test."

"I'll pass along your order, *Unum*."

The Unum proceeded down the concourse, noting the undertone of contempt in Pyros' utterance of the honorific title. Yes, his Primae Jiren was worth keeping an eye on. Commander Cang had as yet uncovered no suspicious activity, but tasking her to conduct the investigation was the right decision.

He stuffed the plug back into his ear, welcoming the silence.

———————

LAOSHI HELD HEQET on one of the Temple's two glass divans, stroking her hair. Her tears still flowed, but the cuts on her cheeks had stopped bleeding. Her sobbing had also ceased—another improvement.

It had been a long night.

She'd spent most of it relaying the wretched story of what had befallen her and Daoren outside the Librarium's southern archway. Laoshi couldn't recall a time when a prospect had struck a Jiren and not been immediately culled for the offense. Daoren had known the potential consequences of his defiance and acted, regardless. It proved the boy's willingness to sacrifice himself for Heqet, just as his grandfather had done to protect those he loved. Dominus would be proud.

Heqet had taken the better part of an hour to describe what the Jireni had done to her after Daoren fell to the twitchgun. When she finished, Laoshi had to excuse himself for ten minutes. Outside the Temple, he'd sat and wept on the tapered steps. He'd also expended every reserve of self-control to stop himself from marching to the Assembly and culling the Unum with his bare hands.

Even now the urge to exact revenge burned slag-hot in his chest. The Unum's day of reckoning would come soon enough though. For now, his granddaughter needed him. "Be still, Heqet," he whispered. "Be still."

"He was trying to protect me." She sniffled. "Will they cull him?"

"No, but they'll hold him in the Rig until the S.A.T."

That, of course, presented a serious problem. He was about to voice his concern when Heqet rendered it moot.

"The insulating glass . . ."

He smiled despite the ill predicament. His granddaughter was no fid. "I know, child. I won't be able to apply it before he sits the test."

"Can't you do it in the Center?"

"Libraria aren't allowed inside if their kin are taking the test."

The edict was as old as the test itself, designed to eliminate the possibility of collusion. It seemed comical now, given the travesty the Unum had made of the S.A.T.

Heqet's brow crinkled over the bridge of her nose—her telltale sign for the birth of an idea. "Can you show me how to apply it? I'll find a way to get to him before the test begins."

Laoshi kissed her forehead. His son and daughter-by-union may have been taken, but their courage lived on. "My brave, brave girl. Your mother and father would be so proud."

"And there's one more item I need for the test."

"What's that, my dear?"

Her voice resonated with resolve. "A dagger for Daoren."

18

A RECKONING

G USTAR RODE IN the levicart's forward passenger seat, hands wedged under his thighs to stop them from trembling.

Plasmonic-map symbology glimmered above the dash-panels before him, none of which made it easier to determine his precise location. Worse, staring at the three-dimensional depictions of transways while moving induced mouth-sweats and creeping nausea.

He'd spent the last half-hour gazing through the side window, pretending to watch the administrative structures glide past as twilight stained the eastern horizon. Of course, he couldn't focus on them either due to the events of the morning.

The Unum had not only summoned him, but he'd also dispatched a Hexalite levicart and three Jireni as personal escorts. They were heading to the Eastern Mound on the edge of Zhongguo Cheng. The moraine covered five square-miles of Daqin Guojin's most pristine territory . . . and most dangerous. For ordinary denizens, one unauthorized step on the elevated ridge risked death. The Eastern Mound was the home of the Unum's palace.

Gustar could barely comprehend it—*he* was going to the Unum's palace. At any other time the invitation would have sparked unbounded joy. Today it spurred unceasing angst. Meeting the Unum in person was a break in the communications protocol. Indeed, it was much more than that.

It was a *fracture*.

When it came to the test-manipulation scheme, the Unum had been cautious to the point of paranoia. Their method of contact relied on anonymous third-party proxies, using quantum messages safeguarded by the most robust encryption. They'd met once, five years ago, in Nansilafu Cheng. At the end of that forty-minute meeting he'd received explicit orders to never make direct contact with the Unum again.

He'd taken the order to heart, even sending his gift through an intermediary. Narses was happy enough to transport the Newton's Cradle to his father following one of his dismal prep-tests at the Spires. Gustar's sole concern was whether the clumsy fid would smash the precious device before its delivery. So what to make of this unexpected invitation?

His escorts pleaded ignorance as to the reason. Either they didn't know or their nature tended toward the obtuse. He wasn't sure which applied. As a Librarian, he'd experienced limited contact with Jireni. They were a foreign territory—as unknowable as the decayed western continent that lay across the acidic western ocean.

He glanced at the driver, a cleft-chinned and callow youth whose vacant eyes in all likelihood fronted a vacuous mind. The boy looked barely competent enough to walk without stumbling, never mind pilot a levicart. He also had the disconcerting habit of taking his hands off the steering yoke during their passage on the straightaways. At this speed, an inadvertent bump would send them careening off the transway. Gustar tried not to dwell on it.

The two Jireni riding in the rear troop compartment were older, but no less shells of men—automatons who needed curt orders and specific directions to function. They announced their presence through the occasional cough or belch. Neither had spoken since their pre-dawn departure from the Librarium's southern entrance an hour ago. Still, it was worth another try.

"I won't mention that you told me," he said to the driver, the most sociable of the three, if only because he'd mumbled a dozen words so far. "That I promise you."

"All we know is that the Unum wants you delivered to the palace before he escorts his son to the Center," the driver said without taking his eyes off the transway.

Gustar forced a smile. On the inside, he cursed the useless fid. He loathed venturing into situations about which he had no fore-knowledge. Foreknowledge was his stock-in-trade.

Foreknowledge had led him to send excerpts of Laoshi's seditious writings to Zhongguo Cheng's district commander—that and the Primae Librarian's snooping into the prospect databases after the January S.A.T. In the face of a mounting insurrection, reporting dissension could generate considerable rewards. Uncovering a dissenter of Laoshi's influence ought to be worth fifteen thousand pounds of grooll. As a bonus, it would remove a dire threat to the manipulation scheme.

The discovery of the two excavation tunnels leading into the subterranean site where Laoshi spent most of his time ought to be worth even more. Commander Cang needed an ally unencumbered by the Jireni's black armor to investigate the Primae Librarian's activities. She'd soon accept his proposal to perform the task. Forty thousand pounds of grooll may be a huge sum, but no one was better positioned to carry it out.

His foreknowledge had also fashioned the test-manipulation scheme into reality. Hundreds of Libraria had access to prospect prep-tests and biometric data. He alone had the foresight to see the information's tremendous value. Over the past five years, the scheme had proven successful on more occasions than he could count. It had enriched the Unum beyond measure and saved his niece from certain death, but today it would pay off as never before. Thanks to Gustar's fortuitous discovery of Daoren's perfect prep-tests, Narses stood an excellent chance of becoming Unum Potentate.

The heady realization provoked a gasp. . . .

The Unum must be summoning him to the palace to bestow his reward in person. That had to be it!

No sooner had the thought solidified than they were passing through the gated entrance to the Eastern Mound. One thousand feet ahead, his destination resolved. He'd viewed countless quantum images of the majestic structure, but laying eyes on it for the first time from such proximity culled his breath.

An expansive oval piazza fronted the palace, its perimeter bounded by a grand colonnade. The colonnade's triple ranks of bone-white ceramic columns rose two hundred feet above the piazza. They supported dazzling entablature embellished with bas-relief renditions of Unums dating back to Daqin Guojin's founding.

The colonnade terminated at the sumptuous portico of the palace proper. The portico's triangular pediment vaulted one hundred feet higher than the surrounding entablature. It fronted the structure's most magnificent architectural element.

The Great Dome.

Polished to a blinding gloss, the off-white dome was rumored to be infused with flecks of a rare, ductile metal. Hoarded and traded in antiquity, the metal took its name from its color. *Gold.*

He leaned forward, hoping for a glimpse of the Imperial Regalia topping the dome, but it proved too high. Beyond the palace, however, a mesmerizing panorama unfurled. Daqin Guojin's glass and crystalline structures twinkled like precious stones set in a boundless bed of sand.

Gustar blinked back tears. Never had he beheld a sight so ennobling or empowering. He'd entered the very epicenter of creation and grappled to find the words to express his awe.

"Sapient Sha be praised," he whispered. "It's more gorgeous than its quantum images."

"S'nothing compared to what you'll see inside," one of the Jireni in the troop compartment said in a listless monotone.

The driver guided the levicart across the piazza at a more sublime pace. Instead of stopping before the portico, he diverted down a laneway skirting the palace's southern wall. The levicart followed the laneway for a full minute before stopping by a plain door.

Gustar eyed the fifty-by-fifty-foot crystalline slab, more plebeian than palatial. The Jireni in the troop compartment exited the vehicle's rear hatch without saying a word. The driver opened his door.

"Where are you taking me?" Gustar asked.

"The Unum wants you to see a special chamber before you see him," the driver said.

———

INSIDE THE PALACE, Gustar and his escorts transited a corridor large enough to accommodate a levicart's passage. By its appearance, many had already taken the journey. Gouges scarred the walls. Swaths of sandy grime blighted the floor. An acrid odor tainted the air.

Gustar scoffed at the squalor, embittered by his first taste of regal splendor. Doubtless the Unum never ventured into this shabby locale.

They arrived at another huge crystalline door with a glowing inset tile. The driver tapped a lengthy passcode into its screen. The six-inch-thick door rolled upward on a guide track, unveiling an immense storechamber. Chilled air wafted over Gustar, prompting a shiver.

Inside the storechamber, groups of Jireni maneuvered

huvvadollies. The huvvadollies cradled opaque crates rivaling the size of private abodes.

Near the door, a Jiren lowered a crate onto a rectangular floor scale.

Another Jiren checked the scale's readout. "That's ten thousand and six pounds," he said, the spoken words condensing into clouds. "Rounding down."

The Jiren activated the huvvadolly and raised the crate, whistling. "There's more grooll in this crate than we'd earn in ten years."

The Jiren beside the readout rubbed his hands together. "There's more grooll in this vault than we'd earn in ten lifetimes."

Gustar couldn't believe his eyes. Similar crates lined the vault, stacked five high and at least fifty deep on both sides. They must contain hundreds of thousands . . . no, *millions* of pounds of grooll. "Is this all the Unum's grooll?"

"Hardly," the driver said. "It's one of ten personal vaults he keeps. The smallest one."

For the second time in ten minutes, Gustar blinked back tears. More grooll than he ever imagined lay within the vault. Was this his reward? Dare he dream it? It was all he could do to maintain his composure in front of the Jireni. "When do I see him?"

"Now," the driver said.

IN THE PALACE'S Hall of Mirrors, the Unum adjusted the pyramidal implants in his forehead for the third time.

He loathed the black studs. They always worked themselves loose and needed frequent realignment, but it had become a tradition to wear them to the S.A.T. Beside him, Julinian and Narses performed their own preening, fussing with their garments before the floor-to-ceiling mirrors.

Julinian had acquired a new shenyi for the occasion, a grand purple design that accented her expanding waistline. The cut suited her well and must have cost several thousand pounds of grooll. It proved a vexing match for her collection of sashes though. She'd tried on six so far and had yet to find a complementary hue.

His niece had slipped into her role as a member of the Cognos Populi with equal style. She'd make a valuable asset if her appetite for power could be suppressed. Deep down, he wondered how long it would take before Julinian made a grab for ultimate power by overthrowing Narses. Not while the Unum still drew breath, to be sure, but before his body grew cold and stiff? He'd need to discuss the issue with his son, and soon.

Narses had also selected a new gleamglass ensemble for the S.A.T., albeit white in keeping with his social status. In a little over eight hours, however, he'd be trading a prospect's pienfu for the purple mianfu of the Unum Potentate—assuming Daoren played his part.

His son executed a twirl in his blinding apparel. Evidently, he desired feedback.

"Splendid, boy. You look ready to undertake the duties of Unum Potentate."

Narses mouth-breathed, struggling to attach a grooll pouch to his tunic's receiver loops. Even from ten feet away, the Unum could see the pouch was backward. Its reflection in the mirror must have confused the boy. The Unum sighed; so much for looking ready.

Julinian must have spotted the error, too. She sniggered into her hand.

Narses caught his mistake and attached the pouch. "Are we going to the Center now?"

"Soon."

Three Jireni entered the hall. They escorted a bloated man in a yellow lanshan. The Unum grinned. Their timing was perfect.

He'd met face-to-face with Gustar al Vlodisar once before, two days after the Librarian contacted him regarding an enticing proposition. As one of the Librarium's senior datakeepers, Gustar had unparalleled access to prospect databases. He also had an unparalleled appetite for wealth, one that a meager grooll ration couldn't satisfy. His transformed body testified that he'd eaten more than his fill in the ensuing years. Test manipulation had been good to him.

It had been even better for the Unum. Providing guarantees of passing S.A.T. scores to the doomed children of desperate parents had harvested untold riches, but it was time to end the scheme. He'd amassed all the grooll he needed. With Narses' position as Unum Potentate secured, he'd never have to worry about losing it. None of this would have been possible without Gustar. Of course, the Librarian expected a reward for his most recent efforts. Today was the day to settle the account.

The Unum led Narses and Julinian toward the center of the hall. He beamed as Gustar halted before him. The Jireni escorts halted two paces behind Gustar, driving their sandals into the tiled floor. The sharp-edged report caromed off the mirrored walls and crystal ceiling, reverberating through the hall. The Librarian flinched.

The Unum grasped his shoulders, grip firm to match his authority. "Relax, my friend, relax!"

He pulled Gustar forward to touch foreheads. Contact proved difficult thanks to their protruding bellies. The Unum laughed when they finally connected.

Gustar's puckered smile only heightened his anxiety. "Survival through sapience, Unum."

"And to you, Gustar. I won't keep you long. I just wanted to make sure that everything is ready before I grant my final reward."

"It is, Unum. Daoren's score will be switched with Narses'

score as ordered. It will happen without any further intervention on my—"

The Unum raised his hand. His clearest recollection from their meeting in Nansilafu Cheng, besides realizing how much grooll the manipulation scheme could accumulate, was Gustar's inability to stop talking once he started. "Excellent! I can't tell you how much I appreciate your work over the past month. I know it wasn't easy to make the preparations on such short notice."

"I'm happy to be of service," Gustar said.

"What if Daoren intentionally fails the S.A.T.?" Julinian asked. "What happens to Narses then?"

Narses expelled three jovial snorts, then fell silent. He paled as though the notion had only just occurred to him.

"I've reprogramed the Center's tabulator to assign the highest test score to Narses," Gustar said, "regardless of which prospect has written it. There's no chance of him failing."

"You're certain?" Narses asked.

"I'm certain." Gustar leveled his gaze at the Unum, exuding confidence for the first time. "Your son's in safe hands today. That I promise you."

"Thank you, Gustar." The Unum lowered his hand, but kept his smile warm and welcoming. "Then again, I recall a time when you promised you could manipulate S.A.T. scores without raising any suspicions."

"Yes, Unum. I did."

The Unum stepped back. "In that respect, you were wrong."

The Jiren behind Gustar already had the wireglass coil in his hands, cued seconds earlier by the Unum's raised hand. Upon the hand's lowering, he merely had to step forward and loop the coil around the Librarian's throat. The boy reefed the wireglass backward, teeth gritting above his cleft chin.

Despite being in a hall adorned with six hundred mirrors, poor Gustar didn't react to the garrote until it was too late. His eyes popped, reflecting the gravity of his predicament, an instant before the barbed thread sliced into his windpipe. He gargled blood, flailing his arms like he was winding an internal spring, and flopped onto his back.

The Unum glanced at Narses.

His wide-eyed gaze fixed upon Gustar's twitching body and expanding blood pool.

Curiosity rather than revulsion lit up his son's eyes—a promising sign. An Unum Potentate couldn't afford an aversion to bloodshed. "Now we can go," the Unum said. "The Jireni will clean up this mess."

19

THE MAY S.A.T.

L AOSHI HUDDLED WITH Heqet and Cordelia near the top of the second flight.

The sun peeked over the horizon, its ruddy orb bracketed by Zhongguo Cheng's tallest administrative structures. Crimson rays sluiced through the glass canyon and washed over thousands of denizens and prospects on the Center's southeastern stairway. Three Jireni aeroshrikes transited the canyon's mouth in close formation, five hundred feet above ground-level. Their elongated shadows caressed the throng like macabre fingers.

Laoshi couldn't shake the surreal aura that came with standing among the masses. For the past twelve years, his position as Primae Librarian meant his place was inside the Center during the S.A.T. One hundred forty-four times he'd watched thousands of prospects face their greatest fear. One hundred forty-four times he'd done all he could to ease their nerves and still their minds. Today, a lone prospect called for his calming manner—except she didn't need it.

Heqet's face evoked serenity in spite of the cuts still healing from her encounter with the Jireni a week earlier. She'd said little since waking this morning. The few words she had spoken trilled with reason and rationality. Even now, less than thirty minutes from the start of the test, she appeared composed; so composed that he questioned whether she understood the scale of the challenge she'd soon be facing.

Cordelia, on the other hand, had been a nervous ruin the entire week. The news of Daoren's internment at the Rig had unleashed debilitating anguish. Laoshi's best efforts to reassure her had been for naught. Weakened by malnutrition and distraught over the potential of losing another son, she'd spent the better part of the morning wavering between hysterical rants and vehement oaths to cull the Unum when she laid eyes upon him. At the moment, her tormented gaze scoured the crowd.

Whether she was searching for Daoren or the Unum, Laoshi didn't know. He needed to focus on his granddaughter. "Remember to breathe," he said. "It will help calm your mind."

"I know," Heqet said, twisting her twin hair braids.

"Daoren will be in the seat behind yours. Apply the insulating glass as soon as you can."

"*I know*, Grandfather."

"You might have no more than a few seconds to interact with him. Don't delay or—"

A high-frequency hiss emanated from the flight below.

At the base of the stairway, five gloss-black levitrans of the regal fleet whisperglided to a stop and settled onto the transway. Armed Jireni exited the leading and trailing levitrans. They converged on the second vehicle. One opened its rear door.

Daoren climbed out.

Laoshi gasped. Purple bruises marred the boy's face. His stiff movements hinted at joint pain. Glass chains glinted, binding his hands.

The Jireni guard encircled Daoren, dart guns held at the ready, and marched him up the stairway. Denizens and prospects parted with a muted blend of confusion and curiosity.

Cordelia aired a pitiful moan and took a step down the flight.

Laoshi caught her sleeve. "No, Cordelia! You'd never get near him."

They watched, impotent, while Daoren passed by within fifty feet, his clipped gait and rigid face bereft of emotion. Laoshi reckoned he'd retreated to an armored place deep inside himself—an unassailable psychological redoubt.

"Daoren!" Cordelia said, waving.

Heqet added her own frantic shouts and waves. "Daoren! Over here!"

If the boy heard them, he gave no indication. He kept his head down while he ascended. Two minutes later, he shuffled through the archway and disappeared inside the Center with his Jireni escorts. Other prospects followed; some of their own accord, others thanks to the physical intervention of their parents.

Laoshi surveyed the immediate area. Nearby families engaged in the ritual of farewell, touching foreheads and uttering petitions to Sha. No Jireni were visible.

It was time.

He beckoned Heqet closer and pulled a small vial from his satchel. After another quick scan, he upended the vial and coated his index finger.

Heqet kept her head lowered while he smeared the liquid glass over her temples, keeping the movement natural, working the film in expanding circles. It glistened for a few seconds before fading.

He transferred the vial into her grooll pouch and gripped her shoulders. "Remember to apply an even coverage to Daoren's temples, like we practiced. And don't touch your own temples lest you rub the film off."

She lifted her head. Crimson sunlight kissed the micro-studs in her cheeks. They sparkled with unsullied promise above her knowing smile. "I won't."

"Cordelia and I will meet you in the Void afterward," he said, voice thinning. "We'll—"

Laoshi's throat fused shut, pinching off his vocal chords—this might be the last time he held his granddaughter. He swallowed the throttling dread, but it vented from his eyes. He forced the words out between his tears. "You are my heart, sweet Heqet. May sapient Sha protect you."

Heqet's eyes welled, magnifying her pupils. "I'll see you again . . . Papa."

He leaned in and touched his forehead to hers, mindful not to disturb the film. "I am your grandfather."

"And I am your granddaughter."

The resolve in her voice swelled his heart—a good portent. He let her go.

Heqet embraced Cordelia, trading silent farewell, then proceeded up the stairway. She didn't look back. Cordelia stifled a sob.

Laoshi draped his arm around her shoulder. "Don't worry, Cordelia. She'll save Daoren, and he'll save her."

PYROS FIDGETED BESIDE the Unum in the central levitran of the regal fleet. Outside, members of the personal guard cordoned off the vehicle, dart guns trained on the teeming southeastern stairway. Inside, the temperature had crept up ten degrees thanks to the rising sun.

He dabbed sweat from his upper lip. The thought of spending the next eight hours in a stifling levitran, inches away from the Unum, incited the urge to gag.

The Unum gazed through the side window. He'd been humming to himself for the last five minutes, from the moment the Jireni escorted Daoren into the Center.

Pyros had never seen the man so happy. Parting company with Narses minutes earlier didn't dampen his mood one bit. Julinian had accompanied her cousin to the southeastern archway at the Unum's insistence, and would hold vigil there until the end of the test. The ruler of Daqin Guojin refused to leave the levitran. Pyros suspected he feared venturing out among his malnourished subjects.

"I had them a second ago," the Unum said. "Where did—" He stabbed a stubby finger into the window, leaving smudged fingerprints. "There! Top of the second flight. The old duffer has his arm around her, the rascally cudd. You don't suppose she's warming his jackstaff, do you?"

Pyros leaned over to gain a sightline up the stairway.

"Do you reckon Laoshi can still raise his jackstaff?" the Unum asked.

Pyros ignored the question, wagering it was rhetorical. He spotted the pair on the second flight, aided by the sheen of Laoshi's yellow lanshan. "I see them."

"Good. Have your men detain them. If they resist or try to run, cull them."

"Cull them?"

The Unum abandoned his scanning. "I have no intention of letting them live, Pyros. The question is how long they'll take to die."

Pyros squinted. Cordelia he could understand if not agree with; robbing her of two sons created a threat that couldn't be ignored. Culling the most popular Librarian in Daqin Guojin was another matter. Commander Cang had recognized the risk to public order that would arise from simply interning Laoshi in the Rig.

"You have an issue with my decision?"

"With respect, Unum, do you think it's wise to cull Laoshi?"

"I think it's necessary! Are you going to relay the order or shall I do it for you?"

Pyros' skin dimpled despite the temperature. The Unum's

question conveyed a cold truth; disobeying the order would render his Primae Jiren useless, and the ruler of Daqin Guojin discarded useless objects. For Pyros, that would mean forced retirement at the wrong end of a dart gun. He grasped the door handle and cleared his throat to strip the disdain from his voice. "I'll relay your order."

"Bide a moment." The Unum cast his gaze back up the stairway. It stayed there for close to half a minute while he hummed. "Let them hold their vigil for their kin."

"You don't want them taken now?" Pyros asked, still gripping the handle.

"Tell your men to monitor them. Don't detain them until after the test concludes." The Unum sketched a random pattern on the window with his finger. "Let Laoshi and Cordelia enjoy eight more hours of freedom."

The rationale for the small mercy escaped Pyros, but he had no desire to argue against it. "As you command, Unum."

He exited the levitran.

HEQET TURNED A giddy circle inside the Center, her senses toppled by a gyrating mass of prospects, Jireni, and Libraria. The air boiled with laments, shouts, and curses. She hadn't expected this much turbulence, this much chaos. She'd been inside for five minutes and still hadn't found her assigned seat . . . or Daoren.

She stalked up the row for the second time, scanning names on the red-and-gold touch-screens while keeping watch for him. She kept her pace controlled and deliberate. There still enough time. There was no need to panic.

An Asianoid Jiren stepped in front of her, dart gun slung on his shoulder. The leering brute offered what might have passed for a smile if it wasn't for his deformed upper lip. It must have been bitten off and sewn back on in the haste of battle.

Heqet quivered with disgust and tried to step around him. The Jiren side-stepped, blocking her. "Where might you be going, my glinty Hyphenoid?"

"To find my seat," she said, avoiding eye contact.

"I'm not above helping slags, especially the tasty ones. What's your name?"

"Heqet alum Fengsei."

He swiped a calloused finger over his quantum tile. "You're two rows over."

He grabbed the collar of her tunic and shoved her through knots of wandering, wailing figures to a seat. The name floating over its touch-screen read *Heqet alum Fengsei*. Prospects occupied the surrounding seats.

None of them were Daoren.

Heqet gasped. A leaden shroud pressed down on her. Flutters of dread brushed her stomach. Within seconds, they grew so intense she couldn't hide their physical signs.

"Stay calm, my glinty. It'll be over soon."

She reeled, mind flooded by a muddling torrent of questions. Hadn't her grandfather said that Daoren would be in the seat behind hers? Had she misunderstood? How was she supposed to find him in this writhing cauldron of disarray?

The Jiren clamped his hand around her forearm. "Let's get you tucked in."

Heqet stumbled forward. Once secured by the restraining straps, she'd lose all hope of finding Daoren. Nearby prospects begged for their parents, magnifying her mental turmoil. Others pleaded for one last chance to see their siblings, their girlfriends, their—

The solution crystallized with breathculling clarity. It bore the slimmest odds of success, but no other course of action could lead her to him. For it to work, she'd have to channel her best performance.

She dug in her heels and leaned back, jerking the Jiren to a stop. "My boyfriend is in here!" she said. "Please! I must see him!"

"You'll see him after the test." The Jiren cackled. "Unless one of you fails, that is."

Behind them, a snarl of shouts and curses arose. Heqet swiveled her head to the clamor.

Four seats away, three Jireni grappled with a prospect, forcing him to sit.

Her heart swelled. She squirmed free and dashed over. The struggling Jireni parted, unblocking a wild-eyed boy.

A wild-eyed *Indonoid* boy.

Despair crushed her heart. She spun around, scanning the seated faces, petitioning Sha for a glimpse of Daoren's disaffected brow, his impervious cheekbones, his imperious jawline.

The split-lipped Jiren snatched her tunic. His friendly demeanor evaporated. "Take your seat, slag!"

Heqet needed to summon the performance of a lifetime. It required a gesture she would never, ever have dreamed of making to his kind.

She placed a hand on the brute's face. "He's going to fail!" She swiped away a conjured tear and caressed his cheek. "I want one last kiss. That's all, I promise!"

The Jiren scowled, unmoved.

Her chest tightened. Unbidden sobs gushed from her mouth, amplifying the atmosphere of misery. The sobs were genuine—and a genuine surprise.

The Jiren's flinty jowl softened beneath her hand. He muttered a chain of profanities and raised his tile. "What's this boyfriend's name?"

"Daoren al Lucien," she said, stunned the performance had worked.

The Jiren input the name. After a few seconds, he pointed. "This way."

He dragged her to a seat eight rows east of her own. Heqet composed herself and reached into her grooll pouch, palming the glass vial. They came up behind the seat, where another Jiren poised to place a halo on the head of a male prospect.

"Tarry, comrade!" the split-lipped Jiren called out. "This one here wants a final noogle with her doomed boyfriend."

The other Jiren rolled his eyes. He set the halo on the touchscreen. Heqet rounded the seat while the two Jireni traded gripes and grievances.

Daoren glanced up at her, his expression a blend of infinite confusion and unfettered relief. Chest and legs straps anchored him, but the chains that had bound his hands were gone.

Before he said a word, Heqet tipped the vial and doused her finger. She leaned over and touched her forehead to his, working the liquid over his temple like she'd practiced with her grandfather. She repeated the process on his other temple, using up the last drop of glass.

She pulled her head back—the glass' sheen disappeared. So did her sense of dread; it eased off her shoulders like a flexglass quilt. "I had to see you one more time," she whispered.

Daoren's smile revealed blood-flecked teeth. "I'm so glad you did." His gaze flicked over her cheeks. His smile dissolved.

Heqet ran her fingers over the scabs still healing from their encounter outside the Librarium. "They don't hurt anymore."

"I'm . . . I'm sorry I couldn't protect you," he said.

She peered into his clouded eyes, looking past the purple bruises and their many arguments, and glimpsed genuine sorrow. In that instant, his sterile surface crumbled, uncovering a part of him that had always laid buried. In that instant, he was *human*.

Without thinking, without hesitating, she leaned forward and pressed her lips to his.

Daoren gulped, no doubt caught off-guard by the kiss, but he pressed back.

She let her lips part, let her tongue find his. A sublime glow flushed her core, filling what had for so long been a numb void.

For a delicious moment, the Center, the S.A.T., and the Jireni melted away. For a delicious moment, she felt *human*.

"All right, leave some for me," the split-lipped Jiren said. "Let's go."

Heqet slipped her right foot out of her sandal. She pulled away from Daoren and dropped to her knees. She yanked the sandal off his right foot and smothered his instep with kisses. "No!" she said, channeling another performance. "I can't live without you!"

The Jireni's hands tightened on the back of her tunic, two on either side. She donned Daoren's sandal, leaving hers next to his bare foot. The Jireni hauled her off the floor. She locked onto Daoren's baffled gaze and nodded at the sandal.

Daoren caught the signal. He edged his foot into the sandal and gave her a hint of a smile.

The split-lipped Jiren hip-carried her away, muttering more profanities. Daoren called after her. "I'll see you again, Heqet!"

Her heart swelled. Now that they were both protected from the stun shot, she knew that he would.

Heqet smiled when the Jiren heaved her into the seat. She smiled when he cinched her chest and leg straps, extra tight. She smiled when he loomed over her with murderous intent in his eyes.

His nostrils flared. "Give you prospects a finger and you gobble the entire hand!"

She gave him a defiant grin.

The Jiren clamped both hands around her cheeks. He crouched so they were eye-to-eye. "Now you're going to give me a taste for my trouble."

His rough fingers scuffed her cheekbones. She jerked her head back. "Don't!"

He tightened his grip. His thumbs rubbed back and forth across her temples.

"No no no no no no!"

He leaned closer, aligning his grotesque lips with hers. She squeezed her eyes shut and sobbed, knowing full well he'd condemned her.

"Come now," the Jiren said, "it won't be as horrible as all that."

His lips met hers, his breath an open sewer.

Heqet screamed into his mouth.

———

EIGHT HOURS LATER, Daoren skimmed through the proof for the final question, ignoring as best he could the incessant whimpering of the prospect seated to his left. The Africoid had been crying for an hour, moaning *no ... no ... no ...* at intervals random enough to create a distraction. At least the group of taunting Jireni had moved on; they'd spent a solid fifteen minutes asking the boy what he tasted like.

Daoren completed the proof and tapped his touch-screen. A new screen opened.

Submit Answer?

He hesitated, tapping his lips. The mass-gap derivation was by far the most difficult question on the test. Its quantum-field calculations encompassed thirty-six screens, its solution dependent on forty-one variables and worth twelve-hundred points. He was sure he'd derived forty of the variables without error. He glanced up at the nearest chronoglyph.

00:00:53 ... 00:00:52 ... 00:00:51. ...

His gaze returned to the question on the touch-screen, but his mind returned to the Unum's threat in the Rig.

Should you score one point less than thirty thousand, your lovely mother will be mounted in her own rig before you receive your stun shot.

The meaning couldn't be clearer. It wasn't enough to write an S.A.T. that would guarantee Narses' ascent to the Cognos Populi.

It had to be an S.A.T. that would grant him the irrefutable right to be named Unum Potentate.

It had to be perfect.

The *Submit Answer?* screen waggled, vying for his attention. No time remained to review the final variable; he had to trust his instinct. "Yes," he whispered, voice clotted with angst.

A new screen opened.

Response Not Understood. Please Repeat.

He tensed his abdomen. "Yes."

The screen refreshed.

Response Not Understood. Please Repeat.

He rocked forward, stretching the flexglass chest restraint to its limit, and placed his lips inches from the touch-screen. "Yes! Yes! Yes, you useless piece of—"

A new screen opened.

Test Complete.

Daoren rocked back and released a whooshing breath. He craned around in his seat, twisting his torso as far as the restraining straps allowed. The effort made him wince. After six days in the Rig, every joint throbbed. He could just make out Heqet in the corner of his eye.

She sat with her arms crossed, head lowered as if weighted by her glass halo. She'd held the same pose throughout the test, announcing her complete surrender. Compared to her brashness and confidence before the test, the contrast was unsettling.

What had affected her mood? Maybe the Jiren who'd lugged her away had been taunting her. Maybe the countdown to their appointment with the grooll mill had sapped her spirit. Whatever the cause, she'd need to tap into every ounce of brashness and confidence she possessed to survive the coming challenge.

If that weren't enough, he'd have to find a way to get to her. Laoshi's plan to have them sit together hadn't worked. Instead of eight feet separating them, it was eight *rows*. He'd spent at least an hour of the eight-hour test puzzling through the problem.

He gazed at Heqet for a few more seconds, but never made eye contact. She never looked up. A few seats in front of her, however, Narses stared at him through a tangle of red bangs, emitting an air of idle smugness. Not once had Daoren seen his fingers on the touch-screen; he'd spent the eight hours focused on anything but his test.

Daoren knew coming into the Center that his final score would reflect Narses' effort and intelligence. He knew now it would be a resounding null. Daoren repressed any sign of concern; he wouldn't give the smug fid the satisfaction of seeing worry.

The automated voice swelled. "*The Survival Aptitude Test concludes in five, four, three, two, one . . .*"

The touch-screens turned black, triggering a collective groan throughout the Center.

"*Now tabulating scores.*"

Though he knew what was coming, Daoren had to confirm it with his own eyes. His touch-screen flashed to life.

A blood-red *FAIL* strobed above a flickering score.

0.

Daoren sneered at the pathetic result. He rotated back to Narses, eager to show him his amusement.

The fid gaped at his own touch-screen. His glass halo projected a white globe; its scintillating light pulses vaporized his hair. If Narses' cringing face and bunched posture were any indication, the procedure frightened the living wits out of him.

The reaction earned a chuckle from Daoren.

The globe encasing Narses' head vanished, but his halo didn't stay dormant. Its luminance intensified, projecting a majestic purple shaft so bright it tinted the entire ceiling.

Jireni and Libraria bathed in the light, mouths flapping open. An Indonoid Librarian clasped her hands, voice tinged with awe. "He's attained a perfect score!"

Throughout the Center, restraints unlocked with syncopated double-clicks. Close-cropped denizens crept toward Narses.

He clambered out of his seat, his halo still beaming its brilliant purple shaft. The denizens, Jireni, and Libraria before him bowed. Narses folded at the waist, returning the salutation. His halo clattered to the floor and winked out.

A cry rose from the gathering. "Behold the Unum Potentate!"

Frenzied cheers punched the air. Two burly Jireni hoisted Narses onto their shoulders and carried him toward an archway. Within a minute, the Center was empty except for twenty-thousand screeching failures.

The shock generator spooled up. Its whir floated over the seats, as delicate as whisperglass, but the volume doubled each second. Power drained in tandem from the interior lights.

Daoren reefed himself around. His gaze found Heqet in the waning light.

She raised her head. Below the halo, her eyes channeled infinite hopelessness. She mouthed a phrase, but he couldn't decipher its meaning.

The lights extinguished. He lost her in the gloom. The wails of the prospects sank beneath the shock generator's shriek, lost as well.

The whir peaked, its intensity equal to a thunderclap. The stun shock was seconds away.

Daoren voiced the one thought left in his head, knowing full well she'd never hear it. "I love you, Heqet!"

An almighty zap pierced the darkness. . . .

JOIN THE READERS' POSSE!

You can join the thousands of readers who receive email alerts on my new releases, ebook discounts, and awesome giveaways. Please visit MIKESHERIFFWRITES.COM to learn more.

If you enjoyed this book, I'd be tremendously grateful if you'd take a minute to post a review at your favorite online retailer. Thanks in advance for your support!

AFTERWORD

T HANK YOU FOR reading *SURVIVAL APTITUDE TEST: SOUND.*
  If this is your first sampling of my work, I sincerely hope it
marks the start of a journey you'll truly enjoy. For those who may
be wondering where the idea came from, I can say without equiv-
ocation that it sprang from an episode of *Parenthood.* Who says
TV is a waste of time?

You'll find a comprehensive list of my material in the "Also
By" section at the end of this book. You'll also encounter two
bonus chapters before you get there: the first chapters from
SURVIVAL APTITUDE TEST: FURY and *SURVIVAL APTITUDE TEST:
HOPE'S GRAVEYARD.*

FURY is the second book in The Extinction Odyssey series,
picking up where this title leaves off. (Bonus Chapter #1 resolves
SOUND's nail-biting cliffhanger, so you can flip there now and get
a good night's sleep.) *HOPE'S GRAVEYARD* is a stand-alone prequel to
the series, and reveals haunting details from Laoshi's terrifying
first mission as a Jiren.

I support the widespread sharing of stories. (It's the reason I
publish my ebooks without Digital Rights Management.) If you
enjoyed this book, please consider loaning it to a friend or

colleague, or perhaps donating it to your local library. All I ask is you not re-sell it. (Bad karma!)

Anyhow, I'll get out of the way so you can get on with reading the bonus chapters. When you're done, I'd love to hear your impressions on SOUND. Feel free to drop me a line at mike@mikesheriffwrites.com whenever you have the time. All the best!

Mike Sheriff
    London, Ontario

BONUS CHAPTER #1

SURVIVAL APTITUDE TEST: FURY
Chapter 1
The Grooll Mill

LAOSHI HEARD THEM before he saw them—a dissonant medley of shouts and cheers that issued from the archway at the top of the southeastern stairway. Beside him, Cordelia craned her neck, expectant, as if she hoped to see Daoren leading the exodus.

She must have known it was impossible, just as he knew Heqet's fresh face wouldn't be emerging under a freshly cropped scalp. They'd spent the last eight hours climbing the stairway and preparing themselves for this moment. They'd held vigil at the base of the upper flight, waiting to see Narses emerge from the Center. Laoshi wagered it would be worth the risk.

Eighty feet above, a manic glut of Jireni, Libraria, and newly anointed denizens burst from the archway. One denizen strode much taller than the others.

Narses straddled the shoulders of two Jireni. Other Jireni,

Libraria, and denizens circled him, whooping and waving. The unrestrained admiration led to one inescapable conclusion.

"He's received a perfect score!" Laoshi said. "They're paying tribute to the Unum Potentate!"

"Did Daoren write a perfect S.A.T.?" Cordelia asked, reddened eyes rimmed with awe.

He glanced at her. "Yes, Cordelia! Your son is—"

A distant flash caught his eye.

Forty feet away, shadowy forms crept through the crowd, crystalline dart guns sparkling in sunlight. The Jireni's stooped posture suggested they were hunting someone.

Laoshi scanned the other side of the flight.

More Jireni approached, slinking and weaving. They leaned forward with predatory purpose.

"Is everything all right?" Cordelia asked.

He smiled, careful to cloak any outward signs of concern. Jireni tended to open fire if they suspected their prey had been alerted. Maintaining a casual air, he glanced down the stairway.

Six more armed Jireni advanced upward from one flight below. Six pairs of cold, calculating eyes locked onto him and Cordelia.

Tingling adrenaline washed through his veins—the encirclement left no doubt as to whom the Jireni were hunting. The closest group was thirty feet away; they'd be upon them in as many seconds. The stairway provided little concealment besides the human mass, hardly an impenetrable barrier. Unless. . . .

He gripped Cordelia's arm. "When I tell you to move, *move*."

She stared at him, clearly confused by the whispered order. He had no time to explain his intentions. He filled his lungs and pointed at the archway. "Behold the Unum Potentate! Let us advance and honor him!"

Thousands of denizens surged up the stairway, pressing arm to arm and chest to back. They formed a cheering, mobile barrier —exactly as he'd hoped.

"Move!"

He yanked Cordelia up the flight, shouldering through the compressed multitude. Guttural shouts penetrated from the right; the Jireni were issuing orders. He risked a glance.

Twenty feet away, two Jireni aimed their dart guns in his direction.

Laoshi crouched, pulling Cordelia down with him. He climbed with the moving mass, one hand clutching the tunic of the denizen in front of him, the other tugging Cordelia along in his slipstream. He was mindful to stay on his feet; tripping now would risk a trampling, doing the job of the Jireni for them.

More guttural shouts pierced the cheering. A second later, five percussive reports hammered his ears. To his right, five denizens brayed in agony.

He didn't see the dart strikes, but his other senses registered their impact. The crowd reacted as a single organism recoiling from a blow. Panic in a few spread to the whole in the space of a single breath. Bodies pressed in from all sides, grasping and jostling, snuffing the sparks of jubilation. He squeezed Cordelia's hand. If he lost her now, he'd never see her again.

They rushed headlong up the flight.

———

DART-GUN VOLLEYS rippled down the southeastern stairway and slapped the levitran's windows. Pyros leaned around the Unum, ducking to get a sightline through the side window.

Atop the stairway, thousands of denizens separated like scattershot, falling over themselves to escape the threat.

The Unum sucked his teeth. "It appears they tried to run," he said with coarse detachment. "What a pity. I wanted to know how long they'd last in a rig."

On the middle flight, six Jireni raked the fleeing masses with glass darts. Their staggered volleys sounded eerily akin to sporadic applause.

Pyros pounded his fist into the seat. "They're firing indiscriminately!"

"So?"

"I ordered them to minimize collateral casualties!"

The Unum shrugged. "I thought you might, so I countermanded the order."

"When did you do that?"

"An hour ago. When you stepped out to use the waste chamber."

"*Why* did you do that?"

"I've never been a fan of fire discipline," the Unum said. "Tell a Jiren he can't cull the innocent, and the next thing you know he won't cull the guilty. I didn't think you'd—"

Pyros exited the levitran. He raced up the stairway, battering through waves of hysterical denizens. More percussive reports assaulted his ears before he gained the upper flights, within vocal range of his men. "Cease fire!" he said. "Cease fire!"

The men brought their dart guns to the ready position. Pyros surveyed the damage, chest heaving, lungs searing.

Scores of denizens lay dead or wounded on the blood-spattered stairway. The celebratory cheering for the Unum Potentate had ceased. Stunned silence replaced it—one so total that the drone of an aeroshrike miles distant sounded as close as a hundred feet overhead. Jireni wandered up and down the steps, turning bodies and checking identities.

The senior Jiren traversed the flight. He halted before Pyros. "They aren't here, sire."

Pyros motioned to the carnage. "You mean after all this they escaped?"

The Asianoid's squalid gaze fell upon the steps. He offered no answers nor excuses.

"Gather your men. Use whatever resources you need to set up

checkpoints along the major egress routes leading to the Librarium."

The Jiren's eyes flashed back to life, revived by the chance for redemption. "At once, sire. We'll find them."

Pyros had his doubts. Laoshi was a cagey target. He likely knew more off-the-grid ways to get to the Librarium than anyone else in Daqin Guojin.

The Jiren turned away. Pyros caught his arm. "I'm rescinding the cull order."

"Sire?"

"I want Laoshi and Cordelia taken alive."

"But the Unum—"

"Doesn't control your duty postings," he said. "Would you prefer to see you and your men patrolling the Great Northern Border for the next ten years?"

The Jiren stiffened to attention. "I'll pass along your order."

He marched away. Pyros settled onto a step and gazed upon the dead.

Many were Daqin Guojin's newest denizens, trampled or cut down in their prime. Mothers and fathers wept over the battered, impaled bodies of their children. Shock and disbelief contorted faces that shone with joy and relief a few minutes earlier. Some parents glared at him, eyes inflamed with unspoken rage.

He had to look away. He understood their rage all too well— and the end to which it would lead. If the Unum retained power, the people's silent fury would find its voice through sonic charges, dart guns, and sound cannons.

His instincts told him that the Primae Librarian could help avoid that fate. If the Unum wanted him dead, that meant he could play a useful role in the coming struggle. Pyros needed to take Laoshi alive before murderous insurrection consumed the entire city-state. And to do that, he needed to find him.

DAOREN GRIMACED.

A high-pitched hum muddled his hearing. Relentless pressure inside his head sought to force his eyes from their sockets. A strange force pulled his arms upward.

He peered into the murk, searching for a recognizable feature, a surface to orient himself, an object to landmark his—

Lights flared. He gasped.

All around him, rows of stunned prospects hung inverted in their seats, arms dangling above their heads. Below them, ovoid pods gleamed atop suspended platforms.

The ghastly vision landmarked his location. He was in the grooll mill below the Center, hanging upside-down in his seat, still secured by the restraining straps. He raised his chin.

Three feet below his hands, a blue pod awaited. Its reclining seat glinted, smiling in welcome.

Daoren rattled his head, shaking off the after-effects of the muted stun shock. How long had Laoshi said it took before the seat restraints unlocked? Ten seconds? Thirty seconds? A minute?

The answer condensed from the fog. The restraints unlocked after—

The restraints unlocked with a double-click. He dropped onto the reclining seat, landing on his back with a jolting *oomph*. Twenty thousand thuds accompanied him.

One of them belonged to Heqet.

That awareness burned off his mental fog. The preparation and planning of the preceding weeks hardened with crystal clarity. He knew what needed to be done.

The pod rotated, stopping at a forty-five-degree angle, head up. Daoren climbed out its opening and jumped onto the platform. He paused to get his bearings.

The platform's width spanned three feet. Five-foot air-gaps isolated it from the adjacent platforms. Convoluted lengths of glass piping undergirded the structure, ready to transfer slurried prospects into the floor's open mixing tanks. The tanks were empty except for huge, serrated mixing blades.

Heqet's seat in the Center had been located five seats to the south of his own, eight rows to the west. He counted off the platforms and locked his gaze onto her pod. He clenched and unclenched his hands, ticking off the seconds until her appearance.

A breathless tone snagged his attention. He glanced up the platform.

Pods self-sealed, activating one after the other along the northern ends of the platforms. The sequence would take thirty seconds to reach the southern ends—and even less time to trap Heqet.

Daoren refocused on her pod, heart pounding. Why in Sha's name wasn't she out yet? He inched to the edge of the platform.

The breathless tone grew louder as the sequence surged closer. She had only a few seconds. What was she—

His own pod sealed with a sinister whisper. He cupped his hands around his mouth. "Heqet! Get out!"

Eight rows away, a glinting panel slid into place, entombing her.

"Heqet!"

His shout faded as he eyed the mill's floor one hundred feet below. Sha help him if he miscalculated. He backed up and gulped a spine-bracing breath.

Daoren lunged toward the air-gap. He planted his sandal and leaped.

His other sandal found the leading edge of the adjacent platform. Barely. He fought for balance, arms twirling and back snapping, and gained his footing.

At the north end of the mill, pods emitted a dazzling red luster; the skin-slicing procedure had started. He had half a minute at most to free her. He put his head down and charged forward.

Daoren leaped, landed, and leaped again, impelled over each chasm by undiluted adrenaline and unceasing petitions to Sha. He thudded onto the eighth platform.

He sprinted down the platform, squeezing by four pods before reaching Heqet's. Beneath its panel, she lay unmoving upon the seat, lips parted, eyes closed. The cadaverous pose culled his breath. Was she—

Tiny circles of condensation formed inside the panel. She was still breathing.

He clawed at the panel's edges, feeling for a seam to pry it open. His fingernails slid uselessly across the glass, again and again.

Inside the pod, the half-dome lenses activated. A ruddy matrix of hair-thin beams formed inches above her face.

He raised his head.

Up the platform, another pod's photonic cutters angled downward, slicing into a male prospect's face. Sections of his skin sloughed off, revealing fat-marbled squares of flesh.

Daoren gagged. He vaulted over Heqet's pod.

Twelve cables sprouted from its rear surface—the power sources for the photonic cutters. There was no time for finesse. He grabbed a handful and yanked.

Blue sparks spewed past his face, venting the sterile scent of ozone. He grabbed another handful; more sparks arced into the air. A third yank severed the final cables. He scrambled over the pod, petitioning Sha that he'd completed the task in time.

Micro-cuts checkerboarded Heqet's face, but it hadn't been sliced to pieces. A distant whine cut short his relief. The next step in the process had started—the high vacuum. He had to look despite his dread.

Up the platform, the same male prospect's white *pienfu* garment disappeared, sucked off his body by the extreme pressure difference. His skin and digestive tract followed, leaving a bloody, oozing shell with bulging, accusing eyes.

Slag-hot gorge rose into Daoren's mouth. In a few seconds, the vacuum would convert Heqet's petite body into the same monstrous apparition, sliced skin or not.

He smashed his fists into the panel. The blows had no effect. He unleashed another flurry, ignoring the pain in his hands. It only wore him out.

Helplessness seared his throat. He abandoned the futile beatings, eyes welling, and lowered his defeated gaze to—

His sandal!

He dropped to a knee and ripped the sandal off his right foot. He turned it over.

Its sole bore a recessed pattern in the shape of a double-edged dagger.

"Yes!"

Daoren pried the dagger free and sprang to his feet. He drove its hilt into the panel.

The glass held, but the strike shock-fused the dagger to crystalline hardness. The high-vacuum's whine drew closer.

He raised the dagger and drove its hilt into the panel again.

The glass chipped and cracked.

A frenetic whine emanated from inside the pod. He hoisted the dagger, channeling every ounce of rage against the Unum, and drove its hilt into the glass with a primal scream.

The panel shattered. Glass shards showered Heqet. Without a seal, the hoses extracting the air did little more than buffet her hair and pienfu.

He hauled her limp body out of the pod and laid her on the platform. One step remained; getting off the platform before—

A faint, high-frequency whistle announced the start of the ultrasonic-liquifying process. He risked a glance toward the north end of the mill.

Skinless prospects liquified into a smoldering slurry inside their pods. The lurid sludge evacuated from the pods' bases and wound through the maze of piping beneath the platforms.

One hundred feet below, the bloody ooze jetted into open tanks, now filling with tons of powdered silica. Mixing blades thrummed, churning the boiling grooll precursor.

Daoren tore his gaze from the horror. He had a minute to get off the platform with an unconscious Heqet lest they undergo what Laoshi had called *sympathetic liquidation.*

Four feet away, a support cable ran at a steep angle from the platform to the floor. It tracked over a line of four tanks fast filling with bubbling precursor. The angle and route were far from ideal, but more favorable cables were too distant to reach in time.

Daoren gripped one of Heqet's hair braids and placed the dagger's cutting edge an inch from her scalp. He hacked off the braid and tied one end to the receiver loops of his grooll pouch, fingers fumbling.

He willed himself to slow down and tie the knots correctly. He secured the other end of the braid to the loops of Heqet's grooll pouch, short-roping her, cinching it as tight as possible.

The ultrasonic whistle grew louder.

His skin flushed—his body was being heated from within. He had ten seconds at most before the ultrasonic energy did permanent damage to himself and Heqet.

He rip-sawed through her other hair braid, hand a blur. Clamping the dagger between his teeth, he dragged Heqet to the edge of the platform.

He coiled the second braid around the cable and double-wrapped its free ends around his hands. He petitioned Sha for the strength to hold on, for the braid to bear their combined weight, and for it to be thick enough to withstand the friction. He would have petitioned for more, but the ultrasonic whistle was upon them.

He wrapped his legs around Heqet and rolled off the platform.

Daoren grunted against the shock of their whip-snapping bodies, almost dropping the dagger. Heqet dangled from his waist, mercifully oblivious to the view below. The braid rasped against the cable as they gathered momentum and cleared the ultrasonic danger.

A few seconds into the descent, a pungent, scorched aroma filled his nostrils. He looked up.

Gray wisps of smoke curled from the rasping braid.

Daoren ground his teeth against the dagger's blade. He couldn't do anything about the friction—they were committed now. Whether they reached the floor depended on the braid's density and thickness.

Midway down the cable, they streaked over the first grooll tank, then the second. He locked his gaze onto the fuming braid. If it parted now they'd be boiled alive.

They continued to accelerate, now forty feet above the mill floor, and cleared the third tank. Smoke poured from the hair braid.

They whisked over the final gaping cauldron. Flesh-tone precursor gurgled ten feet below their sandals. Its radiant heat clothed him like a funeral shroud. A single thought consumed his mind.

Please hold . . . please hold . . . please—

The charred braid parted.

The nauseating tingle of free-fall ravaged Daoren's stomach. His panicky gaze found the smoldering grooll tank.

He plunged past its lip, missing it by inches. A split-second later, he hit the floor and his mind went blank.

Whether it stayed blank for a minute or an hour, he couldn't say. When his senses returned, all he knew for certain was that he was in pain and that Heqet was lying on top of him. She whimpered the way a person does in the midst of an ill dream.

He spat the dagger from his mouth, tasting his own blood, but he didn't care.

He was alive.

Heqet was alive.

They'd survived the grooll mill.

Daoren closed his eyes and rasplaughed.

ENJOY THE CHAPTER? GET THE WHOLE STORY!

Please visit your favorite online retailer to order
SURVIVAL APTITUDE TEST: FURY
Available in print and ebook formats.

WHAT ARE READERS SAYING ABOUT *FURY*?

"This book blew me away! I can't wait for the next one! The ending surprised the s**t out of me!"
~Amazon Reviewer

"I will not spoil the story; you must white-knuckle your way through dramatic changes of fortune!"
~Amazon Reviewer

BONUS CHAPTER #2

SURVIVAL APTITUDE TEST: HOPE'S GRAVEYARD
Chapter 1
Dagger-Ax Men

LAOSHI RAISED THE sonic rifle to his faceplate and peered through the optical sight.

The dim corridor mirrored the previous two he'd traversed. Opaque ventilation piping and black power cabling hugged its angled ceiling. Canted walls bracketed its narrow walkway, surfaces speckled with droplets of condensation. Scattered junction boxes and other bulky protrusions jutted from the grated surfaces. None were large enough to mask a human being. At the far end of the corridor, a pentagonal hatch glinted.

The objective.

Laoshi lowered the rifle, keeping its bowl-shaped muzzle pointed along the threat axis, and raised his right hand. He waved it from side to side.

Five seconds later, another hand fell upon his armored shoulder-plate. Commander Nehjal's nasally voice leaked through his helmet's earpiece.

"*Proceed.*"

Laoshi edged forward, alert for signs of movement. He tucked his elbows into his sides—bumping a protrusion would violate the whispersilent protocol—and boxed his breathing.

Inhale for three seconds.

Hold for three seconds.

Exhale for three seconds.

Hold for three seconds.

The repeated pattern oxygenated his blood, calmed his nerves, and focused his attention. The pentagonal hatch became his entire world—not that it had much competition. He reached the end of the corridor, ten feet from the hatch, and dropped to a knee. "In position," he said, letting the helmet-mic's compressor compensate for his hushed tone.

"*Dominus up,*" Nehjal said.

Laoshi didn't take his eyes off the hatch's circular handle. The first sign Dominus had moved up came when three fingers drummed the top of his helmet. The signal carried no tactical meaning—his friend simply enjoyed drumming his fingers. He must have decided to do it at the spur of the moment, noise discipline be damned.

Dominus stalked five feet farther before pressing his body against the right-hand wall. He aimed his sonic rifle at the hatch. "*Ready.*"

Nehjal's voice crackled in Laoshi's ear before Dominus' ready call had faded. "*Deploy eavesdropper.*"

Laoshi already had the device out of his web pouch. As thick as a fingernail and a little bigger than his palm, the eavesdropper's tri-horn detectors could pinpoint acoustic sources as weak as two decibels from a stand-off distance of one thousand feet. Densely packed amplification circuitry made the item heavy; each eavesdropper weighed two pounds. He carried six of them among his webbing on every mission.

He covered the last ten feet on the balls of his feet, mindful to not make a sound. The eavesdropper needed to go above the hatch, flush against the vertical bulkhead, just like the other two he'd placed. Its powerful sensors could penetrate ceramic-armor bulkheads, but only when in direct contact with the medium. The third and final device would permit sonic triangulation of the guards inside the command post. The mongrels didn't need to talk; breathing alone would yield a cross-fix. The cross-fix would yield the firing solution needed to cull them before they raised the alarm.

Laoshi reached the hatch. He raised his hand to set the eaves-dropper against the—

The device slipped from his gloved hand. It clattered onto the walkway.

Nehjal's disbelieving groan filled his helmet. "*Oh, for the love of Sha...*"

Heavy footfalls resonated from the other side of the hatch. Its handle spun like a whirlwind.

"They're coming out!" Dominus said, breaking the whispersilent protocol. "Laoshi, pull back!"

He back-pedaled to clear Dominus' firing arc. The hatch swung open with a thunderous crash.

Laoshi hoisted his sonic rifle to his shoulder, heartbeats pummel-thumping his throat.

A sneering mongrel burst through the hatch. Bloody fangs jutted from its mouth and extended halfway down its anechoic chest-armor. The horrifying creature brandished two flaming daggers. It unleashed a breathculling howl.

"Sapient Sha!" Laoshi screamed.

Dominus' breathless rasplaughter cut through the din. "Sha can't save you now!"

Commander Nehjal's voice echoed down the corridor. "Endex, endex, endex!"

Laoshi gaped at the blood-drooling mongrel, now frozen in mid-lunge mere feet before him. He lowered his quivering rifle and gaped at Dominus. "What's this thing supposed to be?"

Dominus raised his helmet's slotted faceplate. Gray eyes sparkled above unshaven Slavvic cheeks. He smirked. "That, my friend, is your worst nightmare!"

Nehjal marched along the corridor and yanked off her helmet. "Terminate the projection."

The sneering mongrel and surrounding corridor vanished, revealing an enormous lumenglass stage. The plasmonic-projection platform was the largest in the Jireni training facility. Its bottomless black panels spanned ten thousand square-feet and could replicate innumerable operational settings. Third-Gen haptic feedback imparted kinesthetic and tactile sensitivity that approached the substantive fidelity of real-world objects.

Nehjal halted before Dominus. Her brown scalp glistened in the ambient light. Darker eyes hinted at annoyance, but her neutral brow and impartial lips muddied the signal. She conveyed a serene maturity more commonly associated with an Asianoid elder than an Indonoid Jiren in her mid-thirties.

"Jiren Dominus," she said. "I've never seen a mongrel with fangs, much less flaming daggers. Would you care to explain?"

Dominus stiffened to attention. The posture wasn't rigid enough to wipe the smirk off his face. "I wanted to welcome Jiren Laoshi back to the team, sireen."

"And you felt reprogramming the training projection was the best way to do that?"

He shrugged. "I felt it was the best way to test his nerves."

Nehjal grunted. "Do Jireni shrug when we're at the position of attention?"

"No, sireen."

Her eyes squinched. She waved him closer.

Dominus sighed and took three shuffling paces forward. Nehjal flicked the bridge of his nose with her middle finger.

A sharp-edged crack announced the strike. Dominus flinched and squeezed his eyes shut.

Laoshi masked his amusement. In the six months he'd been on the assault team, he'd never heard Nehjal raise her voice. He'd seen her raise her hand and flick a hundred noses though.

"I had no idea you possessed so much spare time," she said, still berating Dominus. "I'm sure I can find more constructive tasks to help fill it. Ones involving repetitive physical labor."

"I could suggest a few, sireen," Laoshi said.

She pivoted and leveled a piercing glare. Laoshi slung his sonic rifle and pulled off his helmet. He paced forward without waiting for her order.

The finger-flick rang out just as sharply as the one Dominus had received. Laoshi's eyes watered. When they cleared, Nehjal gazed at him without a trace of ire.

"Is your back still hurting, Jiren Laoshi?"

"No, sireen."

"Do you need more recovery time before resuming your duties?"

"No, sireen."

"Are you trying to get Jiren Dominus culled?" she asked. "If you are, I'd consider promoting you."

Laoshi stifled a chuckle. "No, sireen."

"Then keep a better grip on your equipment. Drop something in the midst of a reconnaissance and you could get us all culled."

"Yes, sireen," he said. "It won't happen again."

"It had better not. The next time you place an eavesdropper, it will be for real."

Dominus' eyes brightened, matching his nose. "We have a mission?"

Nehjal nodded. "Tomorrow night."

"Where?"

She reached out and flicked Dominus' nose again. "What do we say about insertion security?"

Dominus winced. "Never reveal the target until you're on the way to destroy it."

"You'll find out on the aeroshrike," she said. "Pass word to the rest of the team to muster at the northern aerodrome at noon tomorrow."

Nehjal strode across the stage and angled for the archway leading out of the training facility. Dominus slugged Laoshi's arm once she'd disappeared. "An actual insertion mission, Laoshi!"

Laoshi summoned his bravest grin. "Finally."

"I'd wager it's Havoc," Dominus said, rubbing his angry nose. "The southern sector."

Laoshi weighed the prospect of performing his first aerial insertion into the most heavily defended sector in the most heavily defended mongrel colony. Since joining the Jireni six months ago, he'd completed six training jumps in the facility's free-fall simulator. He'd yet to perform one in the atmosphere.

His seventh training jump had ended in a spinal compression when Jiren Vandarian inadvertently reset the windtube's blade pitch to neutral. Without the artificial airstream, Laoshi had fallen forty feet onto the hardened-glass mesh covering the turbine.

That was six weeks ago. Since then, Dominus and the other team members had conducted a reconnaissance mission in Decay. It was his friend's first real-world insertion, and he'd chatterwailed about little else since returning.

"Don't look so worried," Dominus said. "I'll be with you every step of the way."

Laoshi puffed his chest and lied. "That worries me more than facing a mongrel with *ten* flaming daggers."

Dominus snorted. He moaned and reached for his ruddy nose. "Sapient Sha—she might have broken it with that last flick."

"With any luck."

"Is that any way to talk to someone who's inviting you to his abode?"

"Your abode?"

"If you think I'll let you spend the last night before your first insertion alone, you're mistaken." He grabbed Laoshi's arm and dragged him toward the archway. "Besides, Myra wants to see you."

———

THE PARLOR'S WARMTH made up for the abode's cramped, austere decor. So did the company.

Laoshi sat at the table with Dominus and Myra. His hosts wore casual flexglass *shenyi* and no tunics—neither stood on stiff formality. Myra's shadow-black shenyi would have been an ideal match for her hair before her S.A.T. Like all successful prospects, she'd emerged from the Center with a shorn scalp denoting the mark of denizenship. Her sleek eyebrows now served as the garment's sole accent.

Dominus bounced little Cordelia on his knee while Myra tickled her bare feet. Cordelia didn't fuss the way most nine-month-old infants fussed when accosted by their parents. She seemed content to be jostled and tickled.

Laoshi marveled at the incongruous sight. Growing up, Dominus had vowed on countless occasions to never enter union. *No woman can take the place of unattached adventure*, he liked to say.

That was before he met Myra, a fellow Slavv and an adventure unto herself. She'd finished near the top of her cohort last year and accepted a position as a quantum programmer at the Librarium. Quantum programmers were renowned for their problem-solving capabilities. Dominus' metamorphosis had to be an extension of that gift.

"Would you like any more grooll?" she asked, abandoning her daughter's feet. She motioned to the half-empty bowl in the center of the table. "We have plenty."

"No, thank you," Laoshi said. "I'm full."

In truth, he hadn't felt hungry at the start of the meal. He couldn't say what suppressed his appetite more; tomorrow's looming insertion, or knowing that the grooll might contain the mortal remains of his friends.

Myra pushed back from the table. "I'll get some more water." She padded into the pantry.

Laoshi's gaze lingered on the pieces of grooll in the bowl. Each bite-size torus whispered a name to him. Their flesh-tone hue only amplified the murmur.

"Are you all right?" Dominus asked, still bouncing Cordelia.

The question broke Laoshi's trance, but not his line of thought. "Do you ever wonder what life was like before the Cycle of Extinctions?"

"How do you mean?"

"Take our food, for example." He pointed at the grooll. "Imagine having alternatives other than our youngest prospects to eat."

Dominus rolled his eyes. "You're not going to bring up the seed vault again, are you?"

"No, I'm talking about the time when life was abundant. When humans weren't forced to make such inhuman choices."

"We do what we have to do to survive. Sha granted us sapience so we could avoid extinction."

Laoshi nodded. *Survival Through Sapience* served as Daqin Guojin's motto. Four centuries ago, the city-state's brightest minds had synthesized a stable food source using "donated" macronutrients and silica. Two centuries later, the Cognos Populi introduced the S.A.T. In so doing, the ruling caste made technical knowledge the sole prerequisite for denizenship and planted the seeds of the prospect undercaste.

Without the S.A.T. and the grooll it made possible, humanity would have joined the interminable list of multi-celled life forms that had passed into oblivion. Most denizens believed Sha—the Sapient, Heuristic, and Adaptive—had herself bestowed the gift of grooll upon humankind. They called it Sha's Mercy. Few questioned the morality of eating the city-state's young anymore.

"You're thinking about the test, aren't you?"

Laoshi harrumphed—Dominus could always read his thoughts. Even as children, he'd known what vexed his friend well before Laoshi could put a finger on it.

Among their cohort of prospects, fifty-five percent had passed the S.A.T. last year. Dozens of friends—boys and girls he'd grown up with during years of tutelage at the Librarium—had been harvested at nineteen years of age. The appalling ratio's shadow hadn't receded one iota over last twelve months. Dominus hadn't let it mire him in gloom though. He'd joined the Jireni, entered union, and started a family. Laoshi envied his momentum.

"Cast it out of your mind," Dominus said. "You'd be better focused on tomorrow's insertion."

Laoshi spun his empty glass atop the table. He was right—the past was the past. "So what's it like? A real-world insertion."

Dominus' brow furrowed. Looks of contemplation rarely graced his visage—he favored action, not reflection—but an inward focus tinted his expression now. He drummed his fingers for a moment, then shook his head. "I could spend the rest of the evening trying to explain it. It's something you need to experience."

Myra returned from the pantry carrying an iridescent-blue ceramic pitcher. She refilled Laoshi's glass. "So, Laoshi, tell us when you'll be entering union."

The blunt order caught him off guard. He stuttered.

"Sha's silica teeth," Dominus said. "Give him a chance to digest his grooll before you start the inquisition, will you?"

"No better time than the present." Myra set the pitcher beside

Dominus before sitting. She leaned across the table and locked her gaze onto Laoshi. "I'm waiting for a response."

Laoshi chucklebucked—an ill attempt to mask his discomfort. "I don't know anyone who'd want to take me in union."

Myra dipped her chin and hoisted her eyebrows. "Oh, please. A strapping young Asianoid who finished at the top of his cohort and aced his S.A.T.? I could find you a dozen women before dawn."

"A strapping young *Asianoid-Caucasoid*," Dominus added.

"Even better," Myra said. "An exotic Hyphenoid. You'll have to fend them off with a sparring staff."

"I'm just happy to be doing something I love," Laoshi said.

Her sleek eyebrows arched even higher. "You *love* being a Jiren?"

"Yes."

"A dagger-ax man," she said. "*That's* what you love."

"We haven't carried dagger-axes in millennia," Dominus said.

"And yet you cling to the title." Myra flicked him a pained look. "That's the Jireni for you. Thousands of years of tradition, unhampered by progress." She returned her focus to Laoshi. "I saw you as a builder, not a destroyer."

"I was always interested in structural engineering," Laoshi said, hoping to steer her away from the subject.

"No," she said. "Not a builder of things. A builder of minds."

Dominus hooted. "Laoshi the Librarian!"

Cordelia squealed, seemingly delighted by the notion.

"See? Even little Cordelia thinks it's a good idea." Dominus hoisted his glass. "To Laoshi the Librarian. May he have a long and happy life . . . after his insertion into a certain sector of a certain mongrel colony that shall remain nameless."

Myra rolled her eyes and hoisted her glass.

Laoshi joined them. He even conjured a smile.

What was another lie between friends?

ENJOY THE CHAPTER? GET THE WHOLE STORY!

Survival Aptitude Test: Hope's Graveyard
is offered exclusively to members of the Readers' Posse.

Please visit MIKESHERIFFWRITES.COM to learn more.

ABOUT THE AUTHOR

MIKE SHERIFF WRITES accessible science fiction for readers with curious minds and a taste for tension. Besides The Extinction Odyssey series, he also publishes short and snappy sci-fi stories under the LIGHTBURST imprint. When he's not writing, you'll find him mangling Rory Gallagher riffs on his Fender Strat or fending off high cholesterol through (yawn) diet and exercise. He lives in London, Ontario.

Independent authors rely on word-of-mouth from their readers. If you enjoyed this book, please consider sharing it with others or posting an honest review at your favorite online retailer. Thanks in advance for your support!

Want to get in touch? Email Mike at
mike@mikesheriffwrites.com

ALSO BY MIKE SHERIFF

THE EXTINCTION ODYSSEY SERIES

Survival Aptitude Test: Hope's Graveyard

Survival Aptitude Test: Sound

Survival Aptitude Test: Fury

Survival Aptitude Test: Rise

Survival Aptitude Test: Fall

Survival Aptitude Test: Life

The Extinction Odyssey Series: Books 1-3 (Box Set #1)

LIGHTBURST SHORT STORIES

Lightburst: Displacement

Lightburst: Love Like Gravity

Lightburst: The Pastoralist

FORTHCOMING BOOKS

Survival Aptitude Test: Death

Learn more at MIKESHERIFFWRITES.COM

34217357R00158

Printed in Great Britain
by Amazon